And Then She Unloved Me

And Then She Unloved Me

Pratik Sharma

AUTHOR'S INK
PUBLICATIONS

www.authorsinkindia.com

Published by
Author's Ink Publications
Info@authorsinkindia.com
authorsinkindia@gmail.com
Facebook: www.facebook.com/authorsinkindia
Twitter: www.twitter.com/authorsinkindia
Our Blog: authorsinkindia.com/blog
Contact: +91-8950970646

ISBN: 978-93-92665-56-1

Typeset by Nikhil Mahajan in 11 pts Times New Roman.
Printed and bound in India.

If all would have happened,

I could have died,

I none had happened,

I wouldn't be much alive.

- Pratik Sharma

"An intriguing storyline that will take you to a roller coaster of emotions."

- Saurabh Bharat, Writer (Doctor G)

"Pratik's writing has always impressed and touched avid book readers."

- Tina, Managing Director, Speed Records

"Pratik just knows how to touch the soul of the readers with his remarkable writing style."

- Madan Jalandhari, Lyricist (Chandigarh Kare Aashiqui)

To Mahadev,

If it wasn't you holding my hand, I could

have never come this far. Har Har Mahadev.

1.

In the dark room when I slid curtains aside, the light of the full moon fell charmingly on her face and enhanced her beauty. As I joined her in bed, she kept her head on my right shoulder and her left chubby cheek was pressed against my arm which ultimately made her look all the more beautifully plump and cute together. Her warm breaths were touching my neck and she adjusted herself upwards and cuddled there. Though, I was drowned in the sea of love, yet something was missing which I felt continuously.

It's easier to find something when you are aware of what you are searching for. When one box can't complete the Lego, you search that one box. On the other hand, I was unable to crack the code; which is that one box? What was still being missed?

My arm was around her neck and I held her softly from her shoulder. The support given to her that night felt like a support I needed all my life. The love I was exempted from all my life finally randomly knocked at the door of my life and entered uninvited.

I was happy to have her as a part of my life; also, I was shattered to hear her story. A girl who infinitely loved a boy was broken when he got married to someone else. It took her three long years to overcome her last relation and immense courage to begin a new one - this. A relation for me that started with a business point of view was bankrupt today. Neither the heart calculated numbers nor the brain understood emotions that fine evening. The fight between both created an agitated sensation in my stomach. Ultimately, the heart won and the brain had to give up.

"I love you" -I whispered in her ears.

"I love you too" – she replied.

After two brezzers and one shot of vodka I thought she was asleep but her quick reply and smile on her face with closed eyes made me blush after knowing she heard me.

I kissed her on the forehead to which she gave a peck on my neck. I hugged her tightly to show her my love and make her feel more protective.

"I love you too Rohit"— she said after a minute's pause.

This broke my heart, lying down with me and the name of her ex on her lips. I found the missing box of my Lego. I instantly felt suffocated there. I pulled off my arm gently from her head and grabbed the pillow nearby to give her support.

"I love you too Rohit" — the line which was playing in loop in my mind.

I wore my slippers and looked back at her before bumping into the bed's corner and walking out of the room.

Whether I was wrong or right by ending my last vague relationship and beginning this new one, I didn't know but that one line popped a lot of uneasy questions in my mind –"Did she start this to forget her ex?" Does she even know with whom she made love just now?" What if she apologizes tomorrow morning what happened last night was just a one night stand for her?"

"Love doesn't appear with tricks and formulas, for you it might be sexual intercourse and for me it might be just a cup of coffee"- words from my past were audible to my ears without being spoken out aloud.

The amalgamation of all the questions triggered my instinct of having a cigarette after two long years. I quickly went down the stairs of the hotel we were staying and bought a packet of cigarettes and blew one right there.

The need to cry out took over me instantly as both my heart and mind were in dire need of some outlet and composure at the same time. Childhood habit of crying being confined and fortified pushed me to run upstairs on the roof of the hotel and find a dark place there. There, I could only spot a few huge water tanks and open space. Desperate to find my little crying corner, I stood on the slab where the water tanks were kept. One by one, I opened all the tanks in hope of finding one with the least quantity of water or was empty but there was none. I opened one of the water tanks which was big enough to accommodate my height. I managed to climb on and look into it.

"The dark place inside is perfect"- my mind said.

Unaware of its depth and water storage capacity I jumped into it. Initially, I bumped on the surface as my legs wobbled but managed to find its depth and calculated its height which was approximately 6 feet. My height being 5'9", the water level was just equal. I was just on my toes to help my face get some air so as to collect air before going into that hour's required sleep in my newfound shell. I collected enough air and loosened my legs which helped my body to sink. My knees hit the surface and I finally found what I needed.

I never had been draped in such serenity which I felt lying there. After many years I felt the need to hibernate. Though, I couldn't do it for a long time as I knew the girl sleeping in the room would be awakened in some time if I wasn't around.

Hence, I decided to try something different there. It was a bit dangerous and a minute's hibernation there had flashed one memory in a slideshow. JASNEET KAUR - The girl who never admitted to love me but our reverence for each other cleared it and was accepted quietly by both. Initially, I started to hear the sound of ripples in water which merged with the voice of Jasneet, her wailing, and begging me to not leave her—"I am sorry Pratik. Please don't do this. Please don't leave me. I will try to change myself. I am really sorry. Please don't go. Please Pratik "

Focused or selfish, whatever you might call me, but that change in me was the hunger for my dream. Her tears and pleading voice melted my heart initially but ultimately in no time, I reversed the process and disconnected the last call to her after bidding her final goodbye with SORRY and blocked her from my phone.

2.

It was my first theatre performance and after practicing for nearly a month on 10/05/2014 was our D-day. From us, I mean everyone from my theatre group; Vinay, Akhil, Sam, Anu Ma'am, Keshav, Jeet and Payal. To be very honest, comedy was not at all my genre. It was quite difficult for me to perform in something in which I am the lamest but by *guruji's* grace, I didn't only perform well but also won the best actor award.

Undoubtedly, I was phlegmatic at the time of the award giving ceremony and I looked very calm and composed, as I was quite certain that I would lose. But, when my name jingled in my ears when the best actor award was announced – immediately my body shook and my mates started hugging me. Honestly, mixed foul smell of deodorant and perspiration from them burnt my nostril hair and I decided to lock my respiratory system till I stepped out of the room. The passage from the green room to the stage felt miles long as my legs started to shiver, and right then, I heard my name for the second time-"Pratik, please come on the stage".

That's how Shah Rukh Khan might have felt while collecting his Filmfare or Screen award, I mused. My courage got a rebirth and chest got pumped, my legs automatically started that tiger walk and I got a complete star-feel. I decided to blow a kiss once I reach the stage to the audience and will do Shahrukh's signature step after receiving the award. Abruptly, when I reached the stage all my dreams were drained in the same narrow passage where they came from because there were hardly 30 people sitting in the hall out of which 18 were my family, relatives and friends. I hoped to be handed over the microphone for a little thank you note after receiving the award but nothing like that happened. My *guruji* spoke in an undertone-"Chutiye, itna time yahan tak aane mein." (Asshole, does it take so long to reach here?) The short speech that I prepared walking till the stage also remained unspoken and I walked back to the green room. But my felicity rose in no time after I read "BEST

ACTOR 2014" on the trophy.

Although my curiosity didn't hit the right spot but this trophy in my hand accelerated the innate me to pursue my dreams. I walked out of the hall where I could celebrate my first ever win with the inner Pratik who use to often fan the flames of a dead actor in days when I reckoned to give up on my dreams during some of the dark times. As this cool breeze was falling on my face when I felt a touch of Lord Shiva, I guess he too gave his blessings to me on my first ever win. Never in my life had I won a trophy apart from a race I ran in my school. Never on one's jack Jones had I thought of the day that it was a one-sided competition as I wasn't fast but others were too slow. But a win is a win, and a medal hung at home, opposite to my bed always kept optimism alive and steers me clear of pessimistic fangs. As my emotions and thoughts were ten folds in each other, my friends lifted me up on their shoulders and celebrated the win. I saw their eyes which were happier than mine because at last they knew the reason of my existence, or to correct, I came to know about mine - the only member of the group who was still finding the right track to walk on.

Payal on the other hand was being too clingy. After heading back in the green room I saw her arranging my clothes and packing my bags. She even got a whiff of one of my t-shirts. Her act made me feel like puking – What was all this about? I wondered! I walked up to her and thanked her for lending her helping hand. I smelled a rat after she went crimson. I picked my bag and kick-started my bike to leave for home. Mom and dad were very proud after I reached home but happier was my sister who ran into me to hug and snatched the trophy from my hand.

Once I lay down in my bed I picked up my phone and turned it on to call Jasneet. The girl I like. Jasneet is my ex-colleague who I met while I used to work for a company as an IELTS Trainer in Jalandhar. We became good friends back then and her simplicity and modesty draped me in her love. Though she hadn't accepted my proposal till then, I knew in my heart of hearts that she loved me. As presumed, she was near the landline and picked it even before the first bell was over.

Jasneet-"How has it been?"

"Since how long are you near the phone?"

"I was just passing by and picked the all"- the short pauses she takes while lying makes it all the more evident.

"Liar Liar bums on fire" – I sang the song

After a short laugh she accepted- "From last 2 hours"

(Jasneet didn't have a mobile phone. I asked her a thousand times to purchase one or let me gift it to her but she never agreed. The more I thought I knew about this girl, it became tougher to understand her. Perhaps that made it all the more interesting between us! In this era where people are drawn to different mobiles, she used a landline they had in their house since her childhood. Though, her brother is a strong adherent of Apple products and her sister every year needs a new mobile on her birthday. Jasneet was opposite to them and loved her landline.)

"Why the hell don't you buy a mobile?" – I spoke in an irritated tone.

She took a sigh and a pause for approximately ten seconds before answering me– "You once told you had a landline at your home. Didn't you?"

"Hmmm..." – I replied in acceptance. "And where is it now?"

Thinking about the place where we had dumped it, I took some time to answer that-" It might be in the store room"

She smirked- "And how many mobiles have you changed till date?"

Counting on my fingers I skipped a couple of them and replied – "Three?"- But was unsure about my own memory.

"Four" – She corrected me, as we had discussed about my mobiles many times in the office.

Cutting her rapid fire round in between I asked-"What's the point?"

"I always love my first love, whether it's material or a human, it never changes for me, no matter what better deal I get" – She replied calmly to it and her answer accelerated my emotions and the rate of velocity of my falling in her love mushroomed.

Love was something I always ran away from. It is termite which will make hollow. The void created would never be filled, no matter whoever fits in that space later! This was something I firmly believed in and lived by till she entered my life.

Jasneet was one such girl who forced me to fall in love with her. Though, I wasn't very sure about whether I like her or love her. Also, my mind at times reminded me of my dream and told me how important it is to not fall in love if I have to shape my career. This chaos always played a war of words in my mind before going to sleep. In the fight of two, the third was always the winner, which was my sleep. Their argument never reached a conclusion and sleep never negotiated with anyone to wait a few more minutes. I always wished to be as punctual as my sleep to reach office. Precisely, it was 11:00 pm.

3.

Things were bizarre at the theatre; a new discovery everyday was adding more maturity to my experience. Since the play happened, it started to change with every passing day and the events happening were actually nit-picking. I heard till then about this industry of ill repute but with time I was witnessing some scandals. I found that *guruji*, for whom I had high regard, wasn't a good human but a hypocrite. The real man behind the mask he used to wear every day was a swine.

Of the many stories about him I heard, I never believed in any as I never found him Machiavellian. Some alleged stories about his office too were quite infamous like a rape of a girl and a suicidal attempt of one but I found none to be verifiable and declared them rumours to myself.

I left early for the theatre practice from my work and then I found *guruji* and Sunidhi making out in their office. I was taken aback by this and pondered whether there is anything wrong in making out. And on top of it when you are married and a father of two. Secondly, you are a 51 year-old man and a so-called respectable one as per society's norms and thirdly, you are making out with a girl of 22 who till yesterday considered you a father figure in front of us. Luckily, they didn't see me and I pulled myself back with soft feet as soon as I entered the room without knocking.

I decided to blow the gaff and tell my friends from the theatre about this cunning man. But I gave it a second thought of whom to believe. It was just a month that I met these people and couldn't really conclude about them being single or double- faced. Hence, I decided to remain mute and learn more about this industry before moving to Mumbai.

Thinking about all these I didn't forget to place my step softly so that no one could hear me leaving. While I succeeded in not being audible to anyone about my presence, I forgot I am no hollow man and can be visible too. And that was exactly what happened. Payal, in her lilac coloured *kurti* and a *churidar salwar* blushed as soon as she saw me once I was at the gate of the theatre.

"Hey" – She said, leaning her back on the wall.

"Hi" – the uneasiness on my face made me look like a thief as if it was me, who was caught red handed with Sunidhi. I felt droplets of sweat slipping down my forehead.

She passed the bottle of water to me-"Have it."

I slugged down in large gulps and handed her an empty bottle.

She kept passing small mischievous smiles to me which made me twitchy as her eyes made it clear that she too had eyed them in a compromising position.

"Want to go for a coffee?" – She asked.

To run from the situation I moved my legs faster than a predator on the hunt and kick started my bike. We ended up in a nearby cafe and ordered two cappuccinos.

Thinking whether to continue or leave *Guruji's* academy, I constantly was making circles on the coffee's froth with the coffee sucker straw.

"We could have ordered frappe if you are fond of Cold coffee." – Payal mocked my actions.

"No. This is good", was my prompt response.

"It's cool Pratik, everyone has a life and is free to live the way they want" – She started the topic which we both knew but were hiding.

I didn't look into her eyes and moved my eyeballs from right to left – "Hmmm. You are right, I guess."

Gaining her exuberant tone back she asked about my family about which I replied and finished our coffee. The dicey thing to me was that she steered clear on questions about her family, quite easily.

But later that night, I made one thing clear to myself- "Why shall I weigh down my brain about something which is not on my preference list. When push comes to shove I will be in Mumbai, finally. My message to myself was - Be here, learn the tricks of the trade, and be subtle. Taking everything into consideration, it's concluded that, be what you are not, because to survive here in this industry one thing that is clear, naivety won't work.

My regularity of job, theatre, and gym remained unaltered as I decided that, relationship of two; name it anything, won't hurdle my dream of becoming an actor. I decided not to discuss it with Jasneet, as she wouldn't want me to be in connection with people who live lives of *Savdhaan India*, every day!

There wasn't a single day when before going to bed, this thought whether I took a wrong step by joining this new company "Knowledge Planet" crossed my mind. I was busy right from 8 in the morning and got free at 5 pm. The only half hour break I got was during lunch. Soon after my job I had to rush for theatre practice and after getting free from there by 8pm I drove directly to my gym where my childhood friends Babu and Sarabjeet would give me this weird look as if I had asked them to lend me two abs each!

As usual, Jasneet was at the same place at 10pm that night too. But that night I called a bit later.

"Hey, how are you?" – Her voice was so low I wondered if it would be reaching her own ears. It was more of air passing through her throat with a mixture of a few words.

"Why are you speaking in such a low tone?"

"Babaji, dimaag dao es munde nu (Lord, give some brains to this boy) I live in a village and here people sleep by 9 pm. We don't have this night life like yours in cities. If I speak out loud, everyone will wake up thinking I am upset with my somnambulism. Hahaha" — she laughed as slowly as she could, covering her mouth with her palms.

My horses stopped at the point she joked about walking in her sleep. I stammered- "Do Do Do... Do you walk in sleep?"

"Yes Pratik. I do it sometimes. Now it is less but in childhood I would find myself sometimes near the well at mid-night and sometimes on the bark of a palm tree near my house."

My weird imagination ran in nitro mode and I imagined Jasneet hanging upside down on the fan in my room, sitting in a squatting position on kitchen's shelf and walking on walls in the lobby.

And was cut between by Jasneet's voice-"Pratik, hey, you there?" "Haa, yeah, I…….. I am here" – I said as my voice started to break. She asked frantically – "What happened to you, are you okay?"

"Do you really walk in sleep?", the shiver my voice got some pauses to complete the sentence.

Her amusement at pulling my leg and making me panic-stricken made her blossom into an enormous belly laugh.

I cut the call right after she didn't stop her chortle at her own execrable pun.

Within seconds she called again-"Baba ji, enna gussa munde ch" (Lord, this boy has so much anger)

"Will take revenge on this Jasneet"- She broke into a cold sweat hearing my irked tone.

"Okay ji, sorry, won't repeat it, and please don't turn into an angry young man in a snap of fingers."

She would recite prayers at night before going to sleep and she did this thing- talk to *babaji*(God) every night at 12. As per her ideology, *babaji* listens to her prayers more at mid-night when he is done with the day's chores of dealing with the world. This undoubtedly used to make me laugh; her hundreds of convincing attempts with thousands of examples which included ample of ways how Guru Nanak Dev Ji listens to the prayers more at midnight had always confused me.

4.

Where NASA was finding life on mars, where India was still struggling hard to get a place in NSG, where Russia might surely be advancing its weapons, Payal was surely coming up with new and wacky ideas to impress me. At Keshav's birthday party she brought a wrist watch for me. Can you beat that? Why on earth will I get a gift on someone else's birthday! Have I ever asked for one? No. Have I ever told her that watches lure me? Yes. Had I ever asked her to buy it for me? Straight NO.

"Why this?"- Knowing her intentions to gift me this, I acted as if I understood nothing (this new world had started to instil the abysmal trait which I hated the most; hypocrisy).

With blushing cheeks, she adjusted her fringe hair aside of her forehead and had a soft bite of her upper lip.

She opened the box and took out the watch. She held my right hand in hers and was about to tie the watch on it. The absolute still me was actually finding an excuse to explain to her how weird I was finding the entire situation. While all these thoughts were playing in my head, when she was just about to lock the strap I pulled my hand away with a jerk.

"I am sorry... I can't. I just can't accept this."

Payal's eyes bugged out after my repulsion. Though, I wasn't happy with my own act but my ideology was clear not to make someone fall in love with me who I cannot love back. My heart apologised to her quietly but eyes were hard stared with vertical lines appearing on my forehead. The song being played at the café "love has no boundaries"- by Beres Hammond pierced through my ear and I shouted at the staff- "Please change the fucking song".

Payal, packed the watch back and leaned back on the chair with her hands crossed in front of her. Her expressions weren't as she was vexed but was somehow hurt.

That silence of a few minutes made all the noise around enter my ear without any hindrance. Murmuring of couples on the nearby tables, people immersed in work and bashing on their computer keyboards and manual stirring of coffee by the worker at reception which was just a table away from us, all these were very soft and weren't irritating at all. As my gaze fell on the person who was stirring the coffee, he kept the mug in which he was doing so as he was the same person I lashed out a few seconds ago. My attention split by the beep tone on my phone and I promptly pulled it out.

It was an unknown number:

"Reach home and save my number. Finally you convinced me to buy a phone."

It was "the" moment when I felt like calling Jasneet impromptu and blowing a hundred kisses on her as an expression of pure love filled with happiness. I knew she did it for me. My lips parted till their extreme and were locked there for quite a long time. My mind flew from Payal to Jasneet, precisely, back to home.

Payal noticed this and coughed to draw my attention. It took her three coughs to get an eye when her windpipe actually sucked mucus from her lungs, I guess, and she broke down into persistent coughing which lasted nearly a minute. Once it abated, I started to think about what to say or what not to, I decided to be honest and not act as in a smiling mime.

"Payal, to be very honest with you, I like a girl. I don't want to expose any wrong intentions to you."

Though she didn't want to show how disheartened she was after hearing this, I noticed her eyes filled with tears which said it all. She started to bite her nails and looked aside. I was in no mood to understand her and eventually found my heart became lighter after I said that. After a sigh my lungs got enough air it wanted.

"I am sorry. I guess I...." – She couldn't complete it as her throat was filled. "Please, don't be. I think I should have made it clear to you earlier."

"Perhaps"- she sniffed after that and I was thinking words to console her-"What's her name?"

"Jasneet"

"Where is she from?" "Hoshiarpur"

"College-time love?"

Though I felt a little uncomfortable answering her questions as I never had discussed my private life like this at random with anyone. Nevertheless, I decided to speak it out all and let things take their own course. Maybe this is what was required, I pondered.

I broached everything with her in detail. Payal looked quite happy after listening to my story or so it seemed to me. The box of watch she had kept inside her purse was once again taken out by her.

After listening to my story with a short pause and, I believe, some extra courage she asked- "No love… friends?" She stumbled a little and then added, "Let this be a token of friendship."

I took some time before thinking about answering. I could not find any strong reason to deny her friendship. She has been quite supportive and loyal since we met. Thus, I accepted it and wore the red and black sporty look Fast-track watch she brought for me.

My exhilaration couldn't wait till home and I called Jasneet soon after I left the café and sat on my bike. She answered the mobile precisely after the fifth ring.

"Thank you thank you thank you…"- I repeated it and kissed my phone many times till she felt my happiness.

The thought of calling her anytime and sending her pictures of wishing good morning and good night with emoticons of kisses, the thought overpowered me along with ecstasy.

She laughed out loud and kept repeating- "Stop… stop Pratik " but I knew she didn't want me to. After all, she too must resonate with the happiness I felt.

Just between our personal moment, Payal spoke from behind me as she was overhearing the entire conversation- "If you don't like the colour we can go and change the watch tomorrow."

She was louder than required. This was done on purpose and was very evident to me. Jasneet's laughter became silent after she heard it.

"Hmmm…"- I turned and looked at her like a deadpan. After a long pause I nodded.

I could feel the animosity in Payal which was visible in her eyes too. Honestly, my mind warned me of her intentions and somewhere at the back of my head the thought arose-"this is just the beginning."

As my mind was re-reading the day started from entering this café till she spoke to Jasneet, indirectly. I was quiet till then; my eyes were following what Payal was doing. Inserting the keys in her Activa's lock, wearing a helmet and her gaze at me, this said "pity you."

"Who's that?"- Jasneet asked from the other end.

I couldn't take my eyes off Payal as I wanted to kill her for this. "Pratik? Are you there?"- Jasneet confirmed.

"Haan… yes, yes I am here" – coming back to her as I was sweating bullets. "Who was she and which watch was she talking about?

I wanted to make up a story and lie to her that she was just another girl talking to her boyfriend but being known to the fact that, my own lie wouldn't allow me to sleep till I admitted everything to her honestly. I decided to make everything crystal clear and explained to her what had just happened.

Jasneet listened to me patiently and very carefully and was silent for a few seconds after I completed. Even though I didn't interrupt her in between, she decides and says something. Surrounded by the traffic at Model town, chaos of blowing horns and music from a nearby shop I could hear the long breaths Jasneet was taking.

Might she be handling her anger or was in a worrisome situation? She finally spoke- "I trust you."

I was perplexed to hear this answer. I expected her to abuse or get angry at me for accepting it or Payal to give it but her "I TRUST YOU" was indigestible to me.

"Are you sure that you are okay?" – I still confirmed

She chuckled and replied-"Pratik, I mean it if I say it. It's very easy to love anyone but difficult to trust. You many times have said you love me. Today, I am saying I trust you."

"I swear I won't break it"- I assured her. On second thoughts, she really made great sense to me when she said she trusts me.

5.

After several calls from Mr. Surjit Singh Chahal, I finally accepted a second lead in his tele-movie which was to shoot for a local Punjabi channel. Mr. Singh was contacting me ever since he saw my theatre which I performed in May 2014 at K.L.Sehgal memorial hall at Jalandhar. I was least interested in acting as a second lead for him. But Payal insisted on me to do so as she was the one who was the bridge between Mr.Singh for conveying messages.

"Do I even look like a second lead actor to him? I always have played the first lead and won't start my career in tele-movies with a second lead." – making my thoughts very clear to Payal I waved my hand in ignorance.

"Arre Baba, he has this criteria where he judges actors by their work after offering a second lead in their first movie and if they pass and impresses him, then he signs them for three consecutive movies as a first lead"- she explained being as calm and polite she could and held my right hand to act as coolant, which hardly worked.

After what happened as she stepped close to me in a room where only we two were there, I accepted and walked out to give no mixed signal to her.

On 27th, November, 2014 I reached the shooting spot in time at sharp 8:15 am. I had already received the address the night before the shooting day from one of the assistant directors of the movie. After parking my bike under a tree I picked my bag, wore it on my shoulder, and walked towards an old Sikh man, who was wearing a black turban, resting his back on the car and was scrolling Facebook feeds, which I saw through the window glass of the car.

"Can you direct me to this address?" – I took out my phone and after finding the message the A.D had sent to me, I handed over my phone to him. His phlegmatic character illustrated enough when he preferred checking the meme he started to read. He slid his phone in the pocket and stood straight, stretched his arms vertically as long as he could, yawned- which was not less than a roar and cracked his neck's knuckles, moving them from extreme left to extreme right.

The otherwise placid and expressionless Pratik was on the verge of losing his temper but realising his age, the abuses rose from my stomach and reached till my throat, I gulped them with the saliva in my mouth.

"Hi Pratik, your first impression is quite impressive. In 5 minutes" – the old man put forth his right hand in front of me, which I accepted in dubiety. I narrowed my eyes to recall his face, grappling with my memory of whether I have seen him before but I was clueless.

He sensed my topsy-turvy expression and introduced himself- "Surjit Singh Chahal".

My nerves as if they got their blood flow back; I rubbed my hand with my jeans to wipe the sweaty palms and accepted his handshake firmly. With a half-smile he passed, he started to walk towards the location where the shooting was to start.

On the way to the location we conversed about various interests of ours for T.V and theatre and discovered that we both sail on the same boat especially on our choice of director; Imtiaz Ali.

"Do it light, and please no foundation"- I made it clear to the make-up dada.

Relaxing myself on a recliner chair, my eyes were closed for fifteen long minutes. Till the time *dada* was applying make-up with various Indian and western brushes which he was using meticulously, he tried to explain them all as a perfect salesman. Finding it tedious I didn't know when I fell half asleep. My unconscious mind drove me to three short dreams in which I got a blockbuster movie, the best debut award and a kiss on cheeks from Alia Bhatt. Though my eyes were closed and brain dreamt, ears were doing their job well, collecting all the gossips and talks from surrounding and transferring the information to brain. Randomly, the talk got adjusted in between the dreams and the last word I heard was-"Director has come". As soon as Alia kissed, the words which got into my mind were audible to her too and she said-"Have to go, sorry". My eyes instantly opened to stop her and right in front, I found a girl in white shirt and navy blue jeans who was adjusting the halogen light according to the lenses she was to use.

"Perfect, make it a bit dim as I want the light only to fall on the heroine's face."- Taking a pause and scanning the whole area she said-"And I believe she is ready"

Her eyes fell on me and she narrowed her eyes as was trying to concentrate.

6.

"A mixture of white and blue LEDs, if you clearly heard me for the first time"- I called out loud to the person who was installing lights at home, dropping them from the roof.

The decorator, the only intelligent person I found in the day who could understand what I was trying to say, who actually felt the pain in my ass of teaching the morons what contrast means. Be it; the one who was installing lights or the other who installed tents for the DJ party.

A Punjabi wedding house is not less than a random public park where you may find many unseen faces wandering in your house and even using your room - which was till yesterday my kingdom now overtaken by some aunties who were feeding their children and using my bathroom as their five years old grown child has pooped in his pants.

Didi was screaming for a car to drop her to the salon, her fixed appointment in the salon was already thirty minutes late. Not a single chance that she wanted to miss to be bedecked with the most beautiful bride.

"If you need a salon to look beautiful, I would need a plastic surgery"- I said, as I wanted to calm her down after knowing the fact that the car was already taken by papa who went to buy ingredients which will be used during *pheras*.

My not so funny joke did work as my *bhuas and cousins* started to laugh, and tried to calm the volcano in didi which could burst any time. Unaware and proud of my lame joke, I patted my shoulders. Initially I couldn't understand but promptly I did later, from their dramatic manner of laughter which went on even after a minute which very well claimed that neither they found this joke funny.

Not even parting her lips for an inch, didi gave a contemptuous look to everyone which eventually brought everyone's teeth reversing behind lips.

"I'll look for something"- I ran out after saying it.

I didn't get enough sleep for the last two days; I was utterly exhausted with all the running around and wanted to drink something to regain energy. Handling rejections till then had become a part of my life and the cook's denial when I asked for a glass of mixed fruit juice didn't bother me much! In my mind I had already made up my mind to deduct his 1000 rupees but decided not to tell him till then.

I was missing Jahnvi every single minute. Though I was high as a kite for *didi's* marriage, I was still a percent happier from the thought that Jahanvi would be meeting my entire family together for the first time and vice versa.

There were people questioning me about Jahanvi's absence from almost all the family functions whereas I was covering as much as I could. Thus, I wanted to shut them all at once. I stood and was about to walk when the cook called-"*Puttar* (Son)"

I felt the 65 years old man's heart melted and would offer me something to eat when he handed me a piece of paper to buy stuff, it read - "50kg onion and potato each, 20 kg cauliflowers, 35kg tomatoes"- my mind calculated roughly 2000 rupees but I managed to smile and walked away.

My eyes were looking for a person to get the vegetables in the list from the market. Failing in finding one, I took my mobile out of my jean's right pocket. I instantly got a message, Jahnvi it read- "Reached Jalandhar. Hope everything is fine there"

I stopped by and typed— "Yes all good. Everyone is excited to meet you" "Hmmm…"— she typed back.

Even though we were back together, still the bonding was weak. I knew it will take some time to be reacquired.

"Great. Had lunch?"- I asked.

Ever since we started talking again, I noticed her replies were taking longer than usual. She would be online but unavailable to read, type and respond instant.

"Yes, and you?"- She asked "Yes... Hope you are good" "Absolutely fine. How are you?"

Taking no time once again, I replied- "Better now"

My eyes were glued on the screen. This time she took longer than last to reply. With every passing second. As the word *typing* appeared which remained unchanged there for a longer time, I adjusted myself back on the bike's seat as till then I slipped down. My mind started to make a guess what she might say.

Missed you, I also feel better now, excited to see you tomorrow, and many more. Though my eyes were glued on the screen, my mind diverted me to some heart- relaxing imaginations. The phone was on ringing mode, I couldn't hear the beep of the message tone and came back to senses with the vibration I felt on my right hand.

"See you tomorrow"- she sent

Eager of not ending the chat I typed-"Wish to see you everyday"

In excitement I didn't notice that she went offline after sending her last message so half saddened of the conversation being ended abruptly, I erased the typed message and slid the phone back in the pocket.

Another thing which I noticed was my t-shirt being wet from the sweat and I searched for a hanky in all pockets of my jeans. Failed to do so, I reminded myself of the two important tasks to be done. First, finding a car and second to make purchases from the list of vegetables. The first task was completed right there as I saw papa turning right from our street's corner in the car. Thus, vegetables were the only task left. I instantly took out my wallet and started to search for the paper that the cook handed to me. The paper he gave camouflaged itself between the number of ATM slips and a couple of bus tickets I had.

I came across a page that was tenfold that was from primaeval times of our relationship. I very carefully opened it. It read- "PJ" in calligraphy.

Ever since I returned from meeting Mohit, my heart couldn't wait for theresponse coming from his side, positive of course. I

dialled his number a couple of times to ask if he got some good news but disconnected the call myself.

"Helplessness is the best teacher for inculcating patience."

7.

"Isn't the base of the make up too heavy for a hero?" – The girl in white shirt and blue jeans walked up to us and began questioning a veteran make-up artist. To my surprise, he was mute and listened to her without wavering his focus. This entire scenario remained a complete mystery to me until she left the place and I instantly asked dada.

"Who is she?"

"She is your director, a very talented and intellectual girl. She has assisted a few Punjabi directors in music videos and in a month or so her first Punjabi feature movie as an assistant director is about to release. A very hard working girl"

I espied her works and commanding her team members very carefully and minutely for some reason. From giving the light-man instructions about the needful lights in different scenes to showing the cinematographer about the angles of scenes required to take the shots from. I really was quite impressed by her commitment and dedication towards work.

Unintentionally my eyes fell on her sharp curves when my mind questioned me- "Is that 36, 24, 36?"

"Naaaaa... She would be 34, 28, and 32?" – The other half of my brain woke up and measured the best from my eyes. The latter was unshakeable in his belief.

The debate in my head overweight my vision and I started to imagine numbers 34 and 24 were in a boxing ring where 28 was at the side of 34 and asking to give a clap so that it actually can show 24 some smacks.

My lame imagination was jerked awake with a snap of fingers.

"If you are done with scanning my chest and hips, can we continue shooting? We have a long day."- She boldly said it as a matter of fact.

I wanted to say to her what I actually was imagining and not really looking at her waist. But ultimately I held my horses as I was aware that an explanation would be obnoxious because at the end of the day I was measuring and thinking about the curves in her body and she was right on her part. I gulped water down my throat and ended up giving all the expressions I knew.

Her discomfort became evident to me once she narrowed her eyes and gave a very confused look at me. With a pause of a minute she said-"Better use them in front of the camera"

She raised her eyebrows and with her long blink of eyes she shook her head slightly. I heard her murmuring-"Creep!" She turned and walked away.

I ran after her to apologise, not because she was my director but owing to the fact that I had made a woman uneasy with my actions. Now, this was just not me! My rate of velocity was faster than hers and within milliseconds I was standing on her face – "Hey… look… I am extremely sorry… I didn't…" after completing half of what I said my mind gave me some hints on how to escape an embarrassing situation. None I found beneficial, thus, I accepted what I did-

"I am sorry for what I just did; I really had no such intentions". With the pauses I took to complete the sentence and eyes staring down on the surface, my heart a lot lighter after the confession.

Her heart melted the way I apologised and she understood that it was more my heart speaking than my tongue! She smiled and asked-"Look at me."

Her big and round black eyes and adequate lids on eyes with mascara just on the upper lid gave her ten on ten for eyes. Her sharp and pointed nose was shining as it lured the rays of the sun. I could see her chubby cheeks bouncing like jelly while she was speaking. Her both lips needed a lick of tongue after every sentence she completed as they were getting dry. Never in my life had I noticed a girl so closely. She had a different appeal which I never found in any girl and the urge to keep talking to her was not just satisfying my thirst.

"It's totally okay… I think I overreacted."- she said with a lot of patience and calm in her tone.

"That's why you are a director"- I replied instantly in anticipation that she would understand the joke and laugh aloud.

She narrowed her eyes to understand what exactly I said.

"Overacted... well, you can't do it as you are a director"- I exhibited my subtle case of upper and lower teeth with a surge of hope that she will understand me now.

"But I said overreacted and not over acted"- she was prompt to catch it.

"Ha haha ha..." –dramatically laughing at my own joke and chanting "PJ, PJ, PJ...."

The poker face she had for the next few seconds gave me the clue of how several times she might have murdered me in different ways in her mind. Understanding we neither had armours nor swords and the consequences of a murder in a civilised society she dropped down the plan and sniffed in a sarcastic tone- "P and J can never be together," And this was enough hint for me of the picture she had painted in her mind about me!

I knew she gave me the BREAK THE CODE challenge with her wittiness. I cracked the code P as it might be my name; Pratik. "J" probably would be her name's first letter. Recalling my conversation with *dada* in the morning, if he had told her name to me while displaying her accomplishments, my eyes fell on her ID card which hung with a green colour strap around her neck. The ID card had her name on it, JAHNVI SHARMA. Alongside was written her designation: Director. It included her photograph as well but there was a big black spot on her face as it had a splash of black ink on it.

Finally, at the bottom of my heart I was euphoric to solve her BREAK THE CODE challenge within seconds as P meant Pratik and J meant Jahanvi. Clearing the doubt if ever we two could be together I was startled to know she misunderstood my trait of cracking jokes to flirting.

Before clearing off the scepticism which was all around the air that surrounded us, I felt the urge to ask about the black spot. Pointing towards it I asked with reluctance in my voice-"I can see a black spot…"

She bugged out her eyes after I said that. Unable to decipher her reaction I concluded she might be thinking which black spot I am referring to. I pointed once again to the identity card she was wearing.

She clenched her teeth and murmured something. She closed her shirt's button and walked away. Both confused and puzzled, I tried to go through what I just said but found none to be offensive. Suddenly, a meme from Facebook emerged in my mind. "Never try to understand a girl, a girl understands the other and they end up being enemies".

There was consolation after this quote appeared in my mind randomly. The Less I understood her, the easier my acting became through the day's shoot.

Though being unspecified of what happened I made up my mind to apologise to her if I hurt her sentiments, just to be on the safe side, after all she was my director! The lunch break helped me to sit close to her. Filling my plate with the needful food, I dragged a chair and sat next to her. The first thing I did after getting close to her was offer her a soft drink which I bought extra for her.

How she had been treating me while shooting was different from how she reacted after I sat beside her. The persistent ignorance was evident to me but I decided not to give up and execute the task I was there for.

First thing first, and I wanted to show her and explain to her about the black spot I was talking about. So, I looked for the strap around her neck but found it wasn't there. The availability of one such thing which I found there was the actual source from where all the misunderstanding started. As the first button of her shirt was open, again, I peeped in her shirt and found a black mole on her chest.

"Oh My God"-I murmured.

"Ummmm??" – She made a sound as she was chewing the morsel she just ate.

I looked sideways and was extremely embarrassed. A part of me triggered to clear the misunderstanding while the other half ceased the feeling.

While the thought of whether to begin the buried conversation still oscillated within me, from the corner of my eyes I spied she looked at me many times.

Being the ice breaker she initiated-"Didn't you like the food?"

The chaos which covered my mind had neglected what she just said, so she had to repeat, and this time a bit louder-"Didn't you like the food?"

Returning back into my senses I fumbled-"No... I mean it's delicious"

I stimulated my feelings from confession to clarification, so I took the jump and hit on the nail rather than beating around the bush. Taking a long sigh and mustering courage I spoke in a single breath – "Actually, I was talking about the black spot that is in the photograph on your ID card but I think you misunderstood it with the black mole on your right chest and honestly I didn't notice it in morning but just spotted it now!"

She stopped chewing the morsel she had in her mouth and after a few seconds, initially blushed with her mouth full and gulped the food without munching. In no time I saw her changing from smiling to laughing. I couldn't understand the feeling that emerged in my stomach after I saw her laughing as I found it the most beautiful and enchanting laugh ever.

"I am extremely sorry, I misunderstood" – tilting her eyes from me she looked back at her plate and filled her spoon with rice and lentil which she had mixed.

"It's okay, not an issue, or just a smile" – thinking of what to reply when you are stuck in this kind of situation I continuously kept asking what to do to the inner Pratik who replied-"pour more paneer than daal"(pour more Cheese than lentil)

"But it is bad manners to peep into a girl's shirt, don't you feel that?" – she said after clearing her voice, it was low enough that no one else could overhear.

Until I was able to reply to her one statement she had a comeback with her second bouncer.

I felt captivated from all sides with the sin I had committed. Though escaping was the only solution from there, I turned back towards everyone who was having lunch at the table. I wished dada would call me for a touch-up but he was busy licking his finger after relishing his meal.

I scratched my beard and even bit my upper lip to fill the void with actions rather than words. I thanked the almighty who after a few seconds gave me the idea, this time I looked her in the eyes- "Look, I know nothing of these mannerisms, but trust me this was unintentional." I took a long pause and gave a long sigh long before I extended my right hand to her and said- "Let's forget what just happened.

Friends?"

Her half a minute's gaze at my hand I wasn't clear about the thousand thoughts running wild in her mind. Until then my eyes didn't move from her beautiful face.

"As I said earlier, I repeat it, P and J can never be together"- she picked her plate which only was left with two uneaten pickles and walked away.

My hand being at the same position made me realise what exactly EMBARRASSMENT is and I noticed what made her gaze at my hand for half a minute. My index, middle and ring finger were decorated with the curry of *paneer* I just dipped in to fill the morsel. The palm was shiny as it had butter on it because of the *butter naan* I was having.

The other half of the day became more difficult for me on two fronts; overcoming the embarrassment I faced during lunch and less shots which I had as I was in second lead.

"Hope things are fine"- in all this day's chaos, Jasneet's message arrived as a therapy.

I arranged myself comfortably in the chair as her message was a self-motivation to me who till then thought "Nothing good can happen in a bad day and just then love arrived."

"Yes. Everything is good. How about you?"

"Bruno is not well. Have called the veterinarian in the morning but he didn't reach till now"

Her obsession with dogs was one such thing which was completely out of my understanding. This could be attributed to me not having a pet ever. On top of this anxiety, if anything happens to her dogs, I also was aware of her habit of not eating all this while.

"Had breakfast?"

The blue tick appeared soon after the message was delivered but I knew what the answer would be. I was just waiting for her to say it.

" :("

During initial days of our conversation whenever she would say this, I would be the first one to castigate her but being used to this trait of hers; I really wished for Bruno's wellness.

"Send me the doctor's number."-I replied.

I didn't know if she knew it and already typed it but my doubt was wrong as I received the doctor's number before I could blink my eyes.

With just two shots remaining for the day for which I had to wait for four hours made me uninterested to give them on the same day. But after realising the decision maker was already vexed at me I completed my shot and got ready to leave.

After packing my clothes and removing my make-up I shook hands with the crew and the producer Mr. Singh. I waited for a few minutes so that Jahanvi turns towards me and I can actually apologise yet again and bid her goodbye. But my efforts went in vain as she didn't move an inch.

Only two hours of shooting was left so I waited in the nearby park and stared at the gate in the hope she would forgive this time. Wandering on one side of the track from the four in the park, my eyeballs were stuck on the gate. My life taught me one thing till then that the pace of time becomes slow twice; one at the traffic signals which I often experience and second while waiting for someone especially when you want to speak to the person.

She got out of the house on her scooty and in haste, I kick-started my bike and followed her. It didn't take much long and I stopped her at the corner of the street.

Her mouth was left open when I stopped my bike and she had to use all her power to pull the brakes of her scooter. The hour of dusk and no street light made her vision unclear for a few seconds but soon she realised it was me and no stranger blocking her way.

"What the hell man, we almost collided" – she said angrily.

"Hey listen, I am really sorry but I had to do this. Whatever happened today wasn't intentional. It is purely a misunderstanding." – I said in one breath.

I was engrossed talking to her, completely unaware of the surroundings, whether anyone was listening or not. There was a complete silence between and around us. Cool breeze and some insects were all that were making a buzzing noise and just the star-sprinkled sky sprawled on top as the only witness.

As I stood there still, I slowly moved my eyes from her face to the road downwards and she spoke gently-"Look Pratik, you might be innocent at your end and most importantly I don't think much about these things. I have no such hard feelings for you. We worked together today and may not meet ever again."

My heart too wanted never to face her after today but I don't know what thought I had in my mind or was it something else which forced me say-"We will" and I looked straight into her eyes after which she too unmoved, kept hold of my eyes for a few seconds.

My heart hoped she resists it and I never have to see her again but my soul had a different concept and wished for a coffee with her.

"We never will Pratik." She took a pause to complete the sentence. Her eyes remained unmoved and without blinking she continued-"Not as a friend and break it into pieces if you think further. As I said in the morning too I stick to it. P and J can never be together."

I gave her a half smile after that and quickly grabbed my bag from which I took out a copy and a mini marker I had. I tore the last page of the copy and wrote PJ in calligraphy and handed the piece of paper to her.

"What's this?"-she asked with a bewildered look.

""P and J will be together soon. I don't know how but we will only be friends and not more than that." – I assured her.

She returned the paper to me after folding it and said-"Then keep this paper with you and I will take it from you when we become friends, if you are so sure about it!"

8.

"It has been 8 months now Jasneet and we haven't met"- I was louder than usual on her.

"I understand Pratik but also want you to understand that my family is conservative and doesn't allow girls to go in city alone"

"How can this work? I know you like me and so do I but till how long will we continue this technology driven relationship in this way. Don't you think we should take this relationship further into love?"

"You say you like me, does liking have barriers? Can anything halt it? Even if we don't meet in the next two years, do you think liking will be reduced or eliminated? If yes, then it can never transform into love."

God! Why does she always have a super logical counter to everything?- I wondered. Sometimes her being too sorted and crisp in opinions annoys me because I don't get better points to prove myself correct.

Though we never proposed to each other but deep down in our hearts we knew what the other one was thinking. We never felt the need to take help of words to show our feelings for each other. We never felt words could justify what we had in our hearts.

I preferred not replying to her after that, I knew after not having a good reply I will end up the discussion into an unwanted argument just to prove her wrong and myself correct.

Also a message from Payal indulged me in a conversation which was an indirect eavesdrop.

"Hey, I went to Mr. Surjit Singh's office today as I was called by him."

As the message appeared I was thrilled and excited. I didn't plan that way but I sat for a while after reading the message and replied in a manner to give the impression that I am least interested-"and?"

"I actually overheard their conversation as I reached outside his office. Guruji was there too and they both were discussing your performance in the Tele-movie."

Inexperienced in typing messages quickly her speed was very slow. Meanwhile waiting for her message I would pick my pillow and keep it on my lap and then again pick it and place it on my back's rest.

Notification of Jasneet arrived-"Fine. If you want to always run away from discussions I won't stop you. Good night."

I saw the message but didn't open it as the chat window with Payal was already open and I didn't want to be late even by a second to hear the gossip she was to share.

Finally after a two minutes long wait her message finally arrived on my mobile- "Actually the final edit of the movie is done and Surjit Singh was very genuinely impressed by your performance. Guruji's chest got pumped after listening to his words. Jahanvi too was there"

Jahanvi's presence there mattered none to me. After the shoot we never spoke to each other. Though, her Facebook ID appeared to me in suggestions many times but I never felt like connecting with her.

"Proud of you"- her second message appeared on the screen.

Though I had received compliments about my acting skills many times but those were only for theatre. The first ever positive response for my work on screen made me overwhelmed.

The next three consecutive messages by Payal were her quickest response she ever had-"Are you busy?

Jasneet?

We can talk later"

With a minor gap of millisecond I received all three messages. To make things clear to her I replied-"No. Was just thinking of a good response"

"You don't need to think and write, especially when it's me. Whatever you write is always good for me."

Her minced images of still trying her level best to flirt and pass some hints of wanting me in her life was something I neglected as toppers of the class neglect mates' voices in examination when they are asked to help.

I didn't reply to her message she sent but kept my interrogation on- "Why did he call you?"

While the word *online* changed to *typing* my eyes were glued there for quite a long time.

"He offered you three tele-movies in the first lead"

I was happy, actually, happier than I have ever been in my life. I noticed my eyes got a few droplets of water in them. I wanted to spend this time with myself.

Thinking of the dreams of which I dreamt since childhood- a poster of my movie outside cinema halls and receiving awards in yearly award ceremonies as best actor. I seemed myself a step further those dreams and they didn't appear that distant to me now.

Recalling my childhood dreams my heart felt so light and relaxed that I started to see everything that ran across my mind. Just as watching a movie with all the background scores and dialogues, I could see everything crystal clear.

And I got back to consciousness once the phone rang. It was Payal. Firstly, my heart resisted picking her call and talking to Jasneet instead but what if it was important for me- With this thought in my mind, I answered the phone.

Sliding the green call button to the right I lifted it. "I hope I didn't disturb you"- She said politely.

I never forgot her cunning gesture outside the coffee shop when I was talking to Jasneet. So I decided to limit my conversation with her just to work. What I didn't notice was her work related talks started to increase as I could never deny this.

"Naa… it's cool"- I confirmed for her.

"How's Jasneet?"- She asked more softly this time.

"She is good. Was just talking to her"- I lied to her just in case she misunderstood any of my actions.

"Good. And how about Jaaaaaaaaaaahanvi?"- She stressed on the name Jahanvi.

Confused by what she intended to ask by that extra stretch, I replied after rephrasing her own sentence with long pauses and stretching each word-"And what about Jahanvi?"

"I mean.... how is it going with her?"

The statement itself was so confusing, thus, I directly asked her- "I am not able to understand Payal, please clarify."

I heard a small pause from the other end of the phone. After a sniff she said-"don't you talk to her?"

I was assured of her new plot but was unable to understand what exactly it was. I said a bit loud and in an irritated tone-"Why would I talk to her?"

"And why wouldn't you?"-her voice was heavy and prompt.

I was taken aback as I had no answer to her question. She manipulated me into thinking *why wouldn't I speak to her* from why *would I speak to her*?

She asked me a question to which she already had the answer - "What is your goal in life?"

"Undoubtedly, to become an actor"

"Do you think your talent solely will help you in getting work?"

Somewhere she made a point. It was insane of me relying only on talent for work and more roles. To better understand her, I probed further-"And what do you want me to do?"

Her pause made me think of whether she comprehended what I said and understood me being quick-witted. But her answer made me relaxed about being a move ahead of hers.

"You are very innocent Pratik"

"Hmmm…", I uttered, not really knowing how to respond to her statement .

"Jahnvi has worked as an assistant director in a movie, and also she has started to direct short tele-movies. Surely, one day she will grow up to become a director.

Don't you think her friendship will benefit you in many ways?"- A mixture of enthusiasm and excitement mingled in her voice.

She made me think about her point. No doubt, there might be some personal benefit of hers but I was only calculating my advantage in the situation.

This industry works on good terms with each other, I already knew, but from where to begin to pull the strings was something I was unaware of. Having the props in front of me I wanted guidance on how to use them in the best possible way.

"I will send her a friend request on Facebook tomorrow"- my shattered confidence burst out in my voice.

She almost sang the word-"and?"

If an idea lies in the centre of the brain I had taken out the centrifugal force and hit the idea on all sides of the brain to check if the answer to it was lying there somewhere.

Failed in finding any I said-"and we'll become friends and she will give me work."

She laughed out her belly. Her way of laughing made it clear that somewhere what I spoke was not correct. Embarrassed with my answer I too shared few laughs with her and once her laughter abated she was prompt-"You are truly very innocent Pratik"

I continued laughing, not at the same pace but a bit slower. Embarrassment till then had got hold a tight grip of my hand and didn't want to leave it.

"From the word friendship I meant to propose her to be your girlfriend"-she cleared what exactly she meant and this too without any hesitation.

My eye balls till then which were moving from extreme left to extreme right ultimately paused. I understood what she said. Honestly, my brain too showed a green signal to her idea but my heart echoed the name JASNEET. Nothing further I could hear but that one name actually overpowered the brain's call.

Accelerating this discussion further my heart didn't licence me. The whole night I kept turning sides as I wasn't finding comfort anywhere, even tried to sleep on the couch but everything failed. Though, I found Payal's words' worthless but also a part of me fuelled to follow her suggestion.

"Will you betray Jasneet for your dreams?"- The heart spoke.

A prompt reply from my brain came-"Why to tell her? Anyway you guys haven't met for a year and don't know when you will meet her next."

My heart was crestfallen and said to my brain-"Since when have you become so evil?

"For years. I always waited for the right time."

"You are corrupting this innocent man"

"As if innocence has given him success? Huh"- there was a smirk in that tone which was evident.

Seeming my tilt in interest towards the brain, my heart called out-"Pratik, don't listen to him. Don't do anything wrong with that innocent girl."

Till the time I could understand any of the words of my heart I found myself at the brain's side after a tug of war.

I didn't say anything. Brain was happy to see me on its side. Heart was shattered. Life was on Columbus who was taking me back and forth on a swing.

"Till the time you will understand why I was right and he was wrong it will be too late."- The heart said, finally.

Brain totally empowered me till then. I could hear what the heart said but its voice was getting low and vision more blurry. After a time, my heart vanished somewhere in the dark.

9.

The aroma of fresh flowers filled the air, relatives were arriving and DJ was all set with his tracks. The perfect Punjabi wedding with all the sparkle was on.

While looking at Gurveer uncle and Binny aunty, our landlords, I wondered if they had known my family for just the last 4 months. Because that just didn't seem so the way mixed up with our relatives, as they always have been a part of them.

Nikhil, their son, didn't come out of the room if not mandatory; the young and shy lad hardly spoke to anyone. A couple of times I tried to mix up with him by initiating a conversation but every time I failed.

The ambience in the house was no less than that of a local fashion street where all the vendors might be calling out for something. A particular talk could be heard only if carefully focused.

"Rajni *didi* and family have arrived" – I heard Gautam shouting from the ground floor.

My heart beat got faster as I heard it. My body shivered due to the embarrassment of what I did on the last day before I left Delhi. Though, not being completely embarrassed of what I did, I was more engrossed with shame of how I did it.

Things could have been better and simpler but a person sailing on the boat of love is on cloud 9 and feels courageous to face any situation and trouble at his own level without considering what better solution any other person can provide.

As everyone rushed towards the door I stood still in the lobby. People bumped into me from my back but I remained unmoved. A part of me triggered me to run from there and the other half urged me to stay back and face the situation.

The vision between Rajni *didi* and me was covered by many

heads. I saw her hugging relatives coming her way. I caught sight of her eyes which were looking for someone. The movement of her eyes was faster than her legs going to meet everyone. Finally, after a few seconds she saw me standing at the end of the crowd and trying to hide myself. Pankaj *bhaiya* and *bhua ji* too were there but the churning of stomach was only felt once I saw or thought about Rajni *didi* as I knew I was a culprit only of Rajni *didi*.

She kept meeting everyone, shared smiles and greetings. Her lips had a broad smile but eyes weren't coordinating with lips.

When finally our eyes met through in between heads and shoulders neither of us blinked them for a few minutes. Neither she was angry nor was she happy to see me, she just remained cold.

Her gaze from me didn't get diverted even for a single moment. The smile that she wore while meeting people escaped from her lips after she saw me and now she had the same straight face that she had on the last day before I left Delhi.

Life became slower in that one minute. The chaos that was bustling since yesterday and that irritation somewhere flew away and for both of us and the world became silent. Neither could I hear the wailing of children nor murmuring of ladies anymore. I wanted to call back everyone there and request to continue everything. The closer she walked towards me, the faster I wanted to run from the place.

Passing everyone now we both were facing each other. Not even a mosquito dared to pass between our sites.

Half of my soul fuelled me to look down to pretend of being ashamed. The other half fuelled to face her as nothing is wrong in standing strong as an effigy for your love. I followed the latter's opinion.

Pankaj *bhaiya* crossed Rajni *didi* and hugged me- "Congratulations to the brother". Patted on my back twice and was aloud.

My eyes were finally distracted from Rajni *didi*. I too replied to Pankaj *bhaiya* warmly with equal fervour. Now it was my turn to greet *bhuaji* (my cousin aunt). I touched her feet and gave her a tight hug. She held my face between both her hands and softly pulled towards her. She kissed me on the forehead and said-"Hun tu vi vyaah karwalae" (you too should get married now)

I was wishing for someone to speak my name out; the cook, the decorator, the DJ, the stray dogs or anyone. I was desperate to escape from there. Rajni *didi* being the last to meet now, the thought itself opened each and every pour of the body and perspiration started as water flowed after the gates of the dam is opened. I somehow managed to control my wobbling legs but sweating wasn't in control.

"Where is Jahanvi?"-the first question she asked. And I very well knew where that was coming from.

"She will come to the wedding"-I looked aside after I said that.

From her end I didn't hear a single word after that for half a minute. From the corner of my eyes I knew she was looking at me but I didn't look back. I wanted to prove her wrong and was also happy at the same time that *didi* had attended the wedding. As I was thinking all this, Rajni *didi* said in a low tone- "I hope so"- and walked into the room.

I saw Mohit online on WhatsApp so I preferred dropping a message to him— "Hello Mohit, I hope you are in good health. Actually, I am waiting for a response from your side. I had called you a few times but it went unanswered." Though he was still online, he didn't read the message. I felt myhands turning cold because of being over-anxious.

"It's often said rejections are difficult to handle but what's more killing is the wait for the verdict to know whether it's rejection or acceptance."

10.

"Shall I or Shall I not?" – I kept tossing between the two thoughts I had in my mind.

"Do it dude, it's just a friend request and not a marriage proposal"- My optimist brain joke with me.

As I was concentrating on what my heart had to say on this I reminded myself of what happened last night. No response from heart stimulated my will of sending the request.

As soon as I sent the request I got a call from Jasneet- "Hey. What's Up?"

As if a notification was sent to Jasneet of me sending a friend request to another girl, I doubted.

"Nothing just at work"- I replied and pretended not to be surprised by her sudden call at 12 pm as I knew she had a lecture during that time.

"Busy?"- Her tone of extreme soft voice emerges once she is disheartened. Quickly understanding her trait I spoke promptly-"No, no I can manage" "Yeaahhhh…"- she sang in a childish way.

It was the first time when I was talking to Jasneet but was distracted and lost in my own world somewhere, as Jahanvi was constantly playing in my mind.

"Didn't you have a class at this time?"- I asked her.

"Yes. It was but Rekha Ma'am wanted to take the class as she was on leave last week and in a month students have their first semester exams. So, she requested to take my lecture and I accepted as I thought I would get time to speak to you"- her excitement and facial expression could easily be judged by the way she was narrating what exactly happened.

I heard a voice fall in my ears-"and you are going to fool her."

I looked around who that was but found no one. I thought this might be my heart but not, the most confusing relationship I was having was with my heart that already left me but kept working in me.

"Pratik??? Are you there?"- She asked. "Yes. Right here"- the voice was low.

"Is there anything that you want to say or discuss?"

Getting too close to someone is also dangerous. They know when you lie. They just know it.

Trying to act normal, I replied in the same tone as I always spoke to her-"thank God, Jyoti Ma'am was sitting next to me so I couldn't talk comfortably. I was waiting for her to leave."

She laughed at that heartily.

"Even if you get a minutes' time you would prefer talking to me. Isn't it?"- I asked her in my softest tone.

There was a pause at the other end of the phone. Though, the hullabaloo was harsh enough but still my right ear, on which I held my phone, could hear the sound of her thumping heart and long breaths.

A short smile automatically appeared on my lips as I knew what the answer would be-"even if I could sneak a second just to hear you"

My short smile instantly changed into a broad one as I heard it. My cheeks blushed. And again a void was created with hidden love in it which we both could sense.

My imagination of how she would be looking was distracted with a beep of notification. While Jasneet was on call I checked my mobile to see what I received, I dragged down the notification bar from the upper screen. It read a message on Facebook messenger from Jahanvi-

"So as you have initiated to send a request after good 19 days, I thought of messaging and initiating the chat." And after five seconds I received a wink.

The broad smile I acquired from Jasneet changed into a chuckle by Jahanvi.

I took the call back and assured her that I will give her a call after my current class gets wrapped. She as usual believed what I said and disconnected the call.

Eagerly, I opened the chat window and replied –"Good. Initiatives are the foundation of durable relations."

She read it as it was sent to her. I knew she would be thinking of a good reply as it surely was one trait of hers I acknowledged. Because she never dodges before completing what she wants to convey.

"Again a PJ?"- she replied

I was prompt this time too-"*chalo kahin toh P aur J ikathe hue* (at least somewhere P and J are together)"

"LMAO"-she sent.

I had no clue of where to take this conversation now. Whether I should ask her about where she resides which would be too early a question or what is your future plan which would be too late as I already am aware of her career plans.

Having no common topic apart from the movie we did, I preferred playing safe by talking about the same.

"So completed the shoot of that movie?" "You think we would wait for anything?" "Of course, for me. ;-)"

"*Zindagi Kisi Ke liye nahi rukti. Jaane wale chale jaate hai.* (Life doesn't stop for anyone. People who wish to go they just go)"

"Now that was too serious in between a healthy flirt"- I replied what I felt. "How do you exactly define healthy flirting?"- She questioned

"People kill themselves or their partner when they are in love. Have you ever heard two people dying because they were flirting with each other?"

Sent, delivered and read but thinking of an answer - her reply wasn't rapid enough. "Okay. But you haven't answered my question: how is flirting healthy?"

"If it wasn't then why would a broken heart enjoy talking to a guy who is flirting with him? Obviously, the wounds seemed to be getting healed."- I took no time in replying to that and I wished she didn't have an answer to it because if she does then I wouldn't for sure.

My gaze didn't leave its place for the next two minutes and I noticed her typing didn't appear.

"Blunder you have done Pratik. Why are you trying to bat in the open if you are a bowler?"

"Got to go, talk to you later"- she replied and she logged out.

11.

"Keshav has a play in the evening. Would you like to join?"- While I was busy in my class, a message from Payal caught my attention. I didn't reply to her there but kept it unread until I got free.

"What time?"- I replied after the class was dismissed and I headed towards the cafeteria.

She called me and I had to lift it, apathetically!

"I knew you were free as you only reply during office timings once you don't have any class"- Payal said.

"Hmm"- I accepted.

"See. I know you this much now"

Still bewildered about Jahanvi's abrupt reaction of leaving the conversation, my instinct of talking was permeated with despondency.

"So the play will start at 7:30pm sharp. We'll reach there by 7 to cheer Keshav In advance."

"Sure"- after disconnecting the call I again logged in Facebook messenger to check if Jahanvi was online so that I could apologise to her but unluckily she wasn't.

As I was infamous for being an incorrigible latecomer, I was late for the event too by half an hour and the play had already started.

As I entered the hall, I saw Keshav on the stage performing his character as a servant and a few more known faces performing. I felt better to sit than stand in between and distract the actors.

More than half of the hall was empty and only the first 10-12 lines were fully occupied. I sat on the third chair in the last row and messaged Payal- "Reached, sitting at the end."

As soon as she read the message I saw a girl from the first seat walking towards me. Unless my vision of the girl wasn't clear because of darkness I didn't know it was Payal.

I stood from my seat to greet her. She came dressed in a never before look which was quite tempting, I must admit. The black one piece she was wearing surely would have gotten many eye-balls rolling in the hall.

"Wooh. You are looking…S…s … Stunning"- the last word I changed from Sexy to stunning just because like Jahanvi I didn't want her to misunderstand me.

With her never before look I saw her never before blush too through which her cheeks turned red.

Understanding a requisite diversion of the time I asked her to step forward and grab a seat.

"There is no free seat available in front"- she was prompt. "So we have to be seated somewhere in the middle row."

Her hesitation in saying something didn't last long and she said- "Can't we just sit here?"

"No doubt we can, but aren't we becoming two Eskimos living in an isolated igloo?"- She laughed as I said it and offered her the seat I was sitting at and got myself the next.

At every dialog delivered by Keshav, people in the hall clapped loudly. He has gotten better from his first performance. I was well pleased by his acting prowess.

"He is so good. Isn't he?"- Payal in excitement said this and held my hand, which didn't appear like a…………………………… Action to me.

I nodded and was waiting for her to leave my hand.

"I wish you to get the same applause once you get your very first break in movies"- she slid her fingers into mine and held my left hand tightly.

Now my less concentration was on the play and more was on how to release my hand.

"How about Jahanvi? Have you sent the request?"

My mind gave me an instant signal and I withdrew my hand from her and took my phone out of my pocket and showed her the chat.

She read it carefully. I noticed her facial expressions change while reading it. She tried best hiding her exasperation but failed, the hopeless actress she was, I considered. I somehow loved it.

Once she was done she looked at me and made a pity face and the change in expressions made her gain brownie points of being a subtle actress and prove herself-"Awww... you are so cute Pratik." She hugged me, which was a bolt out of the blue.

She was chuckling and saying in my ears-"I always wished for a cute and innocent boy like you". I remained stoned there.

All my senses seemed to be suspended that moment and unable to think of how to react. I didn't even look around to check if anyone watched us. This passed the wrong message to her and she continued what she had pre-decided. She took my face in her palms and looked into my eyes deep. Within a minute she kissed my lips. To put it truthfully, I too was electrified and responded to her kiss. Not even a second after I closed my eyes and Jasneet's face appeared in front of my eyes.

With a jerk, I shoved her off me.

Payal narrowed her eyes to understand my reaction. I walked out of the hall and stood in the corridor where I felt captivated by guilt and was watching the lighting of the city.

I wanted to talk to Jasneet that very moment, so I put my left hand in the left pocket of my jeans to take my phone out but found it wasn't there. I checked in each and every pocket and found it nowhere, where could I have left it! With every pocket I was looking for it, the search was making me more frantic.

The thought of whether I could have left it in the hall made me turn out to go back and look for it, but the moment I turned, I found Payal standing with my phone in her hand- "Here it is"

I took my phone from her and slid it in the pocket. She came and stood beside me. There was a complete awkward silence between us. I wanted to make her clear about my feelings for her which was just nothing beyond friendship and my brain urged me to immediately leave that place.

The only noise which was killing the silence between us was that of the hall's hubbub. It too was volatile and flew away as the door was pressed closed.

"Look I am not sorry for what I did…"- Payal said without looking at me.

From the corner of my eyes my vision fell on her and without turning my face towards her I completed the second part of the sentence-"but I am"

A clearance from my side was required and once again the silence prevailed and was persistent for a longer period than before.

A beep on my phone filtered Payal from my mind and helped to centralise on mobile.

"Reached home?"- Jasneet messaged.

After her message the guilt in me clutched my hand again. "Not yet. Will call you once I am home."- I typed.

I accelerated towards Payal and in rage and I said-"look, I had cleared you this before too that I have no such feelings for you and please don't cross your line lest I would have to end up this friendship here"

As I completed, Payal fell on her knees and with hands joined and pleaded-"Please don't leave me Pratik. I am really sorry. Please don't stop talking to me. Please… please… please."- She kept repeating the last word along with her wailing. Every please was a bit slower than the last but she didn't end up saying so.

Going all berserk with what was happening, I rubbed my face with my hands and took a sigh before speaking-"Get up Payal, don't create a scene here"

She didn't listen to it and stayed there. Thankfully, she stopped crying. I held her from her shoulders and helped her stand.

12.

A week's chat day and night managed to resolve the issues between us. Jahanvi and I were finally meeting for the first time after the shoot. I timely reminded my tongue to speak just when needed and only the most appropriate, taking my experience with her into account.

I gulped a sigh of relief after she replied to me on the third day and ignored what I had said above. Not a single day in the seven we spoke she mentioned about our previous chat.

But deep down in my heart I wanted to apologise, if by any means I had offended her unknowingly.

"You order"- I slid the menu to her to which she responded with a smile.

My gaze remained glued till the time she was looking at the menu. Her soft curls with long locks were highlighted with light red colour. Her heart shaped face couldn't get a better hair cut than that, I mused to myself. Above her sharp edged chin was her heart shaped lips which were little lump. Through the rayon yellow semi stitched *kurti* she wore had ban collar, I could see she had sharp collar bones. The green flowers embroidered on her *kurti* were filled with yellow and red colours which were a never seen design for me. A coalition of red and yellow colour' *churidar salwar* she wore matched her marigold-coloured ballerinas. Her stiletto shaped nails were alluring as she wore sea green paint on it.

"What would you like to have?"

My dropped jaw was repulsed as I heard her asking me. I started to rub my eyes to hide my act of staring at her. She got to know I guess but avoided. Without looking at her I said-"order it double whatever you decide"

"Do you like pastry? They make it delicious here"- I heard her excitement in her voice as she mentioned it.

I nodded and kept steering clear ceaselessly.

I heard her saying to the waiter-"two fudgy stout brownies and Marocchino"

"You seem to be a regular customer here."- I asked her.

She gave a short smile and with a short pause she said-"Yes. Whenever I want peace in my life I come here. Like whenever I want to write I prefer sitting here."

I knew there was something more to its truth, rigid of my trait of investigating in detail I asked-"And?"

The smile disappeared from her lips and I noticed she knit her brows.

"Anndddddd..?"- Her extended tone with a spice of hesitation and anxiousness made it apparent of concealing something.

I took a few seconds to ask her. Also, I was waiting for her to speak up.

She avoided going further on the road we started to walk on. Her twirl from the topic made it evident that something from her past is still pinned to her heart.

Understanding the awkwardness, I changed the topic-"Thank you for coming"

Till then her eyes were stuck on the menu that was on the table between us. Those non-blinking eyes assured me that some events from the past were playing in her mind.

(Awakened from her dreams from which she got a short smile was expanded for replying to me.)

The silence which evaded between us, occupied its space back after a few seconds.

The two of us acted in a way as we were made to sit with each other for an arranged marriage. She as a would-be bride who couldn't overcome her recent break-up was desolated and I was too timid as the fear of being rejected once again had gripped me.

As the coffee arrived we added sugar and she initiated with her first sip. As I got the permission to start, I noticed I gulped half the coffee at one.

There was a time when shadow too set me free but embarrassment of playing the role of best supporting actor had no such plans. It stands straight and still beside me and becomes active when Jahanvi is around.

Silently after finishing our coffee we were waiting for the other to start eating pastry and leave the place.

A little about the next projects, about our interest in films, and we called it a day. Nothing personal we discussed.

A wave, handshake, or a half hugs…? I kept thinking of how to bid her goodbye after we stepped out of the café and reached the parking area. I noticed she already was on her wheels and stopped beside me and said-'Goodbye" with a short smile.

13.

"Who is coming with you to the wedding?"- After contemplating multiple reasons in my mind to initiate a conversation with Jahanvi, I finally found one reason which seemed to be authentic.

She appeared online later than she usually does. Passing on the chores to my cousins I sat in the *verandah* and waited for her reply.

She read the message but didn't reply promptly. Rajni *didi* arrived earlier than Jahanvi's message.

"So how is she?"- She softly asked me.

I turned towards her but without looking into her eyes I replied- "Good enough" "I hope things are better between you two."

She understands me quite well and knew my act of avoiding her when I would lie.

A lie we both had known but it was unspoken as it was laced with hope; a hope that it might become a reality with a snap of fingers.

"Did Udit unblock you?"- She asked a question which had been a mystery for us both.

I shook my head as I didn't have an answer to this.

Silence sustained once again between us. All of a sudden I couldn't hear any hustle bustle around me. Though, I could see the children playing around me and also the cooks who were deep frying fritters. The vision was of the present but audio of the past got mixed up and I could hear the voice of Jahanvi and me screaming at each other.

"You doubt me Pratik"

"I doubt you? You give reasons to do so" "He is just a friend"

"So? Does it mean you can go to a hotel to sleep together?" "We were stuck"

"Wow. Why did you lie then?"

I was shaken by Rajni *didi* many times before too as I became numb-"Pratik Pratik… Are you okay?"

"Huh…"- I turned my head to all corners of the surroundings, all jerked back to reality. Whether I was searching for Jahanvi around me or for the answer which still haunts me I couldn't understand but smarter was *didi* who understood my situation and took me upstairs to feed me.

She brought a plate of rice and *rajmah* with some mixed vegetables that was cooked, exactly the way I Loved it and the same manner as how we used to eat together in Delhi.

We both silently ate food from the same plate. No one initiated any talk. There was a gap that acquired in between us; a gap that got space because of me.

While we were eating I heard a beep sound on my phone and in haste I took my phone out of my jeans' pocket as I knew it would be Jahanvi.

"Congratulations for didi's marriage"- the phone number was unsaved so I replied to the person-"Thank you so much. I guess I lost your contact. Can you provide your name?"

Though in no time the message was read, the reply didn't depart from the other side. I too after waiting for a few minutes dropped interest in knowing the identity of the person.

Dixita *didi* came home from the parlour and I saw no change in her! "What have you undergone?"- I asked with my brows narrowed.

The enthusiasm with which she narrated about the long session she had in the salon as if she always waited for someone to ask this question.

"A lot of things, for my face I had to clean up, basic and advanced facial, face mask. For my body I had body massage, body polishing and *ubtan*. For hair…" she couldn't even complete it when I stopped her mid-sentence. So many things she had got done but still looked just the same because she had always been this beautiful.

I didn't react to that. My expression remained unchanged. This sullen look of me actually bothered her and she threw the stole she was carrying-"Hey… What happened?"

I preferred looking down than into her eyes. Though I was assured Jahanvi was coming in the evening and most probably things are going to re-acquire their place but still a pin continuously was aching in my heart and I was feeling emptiness.

"With *bhabhi* and *bhaiya*"- a reply came from Jahanvi.

This helped me to escape the situation. That very moment, I kissed *didi* on her forehead and I walked out of the house.

As I jumped out of Jahanvi's chat screen the unknown number popped up again and my instinctive reaction was - who is this! I copied the number and pasted on the true caller to check the name of the person but no luck.

I opened WhatsApp once again and checked if the name appears on the person's bio and it stated EKAM. From it, the identity of the person was revealed as it read EKAM; it was Jasneet as she had put this name on her WhatsApp which literally translated to God. Her message after more than a year got me by no surprise as I knew she would certainly message.

Mohit had a meeting today with his boss. He was assured of the project being accepted as it is a yes from his side but a formal discussion with the boss for ago ahead was pending. As it was company's norms and he being an employee has to follow the protocol. The project is extremely close to my heart and it actually meant second innings for me. Every time I would think of calling or texting him, I would feel a churning feeling in my stomach.

Even in our worst days we refill our hearts by saying-"There surely would be something better in store for us". Whereas the heart chuckles, once again, and says- "Another hope to keep me going!"

14.

Two days passed but none among us broke the ice which was stored after our first so-called date. I was guilt-ridden for speaking out something that day which I shouldn't have. I was completely oblivious to the reason for her getting upset with me.

Jasneet was busy with her *maasi* (Maternal aunt) who flew from Canada. Constant messages from Payal were seeking attention which was totally on Jahanvi who wasn't messaging.

Jahanvi secured a quiet cosy corner somewhere in my heart - which I couldn't think any further beyond her all day.

Time and again I was opening Facebook messages to check if she was online and this was certainly making me jumpy.

So ignoring Payal's messages I opened Facebook and started to look Jahanvi's pictures. Her every picture was eye-catchy and hypnotised me.

"Hi"- a message from Jahanvi appeared on the screen.

As soon as I witnessed it arriving I clicked on the message and replied-"Hello. How are you?"

"Great. And you?" "I am good too" *Typing...*

Oasis to a researcher and her message to me had equal meaning. "Look I am extremely sorry for the way I behaved with you that day."

"Ahh... that's totally cool. I understand," I tried to sound as calm and composed as I could.

I read the word typing appeared twice but then there was a pause. I thought she was writing a long message but to my surprise the message I received was-"Coffee today? Same place."

I agreed and reached there before her this time.

"In time, not bad Mr. Sharma"- I heard her voice coming from behind me.

My lips parted as much as they could. From her voice and her way of greeting, it gave me a feeler that this was going to be a special day.

Standing from my seat I passed her the bouquet I had bought for her. She (raised) her brows in surprise- "So you are respectful too, I thought you only knew the art of flirting."

I offered her the seat as I had no reply to the line she just said. "So… what would you like to have?"

She gave a smile before answering my question. After staring at me for nearly half a minute she kept her right hand on her lips to hide her smile.

Though the smile was on my lips too but it appeared after I saw her smiling. "What?"- I asked with an unbroken smile.

She shook her head and looked to her right.

I quickly picked my mobile which I kept on the table and checked my face in the camera if something about it made it look funny. As there was nothing, I checked the second thing which can be the reason for embarrassment for a boy - my trousers' zip. To my surprise the zip too was intact.

"What happened?"- I asked slowly so that it sends a message to her to reply in the same tone.

She turned towards me and answered-"It appears from your face as if you have come to meet a girl for marriage."

I narrowed my brows to decipher her confusing statement.

"Full sleeved shirt which is tucked in these trousers. This steel chained watch and… why have you bought this bouquet?"

I scratched my chin and abused my friend Ashween who once gave me this advice of giving a girl a bouquet once you go to see her.

"Formals in teaching and Hijab in Islam are the same. Some wear it by choice and some don't have any choice."- I wanted to speak in a soft tone but she found it to be harsh.

"I am extremely sorry if I offended you in any way"- she developed a sombre expression soon after she said.

"Hey… it's cool. Take a chill. I was just kidding"- I wanted to explain how clothes have an effect on my outlook and the way I behave. But somehow I knew it would be difficult for her to understand this. The Pratik she might meet at home in pyjamas is poles apart from the well suited Pratik in the office.

She passed a half smile but didn't utter a single word.

"So what would you like to eat?"- I continued the conversation as I didn't want to spoil our second meeting too and let silence overpower once again.

She got her smile back and replied-"Let's see how you arrange things today." She winked after saying that and my soul called out- "Judgement day!"

Arrange something for a girl? This was going to be hilarious. It was like a surprise test on the first day for a student who's never attended a single lecture the entire academic year.

I opened the menu and read the contents.

The biggest task which was given to me was spinning my head. The names I never read before; "Cafe' Americano, Café Latte, Cappuccino, Espresso, Flat White, Long Black, Macchiato, Marocchino, Irish coffee, Vienna, Affogato, Hazelnut and what not!" I just couldn't comprehend what all these names meant! This made my palms sweaty. I could see my friends in the coffee shop who were dancing at my situation and were tearing the flesh of chicken wings with their teeth because if ever I had been out I was with my gang of 6 boys and the only place we had been to was THE BON'O'FIRE – a typical stag hangout.

Being unable to understand any I recalled the name of the coffee she ordered last time and I ordered the same-"two fudgy stout brownies and Marocchinos"

She bit her lower lip to not let them give a full smile. She asked- "Sorry to offend you. Is this the first time you came to a coffee shop?"

Being the first visit with Payal a few weeks ago was something I would not like to be counted so mentioning it to Jahanvi was of no point. Thus, I looked downwards and nodded, without speaking a word. The sweat which till then could be felt in my palms now was rolling down from the back of my right ear and was slipping till the collar, I itched and replied, "Second. The first time was the last time we came together"

She passed a half smile and assured us of our further meetings- "Don't worry, I promise you too will get addicted to this place and will visit alone just as I do."

15.

"Thank you Jasneet" - I replied her message

"Please send me pictures of *didi* as I always wished to see her in wedding attire" – she was prompt with her message.

This made me nostalgic and I remembered the day we had discussed every little detail about her being beside *didi* during every ceremony. So much discussion we had that we even discussed which shade dresses she would wear during all the ceremonies.

After approximately one and a half years when a sudden message came from her, I was happy enough. I wanted to apologise to her for the way I reacted last time with her. In the list of people I was ashamed of I guess Jasneet was on the top.

I was taken back into consciousness by *maa's* voice-"Where are your pandas? I hope you have called them, as you remember you have to go to the resort"

I closed my chat with Jasneet and typed-"Be here in 15 minutes or you guys will be killed"- I sent the message on my WhatsApp group-The Bored Pandas. It was read by two of my friends who further called rest three and all were at my house in 30 minutes, ready to move.

Babu, Sarabjeet, Aarohan, Gagan, and Kanav once reached as usual were with the cooks and eating from one plate which was being carried by Aarohan because we find itikatha khaane *se pyar badhta hai* (love becomes stronger if we eat from the same plate) which actually meant *I am too lazy to use my left hand to hold a plate!*

As soon as I walked to them their ongoing discussion was slackened. Their gestures were obnoxious to me as none of them looked towards me but passed a hello. This is how deeply involved they were in eating.

"These cheese fingers are absolutely delicious. Have you tried?"-

Gagan offered it to me.

I looked at each one of them and somewhere deep down in my heart knew what they would be discussing. I still preferred to clear the doubt.

I took some time to think before starting the discussion by myself but before me it was Sarabjeet who spoke-"Pratik, don't you think something is missing?"

I was satisfied enough that Sarabjeet's move to start the conversation made it easier for me to speak but also it gave me goosebumps.

I knew they wanted Jahanvi to be present during wedding preparations. This was something I dreamt of and even had bet with them on it. As I failed to complete it, so I thought it was quite generous of them to not tease me by questioning and jiggling my beliefs.

"She was supposed to be here with us today but I asked her not to as there is not much work here. Hence, she is coming tomorrow evening"- I assured them the same way I assured Rajni didi.

Babu, Aarohan, Kanav and Gagan gave a look first to me and then Sarabjeet and turned their heads back at me. I saw them switching the sides of their heads with subtle co-ordination as if they had already practised it.

The environment around us became silent all of a sudden. My heart started to beat faster and the lub-dub sound of my heart could be felt in my chest. The way each person gave me that doubtful stare, it literally shook my confidence of Jahanvi coming to the wedding.

I gulped the water that was already in my throat and my tongue was getting dried up repeatedly.

Sarabjeet, who didn't speak anything for quite a long time finally spoke-"I was talking about tartar sauce. I guess it would be better if there was tartar sauce than normal ketchup being served with this"

Though no one dared to laugh at the situation, I simply couldn't hold it. As I started to laugh, everyone followed me which was reminiscent of our good old school days.

After a long time I had such a gala time. After a long time I was convulsed with laughter that too with my old buddies.

As laughter mollified firstly I looked at Babu with whom my cold war had started after the fight we had. His eyes had a blend of emotions; anger, sympathy, happiness and sadness. Anger was obviously because of the impertinent behaviour I showed to him. Sympathy for me somewhere as he was still stuck with his opinion, happiness because I finally was happy as it was a happy occasion of *didi's* wedding and not to forget my patch up with Jahanvi, but I couldn't understand why he had droplets of tears in his eyes. There was a pain which he stored in there which was unclear to me.

Finally, I gathered a colossal amount of courage and took a deep breath – thereafter I messaged Jasneet-"Will you ever forgive me?"

Though the message was read by her without any delay, the reply was not instant. "I already have Pratik"

"I hope you forget me too"

I could imagine how her reaction would be while reading these messages as after reading hers I could hear her voice echoing in my ear.

"Sometimes it's easier to forgive than to forget"

As she said this line I was taken back into 2015 when I proposed Jahanvi. Until then I could hear the voice of Jasneet in her messages but her last sentence I heard in Jahanvi's voice. Strange or beautiful, I don't know what was it?

My perturbation could be easily sensed by anyone passing me. The warmth of my body wasn't only because of marriage's sprints but because of the many emotions which were overlapping. Apart from Jahanvi's concern that I had, I was also concerned about the meeting that was taking place in the same city which was a few kilometres away from my home. My future was being decided in a 20*30 rooms where two people were discussing the approval of the project.

"Struggle is never about walking on the path of your life where you are waiting for success, undoubtedly, Success is certain on that path. Struggle is to perceive the path and wait for that opportunity which lets you start walking on it."

16.

Since I started to date Jahanvi, my interest in talking with Jasneet and Payal plunged. I would still talk to Jasneet at times but to Payal not even a minuscule of me felt like speaking to her. But beyond my knowledge, this entire thing wasn't being taken well by her. This was revealed to me one day when I learnt I was being stalked by whom? Payal – every time and every possible place I would go out with Jahanvi.

"Meet me at the theatre this evening after work."

I read Payal's message while I was in class and didn't reply to her. Once the class finished I replied back-"I have to go somewhere in the evening. Will meet some other day"

As always once she got my instant reply that day too she called and spoke in undertone-"I know you have to go to meet Jahanvi today at 5 but she won't be able to come today as she already has a meeting lined up with a director. So, as you are free I believe you can come"

I was taken aback by the details of her statement. What Jahanvi hadn't discussed with me yet, how does Payal know about it? While thinking about the consequences of Payal's intervention between Jhanvi's and me, my dream was broken with the vibration of my mobile. I took it out from the pocket and opened a message from Jahanvi-"Can't meet today as I got to meet a director. See you tomorrow. Sorry."

****

Payal and I were sitting opposite to each other in a restaurant named Dolphin as the theatre area wasn't free and I needed to clear things with her.

Sitting opposite each other I wanted her to initiate the conversation. My upper and lower eye lashes combated to blink but I couldn't do it. It was my way of controlling my vexation, just at the sheer look of her.

"I know you have many questions in your mind but I want to save you from the witch"

"Mind your language Payal"- Her statement provoked me to yell at her, which isn't a part of my nature at all.

She nodded two times before continuing –"I am sorry. I know that you have started to like her. Also, I won't deny the fact that I have been stalking you two, but honestly I am here to save you."

"Save you!" I thought aloud inside my head - who made her my saviour? My patience which couldn't be easily shaken was fuelled by her and I got up from my seat to avoid any further discussion with her.

"Before leaving I want to tell you one thing. We are good friends and not actually dating"-as I was about to turn and leave she grabbed my right arm and stood along.

"I am really sorry if I hurt you"-in her extremely soft tone she continued-"Please sit, I want to tell you something."

I agreed with her and wanted to finish listening to her and leave immediately after. So I sat there.

Before starting to, what she wanted, speak, she unlocked her phone and kept it in front of me.

I looked at the phone which contained pictures of Jahanvi and a boy when she was a teen. As I started to swipe, the pictures depicted the cordial bond they shared while growing up. Both eating ice cream from the same cup, dancing in a pub, outside a cinema hall and many more similar pictures, which narrated the same tale.

The last picture in the slide was of Jahanvi wearing a black saree whereas the boy wore a black tuxedo, it seems to be a recent click as she looked exactly the same, "He might be the boy she was in relation with"-I thought to myself.

I realised how stubborn I had become till then to prove Payal wrong that I lied-"I already know about him. He was her ex from school. Do you think she hid this from me?

Her expressions didn't change for quite a long time and she spoke-

"I want you to be safe and don't fall in love with this girl. She is cunning. I must warn you. This was the reason I managed to collect these photographs. Use her, get some links and focus on your career."

She added with a pause-"On the way to find the rock, the searcher finds many pebbles on the way. To make the boring road entertaining pebbles may help to kill time but can you compromise rocks for pebbles?"

Though she was correct on her part and I too felt as if I was distracted from my goal I am unlike her and can't really betray anyone.

"Thank you for your concern Payal"- I replied being disagreeable with her.

17.

Two army men died saving a civilian. One in the pack of four rolled over the dead body and got a place to hide himself behind a burnt sedan car. Softly placing his right hand first, the second army man peeped from the barricade he was hidden in which had put strain on his right shoulder on which he was shot by a bullet. But the audacious man managed to fall at the side of the former's and landed safe.

Bullets arriving at this side were persistent and the two were unknown of how many would be out there. Also, the exact way to exit and win this battle was undisclosed. What surety they had was the remaining civilians who were captivated had hopes on the army. They nodded at each other and the two stood at their places and started to fire and throw bombs. They were successful in overweighting the situation and moving further.

"I am so sorry I am late by 15 minutes"- I heard the voice of Jahanvi.

I clicked on the home key and didn't save the game just not to show her how I killed time in her absence. Soon, I adjusted myself upwards on the sofa I was almost half lying on.

While keeping her purse on the table she gazed at me and smiled- "It's okay baba, you don't have to showcase your disciplinary attitude with me. You have a friend around and not a student… Sir"- and she winked.

Without looking at her I slid my mobile slowly in my pocket in the hope she hadn't noticed it.

"And you should have saved this round. I hadn't even reached this far"- she said in a disappointing tone.

In haste I asked-"You saw that… that I was playing?" and covered my mouth with my palm while resting the elbow on the left armrest.

"Oh please come out of the teacher's act and let go of the sophistication"- she said with a right hand on my face.

I started to think that's exactly what I wanted to listen to for a long time and it made me happy. My pause somewhere made her uncomfortable and she cleared what she meant.

"I am sorry if I was rude. I just meant that you don't have any students here so you can act chilled."

The clearance was required from me as well so I leaned forward and said- "Correction there, trainer and not a teacher."

She passed a half smile and nodded.

My heart skips a beat only when she gazes at me and the addition of her smile I feel it skipping several times more.

Being crestfallen after she made me the captain of the ship for ordering food last time, today she had no second thoughts!

While she was busy deciding on the food, my thought was going haywire with the pictures Payal showed to me playing at the back of my mind. I somewhere had the slightest clue of her breaking up her last relation but a clearance from her was required. Also, a part of me poked to know the reason why clarification was such a big deal for me! Being honest to me, my heart reminded of Jasneet but brain anchored my feeling to career.

With the snap of her fingers I became conscious-"Where are you lost?" she asked me.

"Can I ask you about your boyfriend?"

The smile she wore on her lips faded away in no time. I noticed her eye balls started to sprint from left to right and repeat. Her brows were frowned and anxious about her beauty.

Waiting for a reply after a donkey's years I couldn't sanction her more minutes. I firmly asked-"You can share with me. Trust me."

As soon as I completed she was filled with remorse, which was very evident from her face. Her lips were parted as there were some words which existed behind them but she didn't allow them to emit.

With a shake she ignored me.

"See if you don't want…"- I didn't even complete when she spoke without looking at me-"Rohit, my neighbour, the boy whom I loved since childhood. We accompanied each other to school, tuitions, movies, dance classes, everywhere. He proposed to me when we were in Class 10th but it was just a formality. We didn't need those three words to formally begin our already begun relationship."

As she continued I noticed the re-emergence of felicity on her face.

"The best thing was her hobby of photography, which was similar to both of us. We also decided on our company's name. RJ CLICKS. Life was beautiful back then."

On the other hand, I was more interested to hear the synopsis rather than reading every line of the chapter-"Why did you break the…?"

Vamoose of her smile was quicker than the blinking of eyes. As soon as I examined it I paused and decided not to wake up dead from the grave.

Not much time had passed when she initiated herself-"We decided to get married and talk to our families. It was then when we came across the truth about Rohit's younger brother Rahul - who loved me too but only silently. Rahul used to accompany me every time Rohit and I used to go out, but I had no idea that he silently loved me. Thus, their mother denied the proposal of our marriage for the sake of family's bond."

I saw her eyes being filled with tears as she spoke. This unusual story somewhere captivated her dreams and left her in isolation for months. Regular counselling sessions helped her overcome the desolation, but it still lingered in some quiet corner of her heart.

"Why didn't you two elope instead?"- I questioned

She smirked and replied with her brows raised-"Rohit was a pure mamma's boy. He never stepped out of his home without her permission. This thing which I initially thought was sweet made me eventually exasperated at him when I asked him for the same." After taking a sigh she continued-"He didn't have the guts to do so."

"Hmmmm…"- I was so engrossed listening to her story that I couldn't realise that Jasneet had been calling me for a long time. And when I noticed the call was already disconnected and there were three consecutive missed calls from her. For the first time since I started talking to Jasneet, the day arrived when the chance to talk to her didn't fuel me. This divergence from Jasneet to Jahanvi was actually a result of this conversation and the sympathy which arose out of it for Jahanvi.

"How long has it been since you two broke up?" "One and a half year… approximately"

"Why haven't you moved on?"

She politely smiled looking at me and said-"I have moved on"

Her smile threw a clue at me.

A clue is the most unstable state for any boy. His mind oscillates between friendship and onset of a relationship after a girl throws one. If the girl means friendship here and you initiate it thinking of a relationship, the victim card will work for girls and it will make you a culprit for being a creep. If the girl meant relationship and you initiated as friendship the same victim card will be played after years of you being the culprit as she gave a hint and you were dumb enough not to initiate it.

I wanted neither so I further investigated-"Moved… on… as…in…? "My camera is my new partner. We go together wherever we want to. No demands. No hopes. No promises"- there was a sense of exuberance as she cleared it.

"Will you ever forget him?

Her half smile became minimal but this time it didn't escape completely- "Sometimes it's easier to forgive than forget. I cannot forget him ever but at least I can forgive him"

Her line made me think of the deep meaning it had hidden in it. I smirked and softly nodded.

"As we have already telling tales of truth then one more about me that I am an adopted child"

With a frown in my eyes, I Signalled with a nod to -GO ON, she continued-"My real dad and mom are my Chacha and Chachi (Paternal uncle and aunt). They already had two daughters and at the time of my birth they were highly expecting a boy. Unexpectedly when this time too, when a girl was born, they ultimately decided get rid of me by killing me. But it was my current parents who adopted me as they have three sons and had no daughter, thus I lived on."

I was numb and that time with a straight face I was speechless. She added-"My childhood was not easy either. I felt abandoned at times, and had no friends.

Children in school used to bully me for being adopted and it was Rohit who eventually became my best friend. I never needed anyone's support because I felt protected when he was around. Rahul, on the other hand, was more than a younger brother to me. I had no clue of our life-story would turn upside down this way.

Hence, on the day when Rohit met me and discussed his decision of breaking-up I was sunk into agony. I ended up in hospital for 15 days and was diagnosed with stomach ulcers after being in depression for months."- My gaze didn't diverge even for a moment while she spoke.

She continued in her soft tone-"Have you ever loved anyone so much Pratik that when they leave you, your eyes don't cry just because your heart won't accept the truth. I almost lost my soul on that day. And this Jahanvi what you see walking happily is dead within."

After seeing me unmoved there was a twirl in her expressions- "Okay, so we had enough discussion about my life. Tell me about your story now."

Suddenly, imaginary Ashween was back beside me as a guide and I repeated what was taught to me by him-"It's very simple to make a girl fall in love with you. Just play the role of being heartbroken. The girl you loved the most in life left you for so and so reason." While my one ear echoed Ashween's words, the second ear echoed Payal's words-"Make her your girlfriend, fetch links those you need and move on"

"Pratik. Are you…" she hadn't even completed when I spoke-

"She got married"

Unable to understand why those words appeared on my lips, my second task of thinking of the story further in this sentence was what made me fidgety.

Bending my head I dropped my eyes at the newspaper kept on the table between us-"Another couple killed in the town for the sake of honour". I thanked my creative mind who instantly developed a story and I started in my low tone-

"Rajdeep, her name. She was with me in college. I proposed to her after our first year ended. She too loved me and it was going well enough till the third year finished and she had to head back to her village. It was just a message of hers that came one evening. **Getting married. Family is forcing. I hope you understand and try to forget me. I spoke about you at home but dad wants me to get married to his friend's son in Canada as he has already given his word to him.** I tried to reach her number for many days but it was switched off."

As I completed and looked at Jahanvi I saw her changed expression from melancholic to wrath and she threw a hissy fit-"What the hell. I mean how can someone do this? At least, speak for one last time to conclude it well, talk to bye."

"Talk to bye? What is it?"

"Talk to bye is when you end a relation it's better to talk before you say bye so that you don't have grudges later. Every relationship is beautiful in its own way and ending always makes it drastic and painful. Hence, we live cursing the other person throughout. Talking to bye helps to not live in such a condition."

I heard the inner Pratik chuckling after he heard it. Though, I pretended to be a serious listener but my teeth betrayed me and I smiled when the set of teeth played the real protagonist.

Though I came back home that evening my heart still was left out there at the café. Her story and her suffering were revolving in my head.

18.

Late evening when the rest of the members of the family gathered, I was continuously receiving messages from Jasneet of multiple things like "to do" list and "not to do" in ceremonies. I accepted her request which she made during the day about being with me throughout the wedding till the end and later she would never contact me again in life. I accepted it for her happiness as there was a day when the dream of being around *didi* on her wedding was shared with her and not Jahanvi. Knowing well the fact that when Jahanvi would come to know the truth of Jasneet and me still being having a conversation, this would certainly mess my relationship with Jahanvi but I also knew Jasneet that she never breaks her promises. Hence, I accepted her being my side for the help.

"Have you brought pots with decorated lights for *Jaago*? "Check"

"Decorated sticks?" "Check"

"Ordered a *dholwala*??(Ordered a *dhol* player?) "I guess so dad has done it. Let me check the list"

Soon after I was assured of the arrangement a *dhol* done by papa I replied to her- "check"

"Lemme think of something else too"

Till the time I hadn't received her message I ran upstairs into my room to change into my *jaago* night attire. Sliding the wardrobe's door to the right I took out my ethnic *kurta-pyjama* that I had decided to wear. Not taking much long to wear the dress I applied wax on the hair and sprayed my favourite perfume.

Continuous thumping of the door puzzled me and I clicked the picture in haste and shared it with Jahanvi and opened the door. It was Mamta *bhua* who couldn't wait long enough to change. With a push on my shoulder she entered the room and said-

"*Hatt piche. Janaani naalo zyada time lgaana hai tu taan.*"(Move aside. You take longer than a woman to get ready)

"Where is the brooch?"- Jahanavi messaged.

Till the time I could barely ask to pass the brooch, *bhua* shut the door on my face.

"I just got out of the room, bhua is getting ready - will get it in 5 minutes once she gets ready."

"And you think it will take her 5 minutes?"

"Yes. Because I took seven and she taunted me for taking more than a woman to get ready."

"Hahahaha… Pratik. Go get some other work to do. She would not step out before a minimum half an hour."

Though I was disappointed as I had forgotten to wear the brooch she selected for me, nevertheless I was at cloud 9 of making her laugh. It had been 4 long months when we shared some smiles together and this moment would be remembered for years.

"*Chajj*"- Jasneet messaged in between Jahanvi's message to which I became conscious because nothing similar sounding was anywhere written on the list.

"Is it important?"-I asked.

"I knew you would forget something as always. Go run. Get it. *Daadi* would kill you either"

I started looking for my cousin brother, Gautam, who I knew would be around the DJ insisting his favourite Punjabi beats to be played and within seconds I received another message from Jasneet saying-"Your *daadi**"

My legs just froze there after I read her message. This was reminiscent of the days when we referred to each other's family members with the same relation.

I opened the chat box of Jahanvi who became offline and so did Jasneet after she sent the message.

I felt like a child whose parents had lost hold of his hand in a strange place. Evacuation of both at the same time dragged me into an isolated state. The state was, in reality, an outcome of multiple things together as mistakes, circumstances and fortune.

With a hope I would undo the mistakes I did intentionally and unintentionallyboth I tilted my plans for life. I chose Mohit as my coxswain who would help in steering my life into the right direction. I knew the meeting probably would have been over as the day passed and it was 8 in the evening. The last thought which hit my mind was of calling Mohit and checking about the meeting but the latter thought overweighs the former wherein I thought of waiting till tomorrow as it would be absurd to call at odd hours. Hence, I became a strongadherent to the latter's point of view.

"It's foolish to keep walking in the dark no matter how determined you are for your goal. It's better to be late than bumping into things and hurting yourself. Let the sun rise and clear the vision. It's wise and best to wait and plan till then."

19.

"I still don't realise I'm Actually doing it, Pratik"— she messaged

"You are my brave kid. I will be there within the next 10 minutes."— I replied to her with a broad smile on my face.

From a nearby town Hoshiarpur she never dared to visit Phagwara which is mere 37 kms away, without her elder sister. Never had her parents permitted the same, but after a three-day boycott of me for not meeting since she left the job I ignored her. This stimulated her desire of meeting and one fine day, out of the blue, she sat in the car of her friend who drives from Jalandhar to Hoshiarpur as they both work in the same college.

"What have you said at home?"— I messaged her while the bus was on its way to Phagwara.

"I said I am going to Phagwara as Shefeena didi has got some work there"

"And you think they will believe it?"

"I don't know Pratik and please don't make me frantic by asking because my legs are already wobbling."

Waiting for her in the Café in Phagwara, I continued playing the game I left midway when Jahanvi arrived.

As soon as I saw Jasneet entering the café hall I saved the game before clicking on the home key this time.

Light brown suit with a white sweater on top. Her hair was dropped to her left. She adjusted her stole twice as it slipped from her right shoulder on which she had hung her bag. Her eyes were searching for me and I could see her rubbing her hands as they were getting cold; anxiety or weather, no one knows. Very safely keeping every step the movement of her eyes was ten times faster. She took not more than 20 seconds to find me but I lived those 20 seconds to my fullest.

Like a scalded cat her eyebrows were expelled from each other (happiness expression) and her upper teeth exposed (smiled) her beauty along with lips. She almost ran to me and hugged me tightly. In no mood to leave me, she held me tighter when I said—"People are watching Jasneet".

"Shhhhh…"—she murmured.

I softly placed my left arm around her waist and buried my face between her neck and collarbone. Being so engrossed in each other we forgot if there was a world which existed beyond this.

I felt she unhugged me first and later I followed her. As soon as I looked into her eyes, I noticed tears in her eyes and she kept wiping them. Very softly I asked— "Hey… what happened". She chuckled and avoided looking at me. I held her face in my hands and wiped her tears.

Though we never felt the need to use words to express our feelings but there, that time I wanted to say it. Words arose from my stomach but I couldn't speak them. I failed to understand what stopped me from uttering those words.

I made her sit on the sofa opposite to me and she placed her bag between us. The two of us, who never ran out of topics to talk while we were on the phone, were out of words. I realised how comfortable we were in the lives in which we lived via technology and how uneasy it became for us when we were face to face.

The very casual relationship we shared over the phone became formal where we asked only about each other's family in the first 10 minutes. It all looked so phoney to me.

Coffee and cookies helped a little to discuss the same old stories but somewhere I could feel the air of discomfort prevailing over our meeting.

"Want to sit beside me?"–I preferred texting her rather than saying it face to face.

She chuckled looking at the phone and preferred not to raise her head. Not replying via phone she walked near me and sat down. Not much longer after that she rested her head on my right shoulder and I held her from her waist putting my arm around her.

Softly murmuring in my ears she said-"I dreamt of this since months."

The moment we came closer, it helped us experience the radical bond we shared. Even in the hall with 20 people, I could clearly hear the lub-dub of her heart.

"I feel so peaceful here"— I heard Jasneet saying to me. With closed eyes I nodded, took a deep breath, and hugged her tighter.

My mind swayed back and forth which popped the question—"If I ask you what is more important to you; Jasneet or acting, what would be your answer?

With closed eyes I started to imagine what first came to my mind, the vision was clearer in the times when I used to get dreams. A red carpet, paparazzi - I enter the hall where my movie has released - I am being greeted warmly by the director and producer. Sitting in the front row with the team and crew, the movie is about to start. I was clear in my mind of what is more important for me. Abruptly, Jasneet who enters the hall running towards me says-"Sorry, I got late". As she arrives the movie doesn't proceed further and everything becomes standstill.

Frantically, I opened my eyes and looked at Jasneet, who was at my right. Still with her closed eyes she was lost in her own dreams. I could feel how ecstasy would have embraced her as she was smiling like a Cheshire cat.

I felt I was trapped in her love. As soon as the feeling emerged in me, the world seemed a beautiful place. I fought day and night to reach my destination where I can feel success is waiting for me. But never in my dreams have I thought of the long road, that's called a journey I need to walk on. Jasneet's presence assured that the journey would be supportive and easier when she's by my side.

As I kept talking to her she preferred answering to my questions without looking at me. The concealed child in her popped out incessantly when she played with my jacket's zip. I giggled as she was doing it.

"Are you enjoying it?"

Her head till then was slipped till my chest and she nodded with the sound— "hmmmm"

To beguile some of the time we preferred dilly-dallying in the cloth market of Phagwara. The topsy-turvy roads hadn't allowed the rickshaw drivers to ride us further to the main entrance. The extremely narrow roads couldn't help two vehicles pass by together. Jasneet was hesitant to walk around with me. Being miles away from her house the thought of someone watching her, haunted her. She covered her head with her stole and draped it on her face too. I chuckled after I saw her becoming a dacoit but as she looked into my eyes, her brown-green eyes got a hold of me and the world for me stopped right there. I couldn't hear the horn blown by the biker who was coming from the opposite direction but Jasneet was aware enough. She tugged me and made the way for the biker to pass. I wasn't scared but became more fortified. Not for a single minute she left my arm till we entered a shop which sold *phulkaris* (an ornamental cloth or shawl embroidered with silk flowers).

The happiness which filled her heart was exhibited in her eyes. Every *phulkari* she would pick up among the hundreds hanging there, she would ask for my permission before purchasing the same. She raised her brows sometimes when words weren't uttered by her to ask. The raspberry coloured *phulkari* matched well with the suit she was wearing and I blew a kiss to gesture YOU LOOK BEAUTIFUL. She bugged her eyes out as I blew the kiss and looked at the shopkeeper and asked her to pack it. As soon as the shopkeeper turned she nudged me softly to gain attention and reverted with a kiss. I blushed and couldn't look at her.

"Go propose to her. There cannot be any better chance tomorrow to do it."- My heart said, who woke up from the grave it is buried in long back.

I gained enough courage to look back at her and took a deep sigh before turning. As I did so I saw her being petrified and unmoved. Her glare was on her phone and I got butterflies in my stomach to see what she might have got on her phone.

"Jasneet… what happened?"– I asked while placing my hand on her shoulder. She handed her phone to me which had a message from

Aman, her sister.

"Come back home before 4pm. I know you are with Pratik. I told you not to be in contact with him."

20.

Auditions never gave me any heebie-jeebies that day because the casting director was none other than Jahanvi. She called me late in the evening to confirm that the director she had a meeting with wishes to sign her as associate director in the next movie production. As soon as I dropped Jasneet at Phagwara bus stand I rushed home and started to prepare the dialogues she had sent me.

Also, there was no contact with Jasneet since she reached home. It was more than 16 hours that I got a clue of her existence in this world. Whacky thoughts like honour killing crossed my mind.

Reciting the dialogues which I had in my hand, I kept swaying in the corridor and was waiting for my name to be called.

"Hey"— the moment Jasneet's message pinged on my phone, I sat on the chair nearby and instantly replied to her.

"Where were you… and how have you been?"

"I am totally fine. Actually, as soon as I reached home I messaged you and directly went to the kitchen. Aman kept staring at me from the corner of her eyes but didn't speak to me till we went to bed. Later, she discussed it and now everything is resolved. I got up in the morning and in haste rushed to college but forgot to charge my phone meanwhile – then what, my phone's battery was dead in no time."

As soon as I received this message her second message arrived— "Phew… it's so difficult to type this long. I was happy with my old school landline way."

I chuckled as I read the second message and was thankful that no mess was there at her place.

"By the way, where are you?"— another message arrived even before I could reply to any of her messages.

"I am in Amritsar for an audition."

"Oh okay okay… Give your best and send a message once you are home. Ekam will help you"

I smiled and replied- "Sure"

"Pratik Sharma"— my name was spoken aloud by the boy from the casting team. I rushed into the room where there was one person with a camera kept on a tripod.

There were three people in the jury sitting at the left corner of the room including Jahanvi, who passed a broad smile at me when my eyes fell on her.

My confidence immediately catapulted as soon as I got a glance of her. She mouthed-"BEST OF LUCK" and shrugged her shoulders while giggling.

I finished my act, executing A to Z as I planned it. Either it was the first ever time my luck was beside me or it was Jasneet's Ekam who held my hand or Jahanvi's best wishes but first time after giving more than 50 auditions I got a standing ovation by the judges.

Jahanvi's eyes gathered all the happiness of the world and briskingly clapped revealing her set of upper and lower teeth which deluged me with my obscured felicity.

As the day ended, I waited for her outside the building where the audition was held. A message about the day was sent to Jasneet and till an hour later she hadn't read it.

Jahanvi walked out from the building and as soon as she saw me her legs moved faster. She ran towards me with both hands in the air and hugged me.

"I am so so so so so so much happy Pratik that I can't express it to you… you killed it actually"— she hadn't left me for half a minute. I didn't respond the way she expected me to and then she initially loosened me and then un-hugged. She passed a short smile and bit her lower lip. We walked along the road to the bus stand and discussed about the things which weren't common in us; school, college, and family. With every meeting our ardent innate instinct of discussing life couldn't be controlled and that day the rate of falling for each just seemed to increase manifold, unconsciously.

The feeling I had with Jasneet was a lot different than one I was having with Jahanvi. To be honest, I loved both and wanted to live with both these feelings.

"Pratik… I want to tell you something."— sitting beside each other on the bus once the driver pressed the accelerator the discussion started.

"Hmmm" — looking at her I asked.

She smiled and looked away from me. As her gaze was towards the window my eyes followed her gestures. I too started to look through the window. We passed *bhel-walas*, fruit vendors, and a few other buses and reached the main road. Once the bus passed Sangam cinema, which is just opposite the Amritsar bus stand, she looked at me.

"What are you looking at?"— She questioned. "I am waiting for you to show me something"

With her palm covering her mouth she started to laugh. Once it was abated she continued—"I wanted to tell you something and looked out of the bus to think how to commence… and you thought I was to show you something?"— And her laughter resumed.

Embarrassed at my foolishness I punched my forehead and joined her in her laughs.

For the next minute I avoided looking at her, it was then when her words fell in my ears— "I have started liking you"

The smile that I wore evaporated as I heard her. I looked inscrutable blank after she completed. My heart wanted to tell her about Jasneet but I couldn't understand what stopped me. Hearts of hearts, I knew the way my relation with Jahanvi was shaping up, she was certainly more than a friend, yet I also knew with Jasneet it was lesser than a partner. (My confused state of mind could sort the lives of all our three but that's what life is all about-**mistakes.**)

She continued— "I feel protected and serene whenever I am with you. You always make me feel special. No matter how tense I am, or how broken my situation would be, you always conquer it with a smile."

I felt my phone in my pocket vibrating but the tremor Jahanvi gave me in life left me completely bewildered. I was zapped and couldn't utter a word; and my eyes were fixed at her.

The incident was powerfully evocative of the day when Payal elucidated her feelings. The same essence could be felt from Jahanvi too but not venomous as Payal's.

Unmoved and expressionless I was dumbfounded. She continued— "Today I don't think about Rohit but it is you about whom my thoughts fly to. The urge of talking to you never reduces. I…"

And my ears stopped receiving vocals of hers. Rather I heard my heart laughing at me, who warned not to move ahead with this— "Never jump in the ring to fight before learning the needful tactics of the game because it just needs one punch to collapse."

She shook me from my shoulder— "What happened?"

"Huh…"—Getting back to reality, I was shaken and looked around to feel where I was.

She carefully analysed my eyes before speaking— "If you don't like me it won't affect our friendship. Stay cool"— she patted my shoulder and adjusted herself straight.

I didn't utter a word. She kept continuing the topics about her school and college like and how her interest in direction emerged but not a single word fell on my ears.

I took my phone out from my right pocket, hiding from her and clicked the home key to turn the screen light on. A message from Jasneet flashed on the screen which arrived a few minutes ago, it read—"I knew you would kill it. You are the best."

Exactly the same words and expressions were used, it just added to my already convulsed mind!

21.

Peace and I were away from each other as Congress was separated from seats in Lok Sabha 2014 polls. Both wanted the other but it was BJP (Both J's - Jasneet and Jahanvi) and a P (Payal) which weren't happy of seeing us under the same roof!

I switched off my mobile and after completing my day at office I walked to the place which renders a soothing soothes me when no one does.

"Shiv Shiv Shiv Shiv…"— I continued reciting his name with my hands on my eyes. This helps my eyes to cool down and mind to relax from the worries of the world. I adjusted my chair a little and reclined.

Peace which I was trying to gather for myself could not be sustained for long. My eyes opened when I heard the sound of the door of the hall and I uplifted myself on the chair to make my vision clearer of the person entering the hall.

With only shadow being visible initially in the beam of light that was entering the hall, Payal's face was revealed after she closed the door and only the needful light was present. She walked up every step till the end of the hall near me. With a broad smile on her face she asked— "May I have a seat?"

I dropped my eyelids and raised them slowly. The gesture was well understood by her and she passed me and entered in the row to have the seat next to me.

While she was on my left hand, I turned to the opposite and supported my chin with my right hand.

"There is nothing to worry, Pratik. You overthink a lot"— she initiated after a pause.

I never shared my thoughts with her about being ill-tempered but she hit the nail on the head by guessing the reason behind my presence here at this hour of the day.

Now, this certainly made me dubious.

"How did you know I was here?"— I questioned after turning towards her.

She smirked before she replied—"I know everything Pratik about you because I care for you."

I felt hot under my collar as she started but controlling my exasperation was the only way out, I knew.

She continued—"I know what theatre means to you. I know what your dreams mean to you. I know whenever you want to be away from the world, you want to be close to the theatre."

"Hiding things is a bad trait, telling everything is worse"— my heart had the best sarcasm while giggling and speaking aloud.

"Accept her proposal."

The exhausted me was instantly energised as my ears collected her words and I instantly looked at her. I couldn't speak a word but I raised my brows to question her - **how do you know about it?**

She nodded and said—"I was seated right behind you in the same bus when you were coming back to Jalandhar."

I stood from my chair at a breakneck speed — "What the hell. Are you really stalking me?"— I stood for being vexed and frantic to realise that I am being stalked. Before this when she mentioned stalking me, I hadn't taken it seriously but now I certainly had.

"I am not stalking you but just protecting"— she too stood and took a step towards me to explain her unreasonable actions.

"It means just the same, just a change of word. And what the hell do you mean by protect, I DARE YOU Payal to stalk me ever after."— Exhibition of my outrage was shown to her after I pointed my finger at her with a surge in volume.

Not a single word she spoke after I lashed out at her. I could only hear my heavy breathing in that still air which persisted after that.

"Please have a seat"— she offered, being as low in her volume as she could.

As I was trying to reach my goal with each passing day, my head had started spinning by then. My dream of leading a normal and easy life started to haunt me every day. Wiping my forehead with my shirts' sleeves I preferred sitting on the stairs and Payal followed the same.

I was devoid of concentration to think about my goals and felt like having a little distraction by focusing on the girl I like; Jasneet, the girl who likes me; Jahanvi, and the girl who stalks me; Payal.

"Pratik, you are only being selected in this movie because of Jahanvi. This is exactly what I am trying to explain to you. This industry doesn't acknowledge talent but connections."— She had a point, I agreed with her, because not in a single movie did I got a chance to play a character role but all of a sudden these people appreciated a person who made no difference from his first audition.

She continued—"I know you love Jasneet but Jahanvi is your key to unlock the door of success. Accept her proposal and throw her out of your life once you achieve what you desire. Jasneet is not the one but it is Jahanvi who will help you to become an actor."

Jasneet and Jahanvi started to hallucinate me; both standing on the stage opposite to me. While Jasneet was sobbing, Jahanvi stretched her arms as she wanted to embrace me. Never had I ever thought of reaching a point in my life where decision making was so difficult. Till 24, the most difficult decisions were selection of Non-medical over commerce and whether to join NCC in college or not. Life changes once you enter the real world and drag you into situations which make you mature overnight.

Thinking over Payal's suggestion, I rubbed my face and smoothly slipped my fingers through my hair. Though the heart again disagreed with the decision but brain was propelled to infuse the teachings of Payal for a promising future!

She stood and held me from my arm— "Get up, I want to show you something"

Being unspoken and dilemma stricken I just followed her. As every step that I was walking down, I somehow felt how my priority list also started to shuffle; theatre, career, money was interchanged by love, like and stalk. As I was engrossed in my own confusion, I was gently nudged by Payal—"Here is the lady I was talking about."

The girl was not a day above 26 years old. A voluptuous and

pulchritudinous brunette was wearing a striped t-shirt with flared jeans and a pair of clogs. She wasn't lesser than a diva in her attire.

Later, the thought of WHO IS THE LADY struck my mind but initially it was WHAT HAS PAYAL TOLD ME ABOUT HER?

Till the time I could recall the introduction Payal gave me of hers, I found myself being hugged by the lady. Her rhapsody of meeting me was way more than I could ever imagine, maybe even more than meeting SHAHRUKH KHAN —"I can't tell you how much I loved your theatre and how much I love you. I saw your modelling pictures on Facebook as I followed you there. I literally LOVE YOU"— extending the last word "Love you" and making an escalation in her voice and revealing her big smile too.

Passing her mobile to Payal with exhilaration, she asked her to click a picture with me. That was my first fan-struck moment perhaps. I finally found my career going upwards. I smiled my heart out; blush and shyness each acquired one cheek with a sprinkle of red colour on it. The lady had no wish to halt at one picture. She kept changing sides beside me and I kept changing poses from sliding my hands in pockets to the victory sign, keeping my foot unmoved by an inch.

"May I kiss you?"— She asked.

She left me stupefied with her words. Before I could deny her proposal she added

— "I mean on your cheek"— with a short pause of a few seconds she said "PLEASE..." in an extended and soft tone.

Being a poor expeditious decision maker, I threw my glance at Payal who smiled and gestured to accept it.

Being extremely shy to say the word YES I accepted it with a short smile at her.

I felt her fingers slipping around my waist and she put some extra force on her toes to uplift them. Her warm breath rose from my neck till my jaw before she placed a kiss. Never in my life was I this tightly clutched with agitation! And once she left me in a timorous voice I said—"Thank you". That spontaneous thank you was for the picture she clicked, for the love she gave as a fan, or for leaving her me from her clench, I could never resolve the dilemma within.

Till then I hadn't noticed her child who was a toddler playing around with his magna tiles at a corner when she called him—"Raghu, come here"

Imagine a white snow man who starts walking initially but runs at a pace of 0.02km/hour, which is his maximum, with wobbling legs and spongy and bouncy cheeks; a precise description of the child.

His winsome smile stole my heart and I couldn't resist lifting and kissing him.

"Your son is really very cute"— the moment I put him back on the floor, he ran at double the speed of his former, 0.04km/hour precisely.

As soon as they left, Payal and I were back in person, not a single word was uttered by her but the vibes made her evident of my next words, and for that she already carried a broad smile —"I think you are right and I will accept Jahanvi's proposal."

"The biggest mistakes we make are when we start thinking that life is difficult and we have to make some hard decisions. We become imprudent and confuse the word MATURITY with priorities."

22.

Same café, same time, different clothes, different reason and we two; Jahanvi knew the reason deep in her heart of us being there. There was sheer optimism in me while speaking to her in the last few days after I had a word with Payal, without further delay I requested her to meet me. But having a deadline to complete the editing of one of her projects, it took her more than a week's time to arrange it.

These were things I appreciated her for; her professionalism and priority were topmost for her. Admittedly, my priority list too got re-shaped and my career again acquired the topmost position in the list.

I turned my phone to flight mode when I went to see Jahanvi as I also was aware of the fact that Jasneet would be returning from her college and as usual she would give a ring.

Jahanvi's elegance was catching more eyes that day as for the first time I saw her wearing dangler earrings than her usual studs. She even took her back hair from her right ear twice and passed smiles, of course on purpose.

The vibes yelled aloud—"Appreciate it you asshole"

"You are looking fabulous in your new makeover"— I said. She blushed and replied—"Thank you so much"

The vibes which flew away a few seconds ago took a U-turn and patted my back— "Good job you asshole".

I felt the burning of my ears as I was sitting there. Not in any of my interviews I have ever been so anxious but on that day I was. Though, I already knew her answer, actually, I was there to answer hers but still guilt wasn't leaving me from its grip. Never a word that existed in my dictionary– **Love you**, but the unpalatable fact was it already slipped in.

"Jahanvi…"— and I took a long pause after that.

With deep sighs and accumulation of wholesome audacity I continued—"I love you too, Jahanvi."

Her vile expression made the length of smile dwindle, both in excitement and fear— "What…?"— I asked her.

She turned her head to her left and smirked. Though, I found it offensive but couldn't say it. I was waiting for her response with utmost veracity.

"How did you feel that you love me? — She asked in her rasping voice.

Having no answer to her query I tried to make an answer but being inexperienced in expressing love, the person who came in my mind wasn't Jasneet, it was Ashween— "I wish I could have spent more time with you"— I spoke in my heart aloud.

Understanding my condition of being struck into a perplexing situation, Jahanvi persuaded—"You can't love anyone until you spend time with that person. People baffle the holy word LOVE. It's easier to use the word to express feelings but to shore up in long term relationships; that's why people end-up being separated after defaulting the other partner in the names of habits, aura, understanding blah blah…. …"

The prototype structure of love was twisted and obfuscated beyond its etymological origin— "Love doesn't appear with tricks and formulas, for you it might be sexual intercourse and for me it might be just a cup of coffee"— Jasneet's definition of love was recalled.

"We'll give time to this relationship before taking it to the next level. If we are successful in finding compatibility with each other then we'll get married"— She completed.

The chauvinist gene in me felt offensive until then but as my career acquired the top most position in the list, I decided to go with the flow and accept whatever she said.

23.

The DJ was doing its job just right with perfect subtlety because he had already gathered many on the floor within a few minutes. Gautam hadn't left the chair, adjacent to that of DJ's till the time his doubts weren't dispelled. *Chachu* (uncle) selected his duty near the bar, a place he and few other relatives created a world of their own. Thumping of their legs and shaking heads with every beat commenced after each one of them was down with 2 pegs; PATIALA, they call it. The girls were taking more time than estimated and so was *bhua* to get ready. Jahanvi's calculation was better in comparison to mine, and I saw the opening of the door exactly after 55 minutes. Though it wasn't a huge difference, I lost it by just 50 minutes to her.

"Well in time *bhua*, I can never be this punctual."— I commented satirically and at the same time preferred keeping three hands distance with her, also a leg stretched because slaps or slippers can be showered anytime. Hence, I did the same while being sardonic this time too.

Once in a blue moon it's your day when you expect to be yelled by family but your mistake hides itself and your sarcasm misses the target; it was mine on 09/10/2016. She continued adjusting her saree and I rushed into the room to grab my Broche.

As I wore it, the first picture of it was sent to the girl who gifted it to me.

"Now it looks quintessential "— Jahanvi's message with a blush tumbled my redundant despondency.

I heard Gagan's voice while he was enquiring about me. So I kept walking and replied to Jahanvi. — "You always chose the best for me. Love you"

"Uncle told me that you were asking for Chajj. I have kept it in the living area"— he spoke with short breaths as he was heavily choked.

— "And come down quick, everyone is waiting for you at the dance floor."— He completed and ran, not even waiting for me to reply.

The person of whom I hadn't caught a glimpse there was Dixita *didi*. As soon as she saw me, she walked up to me without saying a word and hugged me— "Love you bro"— very softly she said it to me. Without wasting any time, I hugged her back and replied in the same tone—"Love you *bacha*".

Not a word was uttered for a minute and such ambivalent emotions are something we hadn't anticipated. Until then my experience rode me on a road where I felt that, strive of men is more difficult than that of women but honestly it is the other way round. My mind struck me into deep angst with only the thought of her leaving the house, family and belongings from the next day. I was worried as I doubted if she could get a sound sleep tonight?

"I always want you to be happy"— she continued after a pause. I felt a twinge of pain in her voice. Thus, I held her from her shoulder to look at her face. Her grip was so tight that I couldn't loosen it. As soon as I called her —"bacha...Ki hoya? (What happened dear?)", she burst her tears out and clenched me with more intensity.

Many-a-times we fought in childhood, a lot of times we made the other sleep till the tears shed but today my heart-felt being weighed by a gigantic stone. I wanted to cry along with her and for that my throat too got filled with tears but eyes were stubborn as a mule and halted the flow.

"Thank god you are going, at least I will have the entire almirah to myself now"— I purposely told her to tease on which she chuckled and gave a soft punch on my chest. My affinity remained unwavering with *didi,* no matter whatever happened in the last few months. Her affection for me was still the same.

"You look so handsome when you keep smiling"— She said while she was adjusting my collar.

It reminded me of days when while going to school she used to adjust my tie every single day which would tilt towards the left, without my knowledge. For a good nine long years till the time we were in the same school she never yelled at me for not wearing it properly.

Taking her face in between my hands I said—"And I wish smile to never leave your lips"

We hugged each other once again. We were familiar with the truth of both thinking the same; from tomorrow *didi* will have left this house forever to begin another chapter of her life. She might have accepted this before me but as the time of *bidaai* approached, the acceptance from my heart was becoming difficult.

While these thoughts were twirling in my head, a beep sound on my phone pulled me back to the present. It was from Mohit;

```
"Hi Pratik. Just came out from the meeting
with Mr.Soni and heliked your proposal. 99%
it's a yes, still the final meeting will
be held tomorrow and the papers from our
side will be signed. Congratulations"
```

"Men are nurtured to be lionhearted; they aren't allowed to exhibit their tears, their sorrows, and their pain – especially in public. Even if one does, he is hold up to shame. The idiocy of disguising widens the distance in relationships. Sometimes it's good to make the heart transparent, as it saves relations and strengthens the bond."

24.

"I am still wearing the smile you gave me, Pratik"— she said while we were chatting.

The devil which was shining like a spark in me was blown into a wildfire within a few days without my notice; as lying to her wasn't dragging me to self-guilt.

"So am I… It was the best day of my life"— I replied to her.

"I can spend the rest of my life in the same manner. And I mean it"

Smile was persistent while messaging her and after a pause I replied—"I am lucky to have you in my life."

I could imagine her expressions while she would be reading my messages and just by then her reply arrived—"Luckier is me to get a person like you in life"

"I am so sorry to be late today"— Jahanvi arrived and hugged me. She said it in my ears.

I closed my chat with Jasleen quickly and locked it to hide from her gaze in the best possible way. Once she released me she kept her bag on the table and walked to the restroom. My eyes escorted her till she entered and I turned off the data on my phone. To this, I remembered my time as a child wherein one shivers with both anxiety and fear after committing a mistake – as he believes he will be castigated if the lie is caught. My state was exactly the same but the fretfulness inside was building up.

Jahanvi arrived and settled herself after taking her bag back from the table. I hadn't realised that the café staff had started to recognize us till one of them walked up to our table and asked—"Sir, would you like to get your favourite coffee or something else today?" and he bowed forward partly. The unseen face cleared the doubt of a major part of his job experience he served in a Chinese restaurant as the trait was pinned with him but being new here; he had a difficult time in reminding himself. He looked behind the table where orders are placed, at his colleague, who gave a thumbs up to him and the guy passed a smile at me.

"Nothing"— Jahanvi replied to him and continued searching for something in her bag.

My consciousness fell at her and I asked to know the reason for not ordering anything—"What happened?"

Without looking at me she kept searching in state of agitation— "Yaar, actually its Naira's birthday today and we need to go for shopping"

Her three brothers have 5 children; the eldest has two daughters, whereas the younger one has a son and a daughter. The youngest has a son. Apart from these, there is a cousin brother living with them who has a wife and a daughter. So all in all there are four girls and two boys in the entire family. My biggest task was to remind myself to whom Naira belongs. While the calculation was in process, Jahanvi distracted me—"C'mon let's go. Thank God I hadn't forgotten the card at home."

I decided to make a hierarchy tree of her family in my head so that the confusion of her family members is cleared. The second idea also emerged on my mind that was easier; to ask her directly but also was aware of girls' obnoxious habit of adapting misperceptions, like — *"you hardly care about my family and this is the reason why you don't remember if I discuss anything about them."*

To avoid such a war of words during the initial stage of our relationship I preferred playing Sherlock Holmes myself. Meanwhile, Jahanvi kept speaking something which crossed me just as air was crossing my ear and the Activa halted outside a kids shop.

For two year's Naira the minimum range of clothes started from 899/-, a cost at which I buy a pair of jeans! After realising how expensive buying clothes for children is, my age limit of getting married shifted abruptly from 28 to 30, just out of nowhere.

Purchasing clothes ended and after hooking her carry bags to her Activa, she looked at me and after bugging out her eyes she said—"I am hungry now".

As she wanted to try something new, I took her to the place where I often visit with my friends; BON'O'FIRE — a pavement restaurant located on the sidewalks of PPS Mall, Jalandhar. It's a small mobile kitchen where the owners are both chef and waiters. Three friends who used to study together decided to get into this business soon after their graduation.

Their bugged out eyes revealed their level of being surprised for a man who has always been surrounded at 360 degrees with boys, has crossed all fences and not by taking one step further of adding a girl in a group initially and subsequently coming with her in person but going on level 2 directly.

"Why are they looking at us like this?"— Jahanvi said after noticing all the eyes being focused sharply in us.

I chuckled and replied—"Actually, you are the first girl who has come with me to this place which is our all boy gang's *adda*."

She narrowed her eyes firstly and then raised her left eye brow to gesture— "Kindly continue"

I kept my elbows on the table and shifted a bit forward—"My group; THE BORED PANDAS, it has six members in it; Babu Kanda, Sarabjeet Singh, Aarohan Singh, Gagan Singh Atwal, and Kanav Sharma, we all are chicken maniacs, except Kanav, who is a vegetarian. Since our college days we come to this place thrice a week, which is the least count, for their amazing chicken preparation. Rest everyone has been here with their girlfriends or friends once, except me. So, it's just that these people are surprised to see so."

Her cheeks blushed as I completed and she became comfortable after knowing this. She looked into my eyes and said softly so that the voice didn't surpass my ears— "Don't turn around as I am saying this earlier. They all have been looking at us." And she held my hands; to make it visible to them she tilted to her right. Now, it was my turn to go red. The redness of her cheeks was transferred on mine and I smiled and blushed at the same time.

As my favourite *Chicken Banjara Kebabs* arrived which had a delightful presentation and was more luring than ever, I turned to the owner and winked.

It was so mouth-watering that the beauty of Jahanvi faded in front of it. The kebabs were so well roasted that the red chili was camouflaged. Unlike last time, these kebabs were well grilled deeply as I could see through the shallows from where the iron sticks must have been inserted. Each kebab was draped with mayonnaise sauce as a cloak. Just at the sheer look, my vision could easily tear apart the smoke which was emitting from the kebabs.

"Can I ask you a question"— and Jahanvi distracted me from a world where chicken and I were living in isolation.

"Why haven't you come here with Rajdeep?"— She questioned.

The name sounded familiar to me but my head couldn't hit right on the nail to acknowledge. I was assured the name has something to do with me. So, I frowned my brows for better understanding.

"What?"— She questioned while having a bite of kebabs.

"R A J D E E P, you moron"— my mind signalled me her name which reminded me of the fictional story I built about my love life.

This long pause intimated her in terms that "DON'T DISCUSS ABOUT MY PAST" and she apologised for asking. I was thankful to her in my heart for ending the topic before I added another lie to the fictitious list that I had started.

Lie never dies. A lie uttered at night is thought meant to be blend in dark but it re-merges with the first rays of the sun. And we humans aren't clever enough to grab this plain concept.

25.

The story of the kiss between Payal and me started to spread like wildfire among theatre artists. After two months to the incident that happened during Keshav's play, from a few days I started to see everyone's eye at me the moment I entered theatre - lips murmuring something all the time, vibes which weren't healthy. After two days of persistent noticing I came across the truth. I knew Jahanvi's ears would not be exempted from the news so before clarifying people around me I preferred to call her but I was late by a day.

"I came to know about it yesterday"— she said.

Being uneasy and frantic at the same time I sat, stood and sprinted three times within a minute, I clarified—"It wasn't intentional. She did…"

"Ssshhh…"— I heard her saying softly and my legs froze like an effigy's.

Lying was a much easier task than accepting the truth, now this was well understood by me within seconds. Moments after this, all I could sense was the heavy silence which persisted accompanied by heavy and light breaths.

"Pratik, I won't sound like I wasn't hurt after hearing about it but what I also know is that this incident happened prior to the day we decided to be together."

There was a blockage of words in my head and I fell short of it. She continued—"Will you fulfil a wish of mine?"

Without wasting a second I was prompt to reply —"I promise" "Break every contact with Payal."

As soon as her words fell on my ears my heart was the first organ before my ears to feel them and became rapturous at what I heard. I was gratified as I wouldn't be fulfilling hers rather my own desire. But as wittiness had already overweight my naivety, my brain was still dominant in thinking about the pros of concealing this truth and exhibiting that I HAVE DONE THIS ONLY FOR YOU.

****

For Payal my decision of ending this friendship was a dreadful truth to be accepted and this made her stupefied. Over the last 45 minutes call that we were having, not a single minute she hadn't used PLEASE.

"It wasn't my fault Pratik…"— while sobbing she used this sentence for the 15th

time, well, my mind was surely counting that!

"I know Payal but things aren't the same now. I don't want your name to be disgraced in the theatre. Jalandhar is a small town, the story will get fuel if we continue being friends"— I tried to make her understand in every possible way.

Unwilling to listen to anything, she plainly denied everything I said. In her choking tone she said—"Please Pratik… I can fix the mess"

Though, my heart knew the matter wasn't a big deal for me. It can be waived off in a few days by referring it to a mere rumour. But considering Jahanvi's words and my heart's desire I was stuck to the decision of ending all ties with Payal.

"I really love you Pratik. And can't really think of being separated from you"

My determination was firm which hadn't gotten anywhere weak by any of her pleading and crying. My heart constructed walls of its own which couldn't hear any wailings from the outside world. Though, this was due to the ongoing war between brain and heart. Brain being the dominant between the two, suppressed the heart; the latter preferred living in isolation.

"I don't want to Payal"— my voice being firm enough.

And I disconnected the call by wishing good luck to her. The sound of her sentence which was about to start couldn't commence properly when I disconnected the call.

Just when my mind started to accept the fact that I became successful in throwing Payal out of my life, a message flipped the side upside down.

"Meet me in Hotel Country-INN by 5 today." I replied back to Payal—"I won't be coming."

"For the last time, please."

After thinking of the meeting to be for the last time, I finally agreed to it.

"Don't tell Jahanvi about this meeting as she wouldn't like it."

I found her idea quite valid. By no means would your present girlfriend like her boyfriend to meet the girl who he has once kissed.

As I parked my bike in the parking lot of the hotel, I entered the dining side of the hotel from the door which was near to the exit. The large spacious hall of the hotel was almost empty and only a few couples could be seen as the odd hours give them privacy.

I took a corner and waited for Payal to arrive. Exactly, at 5:15pm I received her message stating — "That guy in the purple T-shirt 4 tables beyond you is my cousin's brother, it will be a huge drama at my home if he finds me with you."

Finding her nowhere in my vision, I read this and stood from my seat to leave and decided to tell her better not to meet ever but before I could complete the sentence in my mind, another message from her took me by surprise— "Room 224. Second floor. No need to ask at reception too."

I found this completely obnoxious, how a girl could offer to meet someone in a hotel's room but not in front of her cousin. The second option of going to some other hotel or restaurant was still available. The willingness to end this relationship was more than handling the chaos. Thus, I headed to ROOM 224.

After my first knock at the door, it opened. Through a black coloured skin wear bodycon dress, her tantalising curves were crystal clear as she was walking ahead me after I entered the room. The room was filled with the fragrance of roses. Also, the dim yellow light contributed in making the room no less than a room for a honeymoon couple.

Ignoring everything, I went ahead to sit on the chair. Payal acquired the opposite chair and asked- "Scotch?"

Her intentions were being clear to me so I decided not to have anything with her and focus on the reason for being there. Thus I replied- "Nothing, let's get to the point."

She smirked and crossed her right leg with the left, which revealed half of her naked thigh.

I looked away from what she wanted to show me. "So, you sure you want to end it here?"

"Yes"- I firmly said without looking at her.

I heard a long sigh of hers before she said- "Alright"

The most shocking part in a person's life is not to get what he desires but when it is gotten without any delay. Hence, her "Alright" sounded "not right" to me also.

"But on one condition."

I somehow was prepared for it that the girl will not let it easy to free me without any terms and conditions but was waiting for her to mention it- "And that is?"

"I want to lose my virginity with you"- she was firm with the statement.

"What the f…..? Are you out of your mind?"- I stood up by pushing my chair backwards.

In no time, she was on my face, close enough to touch her lips with mine. She didn't want to lose any chance to convince and lure me.

"Listen… we will not tell anyone about this. Just you and me."- holding my face she said it.

I pushed her away from me being known to the fact how desperately she wanted me and walked out of the room. But, she ran after me and held my hand. We were now at the corridor of the hotel. Once again, the mad girl that she was, she pulled me in the room and shut the door. In no time Payal started kissing my neck. Her reaction completely frightened me. I pushed her once again with complete force and almost yelled at her- "This has crossed limits today Payal. Never in my dreams had I expected something like this from you. Though the decision of not meeting you was of Jahanvi, I am happier I have taken it now. You are a psychopath. Don't want to see your face ever"- and in no time I was in the parking area.

26.

The satisfaction I had after throwing Payal out of my life took me to cloud 9. To make sure by all means that she doesn't bother me again, I blocked her from my WhatsApp, Instagram and Facebook too. Both her contact numbers were blacklisted also. So, from 24 hours my time was equally distributed between Jasneet and Jahanvi. Though Jasneet did notice about my changing sleeping habits, as I started wishing her good night at 10 pm and she questioned it once too, yet I lied to her about my early extra classes for IELTS training. Having no regrets in lying to her I had turned out to be superfine in the skill of making stories as well as fooling.

"Pratik... Don't you think this is having a deeper neck than required"— Looking at the mirror in the changing room Jahanvi asked.

Whereas I was holding her bag and was left with my mouth open— "Damn hot"

She blushed as she heard that and looked at me from the corner of her eyes. Not wasting my chance, I kissed her cheek. Now there was a change in role; her mouth was open and I was blushing.

She hit my chest with her fist and turned towards the mirror again.

The red wine colour one piece that she was wearing had two straps on the shoulder and the back was deeper than required. But I also believed that the designer exactly knew what impact it would have as the result of it was just in front of my eyes.

Not losing the golden chance, and taking complete advantage of no one's presence, I pushed her in the changing room and turned her towards myself to kiss her. My sixth sense was correct as she wasn't surprised at my action which perhaps revealed she was mentally prepared about this to happen.

Our lips touched each other's and could feel the other's warm breath. To judge the distance of the wall, I took my right hand off her neck and touched the wall. Once I found it, I pushed her towards it with the force of my body. Taking my hand off the wall, I placed it on her waist. Meanwhile, our tongues started to mingle with the others'.

"Knock-Knock…"— we heard the sound on the door.

We stopped where we were. Whereas I became a little frightened, she very bravely asked— "Yes?"

"Mujhe room use karna hai. (I want to use the room)"– The voice of a middle aged woman on the other end of the door said.

"Andar aajao, ikathe use kar lete hai(Come in, We'll use it together)"— Jahanvi's replied being louder than hers.

Her reply made me laugh and I started to chuckle. Jahanvi too was giggling after she said that and placed one hand on her mouth and the other on mine.

Within a minute we heard the opening and closing of the next cabin to ours.

As we examined no extra sound coming from the outside, we ran from there and billed the dress.

While we were on my bike heading towards her house, she rested her head on my back. Not a single word was uttered but I knew just as me she too was thinking about the kiss in the trail room.

"Thankyou."— She said after she was outside her house.

As I looked into her eyes, she started to look away from me. But, she noticed from the corner of her eyes that my gaze was struck on hers. She blushed and covered her face with her right hand. This gave a broad smile on my face too.

"Okay, don't embarrass me more and go now"— still looking away from me she said in her softest tone.

Her voice was not matching her words and I understood one habit of girls that day and it was not the words we need to follow but the modulation of voice. Being lucky enough to understand it, I did the same and kept gazing at her.

She burst out in laughter and her voice now became heavier—"Okay, now go before bhaiya comes out"

I needed to hear the modulation of voice and I followed it before it changes to — "Nikal yahan se ab" (Leave now) She kept staring at me till I took right from her street's end.

****

"I saw a dress for you today which I guess would look pretty on you"— I said to Jasneet.

"Acha… How do you know it?"

"I just closed my eyes and imagined you in it"

"How do you even know it would fit me?"— And she giggled after it.

"Do you think I don't know your size?"

"Hwwwww… Badtameez"(Ill-mannered) I started to laugh as she said it.

"So what happened about your meeting with the director?

"I'll have that next week"

"I just wish things go as smooth as silk"

As Jahanvi was busy with her niece's birthday party, I knew it would take her long to get free. So, the time scheduled for her was spent for ME TIME.

I observed and concluded that day that my feelings for Jasneet and Jahanvi varied. The feelings of future, family, dreams were shared with Jasneet and with Jahanvi it was more about movies, fun, different restaurants and shopping. Neither had I mixed it myself nor did the two of them broached on any topics beyond what was assigned to them by me. What more could a 24 years old boy wish for; dating two girls at a time, both were fond of me, I liked both, it seemed as if I was living my dream. I was truly enjoying each part of life.

27.

"Life?"— Jyoti mam asked.

"Uncertainty"— I replied.

"Emotions?"

"Weakness"— and there was a hooting in the room.

"Ahan.. Nice"— she said with her brows up and continued — "Love?"

And then a message arrived on my mobile—"Waiting for you outside your office"

This gave me a smile on my face and I looked at Jyoti mam and replied—"Love is movie time"—I winked, stood up and walked outside the office.

Jahanvi decided to go for a movie when I messaged her in the morning about my broken bike. So she decided to drop me at home, but before that we went to see Ayshushman Khurrana's Dum Lagga Ke Haisha. Honestly, I was least interested to see a movie but it was the first time Jahanvi asked for something and it was the first time ever we were going for a movie together.

While sitting behind her on her Activa, I messaged Jasneet of being late from the office, faking about being with the few students who have their exam in upcoming days and I would be busy giving extra classes to them.

As usual, she never questioned anything and replied—"Don't forget to eat something"

"Sure"— I replied and was about to lock the phone when her second message arrived—"No egg today, it's Tuesday"

This made me smile. I didn't open the message and slid the notification and turned the data off to make her think that I started with the class and didn't get time to read it.

Due to Tuesday there were fewer people than usual and better was our seats which were side corners. But above all, the best part was that there was no one in our lane.

"Should I hold hands or shall I hold her from shoulder?"— having zero interest in watching the movie, my thoughts were oscillating between the two options.

I knew Jahanvi was noticing how uneasy I was sitting beside her. Because changing sitting position every 2 minutes, rubbing hands and laughing after 2 seconds when everyone does isn't normal. She played the part that I was supposed to do. She held my hands in hers and looked at me. I became a stone and couldn't say a word. None of the words of the movie fell on my ears and the world instantly stopped for me. The light from the screen fell on her face and I could see her beauty clearly. I clutched her hand tighter to which she responded equally. Not wasting more time I touched my lips with hers. Taking full advantage of the less audience I pulled her closer from her waist. She too replied to my kisses with intensity and the moment was intervened by interval after a few minutes. The moment we realised that people around us had started to walk out of the hall; we released each other from our clutches and smiled looking at each other. Hands in hands and we, too, left the hall for some drinks break.

"Nuggets, Nachos, White pasta and Pepsi. What would you have? — I asked her. "Just Pepsi"— she said and handed over the money to me.

My male ego was hit left, right, and centre but I smiled and looked away from her.

She touched my shoulder and called me—"I am serious, take the money and pay for it"

The girl on the other side of the counter was not surprised by the argument as if she experiences it every day in front of her. But one thing was clear from her eyes that she had her heart divided in two parts, each one acquired one option; Jahanvi or me, who will win in the pay-game.

Leaning over Jahanvi I very softly said in her ears—"Listen, you have already paid for the tickets now let me pay for this."

Leaving no ray of hope to give up her voice was strong—"Did you decide this movie?"

Not even waiting for my response she continued—"No, I did it. Next time ask for a movie and pay the bills."— She responded instantly, passed me and paid directly to the girl at the counter.

The girl gave a broad smile to Jahanvi and me as she won the bet she was playing with herself.

While Jahanvi went to use washroom, I preferred utilising the time by calling Jasneet before she does—"Hey"

"Did you eat anything?"— After my mother, if anyone asks me this as the first question it's Jasneet.

"Yes… Ycs… Yes… I had, what are you up to?"

"Just entered home after Jackie's evening walk"

"Hmmm…"

"Where are you? Reached home?"

"Not yet. It will take approximately next 2 hours to finish"

And there, silence sustained. My eyes were glued at the women's washroom's door and I saw Jahanvi coming out. Before she could look at me I turned myself towards the counter and said—"Okay, I need to go now. The break is over for students"

"Sure. Message me once you reach home"

"Sure thing. Miss you"— and I waited longer than usual for her response. Getting no answer from her side, I asked—"Is Aman around?" "Hmmm…"— in an extremely soft tone she said.

"Okay. Bye now."

The student who completes the last line a second before his answer sheet is snatched by the teacher is more surprised than being happy, initially, and it takes him a few minutes to accept that he was actually lucky. The same feelings struck me as the moment I disconnected the call Jahanvi stopped by my side and asked— "Let's go."

In the second half we were just sitting hand-in-hand; she also kept her head on my left shoulder and tugged her hand in mine. I kissed her forehead.

This feeling with Jahanvi was a lot different than what I felt with Jasneet. Though it was also hug, it was also privacy but a lot different.

As the movie ended Jahanvi's phone beeped and she asked—"What are you doing tomorrow?"

While walking down the stairs, I replied—"Mmm.. Office" "Let's go to Zirakpur."

"Why… Zirakpur?"— I asked in confusion.

"The movie, in which you are casted, will start from there in three months. I have to go there for a location check. Can you join?"

I was feeling lucky to not only be a part of the movie but also, indirectly, a part of the production team, through Jahanvi. Thus, I wanted no stone to be left unturned and promptly accepted it.

"And one more thing"— She added.

On reaching the ground floor, there was more noise than usual because of the ongoing event by a local radio channel. But giving her complete attention, I halted my toes and turned towards her to listen.

There was something that she wanted to talk about but there was also something in parallel that was stopping her to speak. The event, I thought. So I offered to walk in the parking area. She held my hand and walked towards the parking direction.

Apart from us, there was only a couple in the parking area who were in conversation, just as us, while sitting on two adjacent parked bikes. We too stood beside Jahanvi's scooty.

"May I ask you something?"— She was no more hesitant in asking this question. Noticing her changed facial expression and tone of voice, I nodded.

"Not actually I wanted to tell you something."— I nodded again in a gesture to say go on.

"Pratik, I know I told you we should spend more time before getting into commitment. I want to tell you that I love you"— and she kept silent for half a minute. I knew from her expression that there was something more that she would like to add as she wasn't blushing while proposing as generally everyone does.

I gave a half smile to her and she continued—"I don't want you to feel the same but all I know is I love you."

Remembering the words of Payal and from knowing the fact that the movie is to begin in a few months, I didn't want to risk my career and replied her—"I love you too"

She smirked after listening to my response and said—"Love is a bigger word than four letters Pratik. Loving anyone is quite easy but staying in love is what makes it difficult."

Girls often confuse boys with this juggling of words. Having no knowledge of what she meant, I didn't speak anything and waited for the elaboration—"No relation, be it of employee-employer, lawyer-client, doctor-patient can result fruitful unless both don't pledge loyalty with the other. Same is the case when two people start a new relationship."

And she took a pause again. Until then my brain signalled Jahanvi hearing the conversation of Jasneet and I but waited for her clarification first, she said—"Who was the girl you were talking to on the phone?"

And my guess was right, damn she heard me talking to Jasneet. In no time I accepted being kicked out of the movie and starting again from auditioning for work, I replied—"A friend."

"You sure?"— She asked in a more than usual firm tone.

Brain calculated well enough that Jasneet is only a friend yet, we haven't proposed to each other, never committed to each other, thus, until then she only was a friend of mine technically, I replied—"I swear."

"See Pratik, what happened to me in my last relation broke me but if anything repeats now will only kill me."— I heard her throat getting choked while completing the sentence.— "I know there are girls behind you, in the theatre, at your workplace and might be in your circle too, but before committing anything to me I want a promise of loyalty from you."

This shook me. I was feeling like a student in front of her who was cheating in the examination and was given a second chance before finally being terminated.

"I promise to be loyal to you"— this wasn't what I wanted to say. But somehow these words came out of my mouth. Words rose from my stomach and departed from my mouth without any preparation.

On our way back home not much of the words were exchanged except the directions to my house. Just before turning to my house, I asked her to drop me— "I'll walk from here."

"Okay"— she replied.

The question on my mind needed an answer, so before I bade her goodbye for the day I preferred to clarify—"When did you hear my conversation with my friend, as I know you were quite far."

Tightening the stall which she was wearing to cover her face, she replied—"When did I say that I heard it?"

I narrowed my brows and waited for her answer. She continued— "The girl at the billing counter was my friend, she told me about your conversation with your so- called FRIEND"— she stressed the last word and left.

While thinking about the day, it just slipped my mind to message Jasneet about reaching home because of being busy in tossing between Jahanvi and Jasneet. I knew it would be impossible to carry both now onwards. Where Jasneet was what all men desire as a wife, Jahanvi was what my career required.

The phone rang and as expected it was Jasneet calling. "Haven't you reached home?"— She asked.

Lifting myself on the bed to sit and talk, I adjusted my back resting with the bed— "Hmm… reached half an hour ago, sorry, skipped to inform you."

"Hmmm…"— She replied.

And a pause sustained between us which never happened before. At least, we were at that stage in our relationship where silences also spoke.

In her soft-spoken voice she became the ice-breaker—"You want to say something?"

Coming back to consciousness, the first thing that I did was take a long sigh. "Go on, I am listening"— she said.

"Actually…"— Collecting all the courage from each and every body part, though I started the conversation but was unable to proceed further.

She didn't give any filler and waited for me to speak.

"Actually, I went to see a movie and was not taking any extra classes"— I felt exhausted after completing it. How tiring it can be to speak my heart out, I could never imagine. It drains all the energy one has in him.

Jasneet took no time in replying—"I know, you were with a girl."

The exhaustion that I could feel a second ago was no longer in me; perhaps it was taken over by fear. Her words immediately made me step out of my bed and I climbed the stairs to reach the terrace because sitting and talking was only making my stomach churn.

"How do you know about it?"– Every word was stressed to make it clear to her. The inner me was filled with anxiety and didn't have the patience, so I picked up a broken piece of PVC pipe from the corner of the terrace and started to press it hard to break it into two.

"Aman was there too, at the movies, with her friends and she saw you"— she replied.

This got my mind to think about the time I called her and asked her to reply with a "miss you too" but she didn't because of Aman being beside her.

Telepathy got us connected as she easily could read my heart, no matter even if proximity separates us in miles, she continued— "Aman wasn't around me at that time when you called. I couldn't reply to your "MISS YOU" after knowing the fact that you were lying to me."

Words left me soon after that. Now I wanted the table to be turned and Jasneet breaking the relation instead I have to do it.

She said—"Had I ever imposed any restriction on you Pratik? It would have been better if you could tell me…"— I cut her off between and said—"On what basis could you impose any restriction?"

It took her quite a long time to recall the words I just said, in her low voice she asked—"What…?"

Any reason, any words, any talks, I wanted nothing to proceed but the earth to tear into two and wanted to fall into it. I closed my eyes and clenched my fist strongly.

"What relation do we have?"— I asked her in a ringing voice, which further enhanced the impression of my callous attitude towards her.

Very well I was aware of my words' impact on her but I moved a step in life as well as into breaking the relationship which held us together since December, 2013, knowing very well that it cannot be undone later. My white lie was caught and the priority list in my life too was sorted now. Hence, I knew I wanted Jahanvi and not Jasneet.

Through her loud and clear long breaths, I could sense how broken she might be after hearing me. But hearts in hearts I knew that the only thing which could make her unlove me was a deep seated feeling of aversion.

In her choking and the softest voice she said—"I love you, Pratik."

My heart felt low after hearing her, it even talked to me—"You waited to hear this, didn't you?" Why? What is in your destiny will get to you for sure? Why are you hurting this girl who hasn't done anything wrong to you? What are you punishing yourself for?"

But the brain was clear—"You need to make ways for yourself. No one makes ways for you, if you yourself don't."

And that's when I decided what I needed—"I don't"— in my taut voice I said.

She broke into tears. The words that she knew were about to come in a few seconds when fell in her ears, broke the barricade that was halting the tears to flow. The pinch of her pain was so intense that I also felt being on the other side of the call. Honestly, my throat too got choked. Somehow, one part of me inside wanted to share her pain, as my guilt was killing me inside. But I had to take this harsh step.

I promised myself of giving all the happiness to Jasneet but I failed giving her any, I knew. The biggest sin that we do is when we take away the things a person has in his life, without contributing to add anything. That's what I did there. Giving no happiness but taking hers.

In her choking voice she kept saying—"Please Pratik, don't leave me. I love you a lot."

Standing strong on my decision, I said—"Have I ever expressed that I love you?"

I heard her sniffling and trying her best to hold her tears as her family was asleep and her heavy and wheezy voice could make them awake, she said in her breaking voice—"Was it ever required for any of us to say that Pratik?"

Very well, I knew these words had no place in us. It was evident how much the other person matters, but denying everything she said was perhaps the only way I could think to infuse hatred in her heart for me.

"I always considered you as a good friend Jasneet, nothing more than that, but my girlfriend doesn't like me talking to you. So please…"—stopping me in between to complete my line she asked—"What did you just say? Girlfriend?"

I preferred staying mum on her question. I heard her footsteps as she was walking out her room, she, while sobbing, said—"Haven't you ever, even once, loved me Pratik?"

I felt a drop of tear rolling down my eyes as soon as I shut my eyes, I replied, this time being a little softer—"Look Jasneet, I thought I too loved you but that wasn't love. See, we haven't kissed, haven't touched, just met once in a year's time. This isn't what a relationship is. Right?"

Her sniffles didn't stop and there were two reasons for it; first, the chilling night and her walking up on the terrace, second, her sobbing. When we let our heart cry aloud, the sniffles are less than when we try to hold the tears to flow, she said—"Is that all for you, Pratik? A kiss? The time we spent in that café matters none to you?"

I knew the softer side of me couldn't help her to hate me so I acquired my pre- nature of being rude, I replied—"Hahaha… Do you compare a kiss with a coffee? Is a cup of coffee love for you?"— I chuckled.

And there were no words spoken from her end, all I could hear was short breathes and the breeze blowing. After few seconds she said— "Love doesn't appear with tricks and formulas, for you it might be sexual intercourse and for me it might be just spending quality time with a loved one over a cup of coffee."

I was taken aback by this and was speechless at what she just said. No one can ever win an argument with a beloved who is trying to prove her love. Jasneet was in no mood to give up here and very well I knew that this outspoken side of hers could never be defeated. When words fall short then action speaks louder and that's what I preferred doing there.

"Bye Jasneet, never try to contact me ever."— I realised a pain in my heart after I said that. Never in my worst dreams had I thought of going away from her, above all, saying these words to her.

After listening to what I said, her halted tears burst out and her wailing was loud. I could feel her pain of not being bothered if anyone would hear it. It didn't matter to her what her family would think after they found their daughter crying at 11pm on the terrace.

Until her prolonged high pitched crying sound fell in my ears, I too wanted badly to be a part of her pain. I was in dire need of being thrown to an unknown place and start a new life with all past memories being washed away. But also being aware of nothing such to happen, I did the only thing I could do there, that was to deliberately tighten the fist and there it was, the pipe broke into two.

"Please, Pratik, don't leave me, I beg you. I have just imagined my life with you and no one else. I am sorry Pratik. Please don't do this. Please don't leave me. I will try to change myself. I am really sorry. Please don't go. Please Pratik "— her sobbing and pleading continued and I was aware that this will

surely melt the stone heart I acquired.

Not much I could say in any justification before disconnecting the call because all I knew was I was being selfish in order to make the dream come true that I have always wished for, I said—"Sorry", disconnected and blocked her from WhatsApp and the calling list. I also noticed a deep cut in my hand and it was bleeding profusely.

When at the same time we experience both pain; physical and emotional, it's the latter we acknowledge and leaves a scar that is invisible to the world.

28.

Jasneet was no more a part of my life and there was no door left open for her to make an entry. This is where Jahanvi got all my attention now. In the last one year it was the first time when I woke up and didn't wish Jasneet a good morning message. I wasn't much surprised when my fingers typed her name on WhatsApp where the screen displayed *Blocked. Tap to unblock.* I understood to get rid-off people is easier than their habits. Undeniably, Jasneet was my habit. Physically, I was with Jahanvi in the bus, going to the location in Zirakpur, but unconsciously I was living my day just as I used to do with Jasneet, perhaps this was because of habit. Never had I noticed that her timings of leaving to and from school were printed in my mind, which reminded me about it. 8.00 am when she would leave for college, 8:20 when she would reach, 11.00 am the break time, 2.10 when she would leave for home, 2.30 when she would reach back home. Exactly on these timings my hand took off my mobile from my pocket with a hope to receive a message from her. Though I was the one who blocked her, I was the one who broke the relation, and I was the one to tell her never to contact me, still my habit of reading her messages for satisfaction about her safety provoked me to check the messages. Herein I learnt that neither relations not oxygen should be taken for granted because, we might not feel its presence but the absence suffocates us.

Jahanvi, sitting beside, was extremely happy when she got to know about my breaking every contact with Payal and Jasneet, but I was only happy for the former. What I read, what I heard about love and what I was feeling that day was completely different. Not for a single time I felt like crying for Jasneet rather had urge to run to her leaving all desires and dreams. Clearly, it was because of the fact that we only spent time on messages and calls. I was only cuffed in her habit and not love. Thus, experiencing this feeling and form of emotion with Jahanvi was new to me.

After arriving at Chandigarh's bus stand in sector 43, the

production team of the movie sent a cab to pick us and drove to the location in Zirakpur. While Jahanvi was busy in the talks with the other assistant directors and line producer, I couldn't hold myself from checking if Jasneet too had blocked me on WhatsApp. One side of me was in dire need to know if she had done it, whereas the other advised me of not doing so. Honestly, maybe I wouldn't have done it then but Jahanvi's discussion was going longer than expected, so sitting idle and holding my curiosity gave up at the end and I unblocked her.

Blocking her in the heat of the moment made it way more easier than unblocking her and I could feel my hands shivering in doing so. Finally, when I passed completing the task, my eyes shut themselves in a repulsive reaction. I took deep breaths. Normally when we want to see any result we anticipate something but no such thought I had in my mind. With a completely blank mind I did it and the result did and didn't surprise me at the same time. Jasneet hadn't blocked me. I wondered why she didn't do it but failed in getting any response from me. There was not even a single change in profile, same display picture and same status. It made me doubtful about her not using WhatsApp anymore so to find more about it I turned my last seen on and opened her message page again. It showed her last seen this morning at 6.00 am. Somehow, this gave me a sigh of relief.

Jahanvi was done with her work and called me to introduce everyone. Promptly, I blocked Jasneet again and slid my phone in the pocket. In all there were four assistant directors and a line producer. Memorising everyone's name was impossible for an absent-minded person like me; I preferred not even trying to do so.

Before leaving for Chandigarh bus stand Jahanvi explained to me about the location and how it will be used. The brain had been comatose in Jasneet's thoughts before that. It came back into consciousness and learned all the needful before the movie begins. Neither Jahanvi nor I noticed the timing, which was already 5.00 pm and we had almost a 3:00 hour journey due to reach Jalandhar. As soon as we did so, we left from there in the same cab to Sector-43 bus stand.

In the cab, Jahanvi tugged her hands in my right arm and gave me a half hug. She also kept her head on my shoulder and dozed off. In the 30 minutes duration from location to bus stand, Jahanvi was asleep. Timely, I was doing my job by moving her hair aside from her face and this was being monitored by the cab driver from the rear view mirror.

Not a minuscule of my heart wanted to wake her up, but after noticing that the driver's eyes were repeatedly at us from the front seat, I spoke in sotto voce— "Wake up". Because Jahanvi wasn't in a deep sleep, she woke up on my first call and smiled at me.

The enquiry counter clarified about the next A/C bus to arrive is in 40 minutes so to kill the time a cup of tea in a kiosk, Chandigarh and the sky covered with altostratus blue-grey clouds worked well. There are relations on the earth where people put efforts in order to make them work. Also, there are some relations where no conscious efforts are required. Luckily, we two fell in the second category. 40 minutes were extended to 50 minutes and when it finally arrived, Jahanvi noticed her mobile being missing. We rushed every nook and corner of the bus stand, we were bumping into people, moving them aside, even pushing some to make way and let the vision to the floor become clear. Although there were noises of buses honking, people chattering, an old radio playing classic songs, children crying but still my ears were anchored at the voice of the conductor of the bus we were to board—"Chandigarh-Jalandhar, Chandigarh-Jalandhar, Chandigarh-Jalandhar....".

Our failure in finding the mobile persuaded Jahanvi to put extra stress on her mind and recall where she had kept it. Eventually, she remembered to keep it on the table at the location. Unfortunately, all the numbers of the team were in her mobile and I had no one to contact. Moreover, the address of the location was also in her mobile. Above all, availability of anyone at this hour at the location was unsure.

Thus, we decided to spend the night in a hotel and look for it the next morning.

It all seemed like a typical Bollywood movie where a couple is stuck in a different city for a night due to certain unforeseen circumstances. Jahanvi's decision of taking one instead of two rooms filled me with a rapturous mood, unlike when Payal did it. What was in my mind was executed by her.

The dim yellow light as well as lime scented aroma justified the hotel's name— "Hotel yellow lemons". All the worry vanished from Jahanvi's face in a flash as soon as we entered the room as her exhibition of her teeth illustrated it as soon as the housekeeping staff escorted and left the room. She embraced me in her arms.

Her hug blew every trivial and gigantic apprehension I had. After taking her into my arms, I was only left with ecstasy. In no time we were from each other's arms into the bed and kissing each other passionately. This was more passionate than the last two times we did, due to being aware of the fact that we had no eyes on us.

Honestly, eyes were none but intervention was still. Before expected, the housekeeper arrived with our order, given one Vodka and two breezers while checking-in. And the intervention left us both in a laugh.

Alcohol instigates the topics from our life which we confine in our hearts. That's what it did to Jahanvi—"As my last relation, I don't want this to end up being split. Promise me Pratik, you'll never give up on me, no matter what happens between us."

I nodded in acceptance of everything she told. Little did I know that the acceptance was due to Vodka's effect.

"I want to adopt a child; a girl in my life"— she said in her brittle voice while looking at the wall opposite to us with her head on my shoulder.

Vodka till then engrossed me in her pain too and I, who never gave any thought of adopting a girl ever nodded instantly as I always had this in my wish list.

"My brothers loved me a lot, Pratik. But this society had never accepted me. I was always a left out child in my colony with no friends to play with. Brothers had their friends play cricket, while I kept myself occupied with my small blonde doll. You know the kind of Barbie doll, exactly the same. Once I eavesdropped on children of the society talking pathetic stuff like me being an illegitimate child too, my brothers were always ready with their baseball bat and hockey sticks to kick their ass off."

She continued nostalgically, "Then Rohit entered my life and changed everything. Other children of the school too started befriending me and I was accepted by the society as never before. But it's well known that good days don't last long, especially for me. The eldest brother got married and in six months the family was split in two under the same roof. Many-a-times my eldest bhabhi (sister-in-law) plotted against me to be thrown out of the house and almost turned everyone against me when, without my knowledge, a mobile was found, by her, from my school bag. I begged everyone not to be mine but bhabhi called it a white lie as the mobile had my pictures in it and adult messages being sent by random boys. It was the last day when my family believed me and I decided to earn my own money.

Thus, from class 10th I started taking tuitions and paid my own bills; school and college fees, medicines, clothes and literally everything. Things started to get better later, but when Rohit left my hand and believed in the conspiracy of her mother against me of me being a demon who tries to split families; first my own and then Rohit's. He decided to comfortably take his mother's side. I never blame him for it. But that day my soul too walked out my body and I was left completely hollow inside. For days I locked myself in my room. I don't know why but I started to get frightened of people."

Jahanvi added, sounding devastated, "When my condition persisted, then my family took me to a doctor, I was diagnosed with depression which was the root cause of ulcers in my intestine. For three months I went regularly to hospital and it was then that I found my father crying at a corner for me. This left a deep impact on me and I decided to be resilient and focus on my dreams. Thus, I bought a Canon 6D and took admission in the course of direction."— I felt tears rolling down from her eyes and wiped it.

We humans start loving the other person for a reason; some love others smile, some eyes, some love their nature— these all are the shades of love. One such shade is sympathy. We feel others' pain anddecide to help the person to overcome it. Many of us feel our own selves to believe this empathy to be love.

Though, I had heard her story briefly before too, but this time, with Vodka, I felt it and not just heard it. I kissed her on her forehead and she smiled looking at me with her teary eyes.

"I will never leave you"— I said to her while wiping her tears from her eyelashes. She came closer and sat on my lap. In no time, we took the other's lip in ours.

From slowly licking and biting, it became passionate. It was when I reached the back of her ear, she started moaning and eventually we made love.

****

Opening the tank's cover, I came out breathing heavily. There was still no one on the roof. One and a half minutes of hibernation flash back to my last one year in front of my eyes. I got off the tank and proceeded towards the room. Just beside the entrance of the room was the bathroom, so I headed there. I changed into the bathrobe and gave my clothes to the house-keeping staff for drying.

Jahanvi was asleep and had no clue of my absence from the room. I got into the bed with her and fell asleep.

The next day, she woke me up with a kiss, sitting beside me and wished me— "Good morning" in her soft musical morning tone.

I woke up and looked at the clock which showed 11:43 am. It took me a second to get off the bed in haste. I looked at her and noticed she was ready.

Wearing slippers in haste, I walked towards the bathroom and said— "I'm sorry to be sleeping this late. How could I forget that we have to get your phone?"

"I already got my phone Pratik, chill"— I heard it from the doorstep of the bathroom.

My narrowed brows were in a complete confused state which asked for a detailed explanation. Thus she said—"Actually, Akhilesh - the line producer, called on your number at 9am. Luckily, you had a true caller and the name displayed. So, I noted the number and in half an hour I went to the reception and called him stating to deliver the phone here at the hotel. And he was here in 45 minutes"— she smiled in a childish manner with her eyes closed.

We got ready, had breakfast, checked out and left for Jalandhar. Throughout the journey, the only thought going on loop was Jahanvi's story. And I promised myself to be beside her throughout life.

29.

It was more than one and a half months that Jahanvi and I were in a relationship.

This was evident to everyone from the theatre. Many of them would bet upon whether the two of us were in a relationship or not. But, it was a collaborative decision of both of us not disclosing anything about our personal life to the people in our professional world. So, we let them be sceptical and continue betting.

Two people become closer when they share similar interests. We were lucky in those terms as we didn't waste time in deciding for a place to meet — PVR, it was The Place always. Movies were something we both had passion for. In between this one and a half month, there was no movie we ever missed watching together.

I started to find the real meaning of a relationship with Jahanvi. It doesn't only mean spending hours on call but also spending time together; shopping for each other, discussing about the future, exploring new restaurants and also dilly- dallying.

All these feelings were absent in Jasneet's and my relationship. In a year's time we only used to talk over the phone and the only day we met couldn't steer the relationship ahead. Eventually, we two ended up having a painful split.

What I understood about love and relationships was that we need a friend more than a lover in life because love is boring but friendship brings adventure every day. Jahanvi and I had a lot of things in common; movie, theatre, food etc. So, we never felt like disconnecting the call even after being together for the entire day. The umpteen topics would give us a reason for talking for hours on the call. I found all in one package in Jahanvi and she made my life complete.

On the other hand, my over-obsession for Jahanvi took me away from my friends. As unconsciously, I started ignoring them.

"Take some time for us too; you hardly ever come out with us"— Sarabjeet and Babu yelled at me in the gym when I was asked for a late night movie.

"Jahanvi would be waiting for my call"— I grunted and said after finishing my last rep of standing barbell curls.

Eventually, my constant excuses to them led to poisoning our friendship. Thus, there were times when I would get to know about their group outings from Facebook posts and it wouldn't matter to me at all.

This change in my behaviour was well noticed by my family too. Late night calls and getting well-groomed on five consecutive Sundays before leaving was never in my book, which certainly signalled me getting ready for a date.

The only troublesome part for me was the lie with which I started my relationship with Jahanvi, and it was about me being in a relationship previously with RAJDEEP. Thus, I decided to confess in front of her and give our relationship a fresh beginning. Maturely, she handled it well. and accepted having perplexed feelings between content; for not having any ex-lover, and hurt; for lying. Sooner she let go of her latter feeling too. Also, she wanted a clarification of me being in touch with Jasneet or Payal by any means.

"No. I swear. I am not in touch with any of them"— my instant response gave her satisfaction and mouthed "Love you". This rendered a new faith and confidence in me about her – about us.

30.

After removing my make-up and greeting everyone a goodbye, I sat on the bullet, which I borrowed from Sarabjeet, and called Jahanvi- "I am done with the shoot. Where are we meeting?" On my way to the restaurant we had decided to meet in, the only thing where my mind flew to was as to how the project landed in my hands.

Commonly whenever good things start to happen to an unlucky person, he starts analysing the difference he made in his lifestyle. Either it is the colour of shirt he wore, or the route he took to reach his workplace. However, a person in love reasons his lover to be behind his change in fortune.

Same was the case with me. Day before yesterday I got a call from a music director, Nawab, for a shoot of a Punjabi song. I accepted the offer without asking even a single question. Amongst everyone close to me, the first was Jahanvi I called, to share the news. As expected, she jumped off her bed and blew a hundred kisses to me through her mobile.

"I am going to meet the director after office hours. Will give you a call once free"— I said to her.

Once I reached City Square Market, I redialled the number of the music director and called him to reconfirm the office. He called the security after disconnecting mine and one of the guards escorted me to his place.

With no separate reception, his office space had a waiting area for visitors. The black leather couch almost gulped me as I sat on it. Being concerned that no one acknowledged my presence; I stood up in seconds and preferred to stand. There were pictures of singers Mohammad Rafi, Nusrat Fateh-Ali-Khan, Elvis Presley, Gurdas Maan, Amar Singh Chamkila, Diljit Dosanjh hung on one of the dusky shaded walls. A few motivational quotations of famous artists too were carved on a wooden board hung adjacent to the pictures.

As I completed reading a quote by Bob Marley— "One good thing about music, when it hits you, you feel no pain", I was called by a staff member to the director's office.

As I entered his spacious office, the first thing I wanted to suggest him was to have a bigger space for waiting area with better sitting arrangement. But I controlled my outspoken instinct and greeted him with a warm handshake. His appearance was reminiscent of Bappi Lehri but poor with no gold chains or bracelets.

"Pleased to see you Pratik after I saw your tele-movie"— and he laughed out on something I didn't find funny at all.

Keeping my posture straight, without any change, just as anyone in an interview, I said—"Pleased to meet you sir"— when I failed to recall if I ever had heard any of his songs, I was left with no choice to complete the sentence, I said— "after we spoke on phone a few minutes ago"— in my mind I had covered my face in embarrassment and scolded myself for being an amateur comedian.

But he laughed out loud and said— "I know you haven't heard my name before"— the pitch of his voice was persistent.

My second point of getting embarrassed dragged him along with me when I said— "Of course, I do."

My statement left him more shocked than surprised and he confirmed—"Acha? Where?"—the persistent laugh finally tumbled and hit the trough.

I felt no less than a back bencher sitting opposite to the invigilator during viva who's clueless about the answer but gives immense stress on his eyes as if he just remembered it a second ago.

Acknowledging my mistake of being extra smart he said—"You couldn't do it because none of my work is out yet"— and his pitch while laughing catapulted. This time, I joined him wholeheartedly.

He showed me his recording room and studio. Also, he didn't leave the chance of telling the price of all the equipment as if he was the salesman and I was the buyer.

Returning back to his office, he confirmed—"In total this cost me Rs.17 lakhs for the entire studio set-up."

I raised my brows in order to show him the worth and preferred not using my tongue.

Completing what he started, he continued—"I am starting a label under the name of SOOTHING EARS and this is the first project."

My ears paid more attention at last when he started to talk on the topic of what I was called. I nodded to what he said.

After two clicks on the mouse, music started to play, he said—"This is the song, we will be recording with you."

My heart felt delighted to experience a day when I got the opportunity to listen to a song before its release, but I was in a bit of doubt also as the music didn't match the label. It didn't soothe my ears at all.

But knowing the fact, that it's the only and my first chance to get enter as a model in a song, I exhibited my over excitement in being a part of the project and before leaving, at the door, just to confirm if I was getting paid for the project, I asked— "Sir, payment?"

He looked into my eyes as if I had directly quoted to him some random figure in lakhs for acting in it, but acquired his smile and said—"I truly loved your work bro. Wouldn't take a penny from you". Not saying a word I left from there. It was then when the rumour of paying labels to be casted in Punjabi videos was directly experienced by me. However, I considered myself lucky for not doing so at least.

The location of the shoot was messaged to me in late evening. And everything was falling in my basket with extreme subtleness. My shots were perfect, the director from Chandigarh was impressed, and above all the make-up person was the same from my last tele-movie. After the day ended, I started the bike and called up Jahanvi.

I parked my bike and entered McDonalds at BMC Chowk, Jalandhar. She was already waiting inside. After very long I was on cloud nine. I walked to her and hugged her while she was on her seat. But the warmth couldn't be felt from her. I kept my bag aside and sat on the chair opposite hers. I noticed she wasn't dressed how she usually does when we meet. No eyeliner and her tightly tied hair clarified that something was wrong at her end. Her eyes also seemed to be swollen because of crying. Thus, the smile I was wearing was just torn apart.

Her condition left me perturbed, so I asked her hands—"Hey, what happened?"

The tears which she was holding back rolled down from her cheeks and within seconds she started sobbing. Instantly, I moved from my seat to hers and took her in my arms.

I could not resolve the matter, unless the reason as to why she was in tears was clear to me. Hence, the only way left for me was to console her. So, I let her cry and didn't leave her from my arms. Once she stopped and sighed, she told the actual reason—"The movie that we were doing" and before completing she sniffled. I offered her water but she declined it.

After wiping her tears from cheeks and nose with a tissue, she completed—"I have been thrown out of the movie".

Initially, my ears resisted to believe what she just said and took some time before accepting it, so I asked—"Why in the world would they do it?"

Looking down at her own hands while tearing the tissue into pieces, she said— "The director had been messaging me for a week now. From his talks, I was sure that he wanted me to compromise and sleep with him to which I didn't concede and thus the result."

I closed my fist and clenched my teeth in anger before saying— "Bloody bastard." This wasn't enough, then she threw a second bomb on me—"He has fired you too"

The news came as a bombshell to me and left me dismayed. Till then I understood that joyfulness and desolation were on a see-saw in my life. And these both keep swinging.

In an extremely low voice I asked—"Why me?"

The solace that I gave to her was now given to me. She rubbed my shoulder and said—"It's okay. Keep your spirits high."

For Satan it took nine days to reach in the abyss after being thrown from heaven. But for my spirits it took just these five words to reach that low—"He has fired you too."

"Actually, he got to know that we are in a relationship and were together in the hotel from Akhilesh and demanded that I be with him too. I declined the offer and he threw us both out. "

The irony was I started my relationship with Jahanvi to get connections in the industry and today it didn't matter to me a minuscule when she was the reason behind me losing the project. What more I cared about was Jahanvi, who was in tears. As if only her dreams were broken and not mine.

"I have decided that I am going to Delhi"— she said once we both accepted the truth of being thrown out of the movie after some time.

I couldn't understand why she wanted to go to Delhi. Only if it was Mumbai, I could have discerned. I asked—"Why Delhi?"

She took a sigh, exhaled the air and replied—"For now, I have no contacts in Mumbai. That's why I am going to Delhi. Udit is there and he has some contacts with the advertising agencies there."

Women are stereotyped for being possessive. But in reality, it is men who are more possessive and insecure. Just as from far away we can see water on the extreme end of the road but as we get closer we can see it's just a mirage. The same is with partners in a relationship. From a distance the world would judge a woman being possessive but as you get closer to them, you'll realise it's the man who is over-possessive about his woman.

When a never heard name fell on my ears, I wanted to know about her friend more than her plans in Delhi, so in my firm voice I queried—"Who Udit?"

So she started to tell about Udit, who was her classmate in Jalandhar. He along with his family had moved to Delhi in 2001. Their reconciliation happened during the days of Jahanvi's post-graduation in Amity University. In the next 30 minutes, I learnt more about Udit than Rohit, her ex-boyfriend. He belongs to a business family and after completing his studies from McGill University, Canada, he started to help his father in his business. With his knowledge and genetic business prowess he started to expand his business of bakelite sheets in the African continent which previously was limited to South and East India only. In short, now this person was automatically shifted in my hate list to first position, slipping Rohit to the second spot.

The only thing mattered to me at that point was Jahanvi's happiness. If she had decided to move to Delhi, I was no one to question her on it.

"Shall I go?"— Once she told me her complete plan of what, when, how everything would be done in Delhi, seeking my permission was a formality which I understood well.

31.

The first notification after I switched my internet data in the morning was of Jahanvi tagging me on Facebook. With my under eye bags, I opened them partly toread the post. It read—

"Dear Pratik.

How courageously I am posting this after the striking past only I know about it. Honestly, the only person to pick me up and infuse courage is you. From attentively listening to my problems and resolving it as your own; no one ever could do it the way you handled them. Your optimism towards life makes people around realise that the world isn't that bad to live in. Thanks for being a part of my life and standing strong with me. I Dare you poke your nose into finding any grammatical error. I know you are a trainer but I am no student. XoXo.

And along with this was our picture attached that we clicked yesterday at McDonalds. This brought a big smile to my face. I read the time of the post which was uploaded at mid night. The urge of calling her early morning was somehow controlled and I preferred to message, with the thought she would be asleep, to thank and assure her that I will always be beside her no matter what.

In between my job when it was lunch time, I checked my phone and saw 2 missed calls from Jahanvi. After requesting the office boy to warm up the meal, I gave a call to her.

"Hey... lunch time?"— She said in between the chaos in the background.

Jahanvi and I had a common habit of informing the other before going anywhere. But having no idea of her being somewhere at this hour of the day, I asked a question rather than answering hers—

"Where are you?"

The distortions at her background were making her unable to listen, so she took some time before replying once finding a peaceful place—"Hanji… ab bolo? (Yes… now speak up?)

"Where are you? — My attempt of being louder and clearer to her seemed to be rude to her and she raised her voice more than normal –"Please read the messages before screaming at me."

With her being on call, I went on WhatsApp and read her message—"Going to Model town with Shweta for shopping & the ticket for Delhi has been booked for 25th May."

I hit my forehead in embarrassment and apologised to her and in order to compensate for the damage I asked in extreme politeness— "Till what time are you there, shona?"

I heard her giggle but she too started to act in being dominant and said—"We are here till 6pm."

"Will see you guys in two hours"— I said and she cut the call.

Lovers, around the world, have their own species. A couple in love, everywhere, are more in each other's habit than in love.

I got a gaze of her once I entered the door of Nik Bakers. She, along with her friend Shweta, was seated at a corner, eating our favourite red velvet pastry.

As Jahanvi was facing towards the entrance door, her eyes fell on me. She raised her brows and turned her face dramatically. Without notice of her friend, I mouthed SORRY from afar. Walking down towards her, she stood up and gave me a hug. Her friend rose from her seat to greet.

"Hi… Shweta"— she said introducing herself.

As Jahanvi left me and took her seat, I wished a hello to Shweta and we too seated ourselves.

Jahanvi filled a scoop of the pastry from her spoon and fed me. Shweta, on the other hand, was looking at our loving gestures towards each other. Noticing lately but eventually, Jahanvi started to tell the story of how the two became friends in APJ School, Jalandhar. Her mention of APJ hurtled my thoughts to Rohit, who was in the same school.

In love, there's no end to the hunger of knowing each and every minute part of your partner's life-story. In the illustrations of their life, we live along with them without ever being present. So was I playing the role that day; how the two became friends, who were their tutors, when they both, together, were reprimanded in front of the whole class. I could feel the pain when Jahanvi once broke her leg during learning cycling, I laughed when she mischievously robbed tiffin boxes from others' bags, and I was disheartened when Miss. Monica made Priyanka the head girl when everyone was expecting Jahanvi to become one.

The odd part which I felt was - nowhere there was any mention of Rohit and Jahanvi's family. I wanted to know and hear about them. Due to the fact these two were the closest to her in childhood. Any information regarding both could lead me to understand Jahanvi better. But Shweta's each and every word was very wisely measured without giving away any detail about Rohit.

Jahanvi's phone rang two times in between. I saw from the corner of my eyes of her disconnecting it both the times and getting anxious.

Once we were done with an hour's sitting, we called off after Shweta got a call from her mother. Jahanvi picked her both the shopping bags and tucked them in the front hook of her Activa. Till then, I was waiting for her to mention the unknown calls herself but she did nothing of the sort.

32.

Four days had passed but Jahanvi didn't pick a topic of the unknown calls herself. The doubt became stronger when the day before yesterday I eaves dropped her from a distance, at the theatre, warning the caller to dare call again. My sixth sense popped Rohit's name instantly. Also I pioneered the topic of if she is hiding anything to me but she dismissed it altogether. For the first time in months, she hid a secret from me and this was driving me a little uneasy.

Our fixed Saturday movie plan wasn't skipped that week too. We both had decided to watch 'Tanu weds Manu returns' together when its first trailer was released. But I was least interested in sitting in the cinema hall and watching it. The obvious reason was the unknown caller still circling my mind.

I finally decided to ask on her face when I noticed someone calling you from a few days. Before I did it, her phone rang and again an unknown number displayed on the screen and she swiped the red button to the left.

"Who was it?"— I asked in an aggressive tone.

Without making any eye contact, she answered—"Might be some random company call."

Having no intention of ruining anyone else's movie and creating a scene, I held her hand and took her out of the hall. She released her hand, in force, from mine when we reached out—"You are hurting me, Pratik"

Needing a punching bag to throw a hundred punches on, all I could do was close my fist and clench my teeth. I said—"So are you talking to your ex, Jahanvi"— my wrath was apparent in my red eyes, so it was her who lowered her tone.

"It's not him"— she looked away and said.

All the stories that I made up in my mind since the first time I acknowledged the unknown calls had made me venomous. As I further was in the state of throwing all the poison choked up inside me, her phone rang again. We both shared a gaze at each other. She understood from my eyes that I wanted her to take the call.

Without saying a word, she took her phone out and I asked her to turn on the speaker.

A girl from the other side of the phone said—"Have you considered what I said?"— Without an iota of doubt, I recognized the voice; it was Payal. I couldn't understand what discussion was going on between them. This time rather than questioning Jahanvi, I directly enquired from Payal—"And what is that to be considered, Payal?"

This filled a long pause on the other side of the call. Jahanvi's eyes were glued on me while mine was on the phone. We heard a murmuring voice from the phone.

One was, surely, of Payal, but the other was of a man. The two of them were in an argument over whether to talk over the phone or not, but in hushed voices.

Eventually, after 15 seconds, a man in his baritone spoke— "Madarchod Jahanvi ke phone pe tu kya kr rha hai? (Motherfucker, what are you doing on Jahanvi's phone?)

His abuse worked as a catalyst and filled me with fury. I wanted to drag all his forefathers and abuse them all for raising a child like him. But the call was disconnected from the other side before I could commence anything. Jahanvi constantly was stopping me but the wrath in me had dominated my senses to understand anything that was happening there. I redialled the number again and again but the automated machine said *the number you are trying to reach is switched off.* I couldn't even realise my idiocy was tumbled down to the trough which didn't understand that calling from my phone wouldn't switch on his mobile, but I did call thrice.

The day was already ruined and so was the movie. In anger I didn't pay attention to Jahanvi who supported herself by the wall, was still as an effigy, and was on the verge of crying. Just a gaze at her, and my exasperation dipped abruptly. I took a deep sigh and held her in my arms. Having no knowledge of why Payal called, who the man was, what she said to Jahanvi I decided to ask her in peace about it.

As soon as I opened my arms for her, like a toddler running towards her parents, she embraced me tightly. Her short and fast breaths were an epitome of how frightened she had become by the entire episode.

"What was she talking about?"— I questioned Jahanvi, sitting on the round cemented surface under the gigantic Indian Lilac tree at our theatre's premises, when after nearly an hour she was out of the minor panic attack.

Completing the morsel of the sandwich and gulping it, she wiped her mouth with the last tissue she had. She inhaled enough air to breathe deep and spoke—"Were you ever in a relationship with a married woman?"

I smirked as I knew Payal's habit of persuading stories, I said— "Haha... do you think that?"

Jahanvi turned her face and looked into my eyes and in her firm tone she said—"I know the answer Pratik, but this is just to satisfy my flying thoughts."

"Obviously… never. So that's what she said to you that I had been dating a married woman?"

"Hmmm…"

I was well aware of the wittiness of Payal and deep down my heart somewhere knew that she would attempt something in order to break my relationship with Jahanvi, which was going pretty smoothly.

The thought that emerged in my mind was of the day when she called me to the hotel room and in vain tried to seduce me. I was brought back to present with Jahanvi's intervention and continuation of the story—"I didn't even know it was Payal, I got to know it today. And…"— she held her words. I looked at her and saw perspiration running down her forehead. I held her from her hand and asked— "And?"

"Pratik… I am scared. I seriously am. I never had been in contact with people like these. The man warned me if I ever meet you, he will throw acid on my face."

The words cut the ground from under my feet. My ears couldn't believe what she said. I was dumbfounded at the psychic level of Payal that had dropped to ground zero.

Truthfully, I was more agitated than Jahanvi but could not show her. I held her from her face and said—"Anyhow you are going to Delhi the day after tomorrow. Change your number and have no contact with anyone here from Jalandhar theatre group."

33.

It was 7am and as I was on my way to the railway station with Aarohan, I was captivated with a mixed feeling. My heart was happy and sad at the same time. Sad, undeniably, because of Jahanvi, who was leaving me and moving to Delhi forever for a better career, but happy because she finally met my family at my house yesterday. Taking her home without any prior notice to my family was done purposefully. Firstly, I wanted to keep it a surprise for them and secondly, paucity of audacity to inform them of their son bringing his girlfriend home.

It wasn't that my family was not familiar with the name of Jahanvi. Often they had heard her name from me while I kept narrating things and activities regarding theatre. Regularity of her name on my mouth had already given them clarity of their son's relationship status. And I got to know when I was about to take her name and mom interrupted—"I know, she is Jahanvi".

Like a perfect Indian daughter-in-law she too touched mom's and papa's feet, and hugged *didi*. Standing beside them with a big smile on my face and red cheeks, I was nudged by *didi*, who mouthed—"BEAUTIFUL".

In no time, I found Jahanvi, papa and *didi* at one side discussing my habits of procrastination, laziness over not picking my towel after bath, how I often forget the names of pulses when I am sent to market on my own to make household purchases. But, my mom, like a typical mother, tried justifying each and every mistake of mine.

Jahanvi was a bit surprised when she learnt from *didi* about us being tenants and how our ancestral house was unevenly divided by our *dadi*(grandmother)with the bigger portion given to our *chacha* and the left one - a trivial to us. I never got a chance to discuss our family and financial condition with her. I observed her trepidation when she glued her eyes at me, while *didi* was discussing it with her.

However, her words sorted the chaos of thoughts in my mind once I dropped her at her house—"I know what's going in your mind Pratik and I won't deny that yes I was hurt as you never discussed any of this with me earlier."— I wanted to clarify her that it was not intended to hide anything from her but the thought of discussing it never occurred to me. Somehow, I could not utter a word from my mouth.

She continued—"Financial stability is what every girl desires from her partner. Also, we cannot neglect the fact that families too consider wealth important before giving their daughter's hand to a man. But, you know what, when I met your family today, not for a second did I feel that I am meeting them for the first time. They made me feel as a part of them. I understood today that a house cannot give that happiness which a home can. We'll buy a house later but thanks for the home you welcomed me into."

Aarohan stopped the car at the station and I saw Jahanvi, with her brother and *bhabhi taking* out bags from their car's boot. As Aarohan was busy finding a parking place, I stepped out of the car and dialled Jahanvi's number, standing at a distance.

"Hey… where are you"— she said, walking a little far from her brother. "The red jumper suits you"— I said.

Standing with her back at me, I could see her efforts to find me in every direction through the crowd. Finally, she turned 180° and acquired a big smile on her face when she saw me. She gestured to come and meet her brother and sister-in-law. From their 4 years old son, I guessed it right that he was her youngest brother, who is a doctor by profession.

I was trying my best to control my wobbling legs. My gaze was searching for Aarohan to come and accompany me as going to meet my girlfriend's brother could be risky.

While Jahanvi's brother was taking a handbag out of the car, she said—"*Veerji* (Brother)."

He took his body out of the car's back seat with a purple coloured ladies hand bag, he saw my face for more than 10 seconds before scanning me from head to toe.

Jahanvi introduced—"Bhaiya, he is Pratik, my friend and Pratik he is my bhaiya, Dr. Rajesh Sharma."

Since his brother started scanning me, I didn't let a smile leave from my lips even when they became dry. He forwarded his hand to me as a greeting. Realising soon that my shaken confidence had made my palms sweaty, I rubbed it against my jeans and shook with him. He said—"Aah, the guy with CD Dawn, PB08 CZ 9417."

Jahanvi's and my jaw dropped, at the same time, after we heard my bike's number from him. He added—"Saw you from our home's CCTV couple of times when you came to drop Jahanvi home."

Where I was drowned with embarrassment and discomposure, Jahanvi was blushing standing beside me. Words rose from my stomach like—"Yes, exactly that's my bike's number, oh you saw me before, Ohh doctor bana detective."— but nothing was allowed to come out.

Sooner, I was introduced to her sister-in-law, and niece. As Aarohan arrived I introduced him to Jahanvi.

Aarohan and I were standing at a little distance from Jahanvi and her family. Till the time the train didn't arrive, my stomach started to churn with the thought of Jahanvi leaving me. My eyes were glued at her. She too was constantly looking at me from her eyes' corner and would turn her face towards me at intervals.

The train arrived and I offered her brother help to pick the bags. In no time, we located her seat and placed her bags.

Flying in their own pink sky is not all for love birds. To feed their stomachs, they need to return to ground from cloud nine. Therefore, we needed to separate to take our careers ahead.

I saw Jahanvi's eyes filled with tears but she maintained a smile on her face to boost me. There were several people pushing us, finding their bags, some were finding their seats, but nothing could distract us from watching each other. For the first time I felt a pain in my chest, I was sure the heart became heavier from the weight of Jahanvi leaving me. I realised from the next day we won't be meeting at the theatre, we won't be exploring newly opened restaurants in Jalandhar, there will be no weekend movies together. It just seemed like a big vacuum to me.

The honking of the train was heard and her brother, sister-in-law and nephew passed me to step out of the train. Jahanvi waved at them, standing at her seat, but with her eyes glued on me. I could hear Jahanvi's deep breaths; she too was in the same state of pain for leaving me. As the train accelerated, I heard Aarohan calling my name from the platform. I couldn't resist myself and held Jahanvi in my arms and kissed her. We both were, finally, in our own world; the two of us, our lips, and warm breaths. Jahanvi's controlled tears eventually rolled down her cheeks and touched our lips. She left kissing first, hugged me tightly, before saying—"Go Pratik. Please"

I ran out and jumped off the train. Luckily, a little bit of the platform's area was still left for safe landing. She came at the door and I shouted—"I love you, Jahanvi"

She laughed in her tears and shouted back in ecstasy—"Love you more."

****

The female singer of the song, Ms. Palak, and I were called by 10:30am, at the office by Nawab to show the final edit of the song before releasing it on air. So, Nawab turned the screen of his desktop towards us and dimmed the light of the room. I saw a big smile on Palak's face before the video commenced. Of course it would emerge on any beginner's face whose dream becomes a reality.

Career achievement always comes in two verticals; one with happiness, for people who achieve their goals in a certain time period, and second with satisfaction, for people who achieve their goals late in their life. Thus, the latter is satisfied with what they have achieved but not really happy with the time frame.

Palak and I were nowhere in the second category because what we both desired, in our respective dreams, was finally in front of us. So, at the end of the video clip we hi-fived each other for successfully stepping on the first step of the ladder of dreams; she as a singer and me as a model.

The marketing discussion went longer than predicted. And I realised it was already 12:30 noon. 4 missed calls from the office made me jumpy and I took a leave from there to reach the back office.

As I sat on my bike, I received a message from Jahanvi— "Reached safely."

With my bike on, simultaneously, I dialled her number and accelerated to the office. Just two rings rang and the call was disconnected by her.

Her next message arrived that I read from the notification bar without opening—"I am in the car with Udit and his dad, can't answer the call in front of them."

A blend of possessiveness and insecurity hadn't allowed me to even open and mark as the message has been read. I headed to the office and resumed the class till it was 4:30 pm and my day was off.

I saw my phone and saw a missed call from Jahanvi at 3:30pm. Taking a deep sigh, I called her again and she picked up this time— "Hanji.. kaise ho?(Hey… how are you?)"

Her voice was enough for the evading annoyance, I replied in my soft tone—"I am good… how was the journey?"

"Hmmm… pathetic! This toddler beside me was on a non-stop wailing mode"— she said in her irritated tone and after a pause continued—"Leave it. Tell me how your day was?"

From Nawab's call to watching the video, and finally discussing the strategy of marketing, I narrated each and everything attentively. Her happiness for me was vivid from her level of excitement.

"When is the song releasing?"— She asked. "Next week, probably"— I replied.

34.

Jahanvi and I decided to concentrate more on our careers now and made a choice of not chatting or calling each other every hour as we used to. Actually, it was her decision initially which became ours lately. But I too found it valid as wanting Jahanvi in my life was another goal added in my wish list and to get married to her the only way was to earn a lot of money and secure a bank balance. Thus, career had to be prioritised. Unlike the past, now the calculated hours of our talks was reduced to an hour from ten in a day. We had our fixed timing of calling at 10 pm. She would be busy throughout the day meeting people, showing her portfolios, working as a freelancer editor and many more. I decided to be more focused at work, give my best at theatre practices, give more auditions, and burn more calories in the gym. But with the distracted mind, I was failing in giving even half to what I used to give when Jahanvi was in Jalandhar.

My never seen avatar was witnessed by my students and it would only take a request to repeat what was taught for being a victim of my castigation. This change in behaviour was observed by everyone around me as it wasn't limited to my work but accompanied me in the theatre, gym, and at home too.

I was extremely engrossed in Jahanvi till then. Her not being around was making me eccentric. However, for a person like me who never had pleaded with anyone for being with them, approaching Jahanvi for it was held by my self-respect. I was saved, till then as love had only impacted my heart and not my brain. Thinking was still an active sense in me, sometimes.

The only good thing which happened after a week was the release of my song. When I received the link of the song on my WhatsApp sent by Nawab, I immediately forwarded it to Jahanvi and my family's WhatsApp group — Our World. It was *Didi* who read the message before anyone else and sent a hundred emoticons of kisses and hugs.

As soon as I shared the song with other people in my WhatsApp, my messenger was flooded with messages of congratulations and blessings. On Facebook it was shared by nears and dears and they proudly tagged me in their posts.

Paroxysms of delight were never in my fortune and things were changing now. As directed by Nawab, I shared the link on people's Facebook messenger one by one. An unnoticed surprise waiting for me was Jasneet's profile. Actually, she unblocked me from Facebook and never unfriended. Till the time I could calculate anything, the Youtube link of the song was already shared with her. She read the message, I read *typing on* the screen. The message read— "Congratulations. It's good at least you got benefit out of what you did."

It took me half a minute to understand what I read. Lastly, I asked— "What do you mean?"

Typing appeared…

While she was typing, I read the message once again— "Congratulations. It's good at least you got benefit out of what you did."

Her next message arrived—"All those months that we were talking, I was insecure from Payal, who was the closest to you. She was the one you used to talk about and tell her stories of how cunning she is. But, I was completely wrong. It is Jahanvi who you fell in love, with her only credentials being that she is a director."

Jasneet's vitriolic attack directly hit my heart. Her bitter tone and prompt replies made me clear of her not unfriending me and coming across the truth of Jahanvi was done long ago.

Never after she blocked me from Facebook, did I check her profile because never the thought of Jasneet appeared in my mind as I was engaged with Jahanvi throughout the day. What made me clear was her unblocking me from time to time to go on my profile and check it. Once done, she would block me again. I was sure about this because never had I seen her online on my Messenger.

Nevertheless, one question was hovering across my mind— how had she come across Jahanvi? Who would have told her? Is it Payal who contacted her?"

I replied to Jasneet—"Never got the chance to tell you about her."

"LOL. What could you even tell? Jasneet there is a girl named Jahanvi whom I am dating and falling for?"— Jasneet's urge of spitting her anger on me was obvious from her prompt replies.

Not answering to hers, I typed—"Who told you about Jahanvi to you?"

I wanted to know if it was Payal who contacted Jasneet. I was sure I would slap her on her face for interfering in my life.

But Jasneet's reply was—"Does her picture with you and the caption require any other confirmation?"

It reminded me of the post Jahanvi tagged me in a month ago. It was my idiocy of not thinking anything like that. I replied—"Good for you if you have learnt the truth. I know what I did was wrong but I only have my apologies to give for now."

"I hope and wish sorry could heal pain."— she said. I felt a slap on my face with her message and was left with no answer.

Another message arrived from Jasneet—"Pratik… can you please tell me where I was wrong?" because I have started hating myself more than ever."

I knew well there was nothing wrong with her. She always had been loyal, loving, and empathetic to me—"Nothing. You are a perfect girl Jasneet."

That moment, I realised love is hearing your partner's voice while reading their messages.

Also, I realised that I had stopped reading Jasneet's messages in her voice. All of a sudden I could remember her voice.

It took her sometime to reply—"I know I am not. That's why you left me. Is it just because I am not a director that you broke-up with me?"

It was the truth. I started my relationship with Jahanvi just because she was a director but now it hardly matters to me. I wanted to explain all this to Jasneet but I knew neither I could explain her nor could she understand anything. Not receiving a reply from me gave Jasneet a hint of me being least interested in replying to the question.

She sent her next message—"Please be loyal to her, Pratik. To love someone is easy but it takes enough effort to live and sustain that love."

My heart spoke—"She is right, Pratik. Be loyal to Jahanvi. Intentionally or unintentionally, a girl is hurt because of you. We can block people in our life but can't block *karma*."

I knew what I should do and I did the same, I typed—"I am sorry for what I did. Hope you forget me."— And then blocked her. I knew her instincts would never allow her to control herself from not stalking me. Thus, for her benefit I blocked her so that it becomes easier for her to forget me. What a stupid logic that was to give oneself!

"Congratulations my love. So so happy for you."— Jahanvi message on WhatsApp popped in the notification bar.

35.

The reign, the service, and the career are near its end when the thin line between personal and professional life gets blurred and we forget the art of differentiating between the two.

My fight with Jahanvi had not allowed me to sleep for a single minute. I wanted to talk to her over a call but she refused to do so. Udit and his family were around and they all were sitting in the living area together. I suggested she go to her room excusing everyone of being sleepy. But she denied as Udit's sister too had come to visit her. Throughout the day Jahanvi avoided texting or calling me as she was busy in meeting a production house who was going to start shooting for episodes of 'Saavdhan India' in Noida. I consoled my heart about talking at night and her denial made my anger burst at her. For the first time, we ended up being in a war of words for the next hour on messages. In the heat of the moment I abused Udit too which stimulated our fight and she blocked me from WhatsApp.

The outrage was more on Udit, whom I had never met or seen any picture of, than on Jahanvi. Till 4:30 I was changing sides in order to get some sleep. After which I woke up at 11 am and noticed 7 missed calls from the office's landline and 4 from Manager's mobile.

With a heavy head and swollen eyes I reached the office by 12:30 noon, and was called directly into the manager's office.

Be it relationships or profession, one big mistake reminds of all the small mistakes which were ignored.

"From last week I can see you being careless towards students."— The manager shouted at me.

With my head down I was listening to her but being non-respondent.

"Do you want to check the weekly feedback form?"— Not even waiting for my yes or no, she continued—"Every student had a common concern of writing tasks not being discussed in class; neither pre nor post-discussions. No notebook has been checked in this entire week. Do you have any reason to defend yourself?"

The absence of Jahanvi to face my exasperation made my manager a victim of it, I replied—"Only if you are in a mindset to listen."

My reply made her more enraged and her pitch of voice rose—"Do you mean I don't listen to you guys?— Again, caring the least for my answer, she continued— "You know what, if you want to work in this company you better change your attitude."

Not thinking for a while, I said—"I quit."

Her mouth was left open after listening to it. Quitting the job as an answer was out of the syllabus for her. I left her cabin and came with my resignation letter with a 15 days' notice, as per company's norms.

Jahanvi was briefed about the incident after two days when she unblocked me. The preparation of lashing out at her was done by her after hearing the news. Bike's EMI, my sister's marriage, our future, and every responsibility was reminded to me in the next 10 minutes.

Once she finished I replied—"I have a better back- up plan." "And in God's name will you enlighten me on it?"— She said. "I am moving to Mumbai."

She was silent after listening to my reply. I knew she expected to be offered by some other company in Jalandhar but after listening to Mumbai she became speechless.

I continued—"I have spoken to papa about it and he discussed the same with his friend in Mumbai. Everything has been finalised."

After a while she spoke in her soft tone—"Mumbai isn't easy Pratik, you know that well."

I too was well aware of the fact but the under-confident me spoke confidently—"I know it but I know it's the right time. "

36.

Abhilaskshya, my uncle's son, came to Bandra Terminus to pick me up at 4.05 am. I finally was in the city of dreams. What I never told Jahanvi was after my birth in Jalandhar, papa took Mom, *didi* and me to Mumbai to live with him. My childhood days till age nine, I studied in St. Theresa's High School, Bandra. After my father's business crisis in 2000, our whole family shifted back to Jalandhar, our hometown.

When papa moved to Mumbai in 1983, it was Shankar uncle with whom papa did business. Both saw the ups and downs together. When my uncle decided to stay back in Mumbai, papa packed his bags and we came back to our hometown.

The last time I saw Abhi was when he was 8 years old. The tall 6 feet 1 inch boy was, now, working as an art director in a production house. I knew that Abhi was my key to enter Bollywood.

The responsibility on me multiplied when, while boarding the train from Jalandhar to Mumbai, my friends and family members came to see me off at the station with "Good luck Actor" written on the cake. I had no knowledge of where my destiny would take me but what I knew was that I had to give my best and stand up to their expectations.

Shanker Uncle and Meena aunty greeted me warmly at their house. Once the sun rose, I gave a call at home about my safe travel. Once we were done with breakfast, I requested Abhi to take me outside Shahrukh Khan's house.

Like every aspiring actor, I was always a big fan of Shahrukh since childhood. *Mannat* to me was equivalent to Mecca to a Muslim. I spent an hour clicking pictures with the name plate and watching his house. The blurred memories of my childhood appeared to me of how I used to run along the Marine Drive with didi. While coming back home, I visited my school too. It was as if I wanted to live all my childhood in a single day.

While Abhi went to his office and Shanker Uncle at his Supermarket, aunty and I discussed the gone away days; when my dad and uncle decided to shut their business and split their ways. She had teary eyes when she recalled those tough times. Today, when I saw uncle returning back to where he lost everything, dad was still struggling to earn hand to mouth. Aunty also told how Shanker uncle and all their business clients had tried to convince papa to stay back in Mumbai, but he was shattered after losing everything he had earned. The good move uncle did was buying a house during their business' peak and papa used to send money back to his family for supporting them. Hence, he couldn't purchase anything for himself.

Abhi too wanted to become an actor but after wasting his 5 years after graduation in giving auditions and getting no success, he gave up on being one and decided to give his career a different shape. This story was also narrated by aunty to me.

Abhi had looked for a room for me in Bandra, not very far from his house but 20 minutes away. We went to drop my bags there and noticed six mattresses on the floor in a 1BK flat. What surprised me more was that it cost 4000 rupees per person as rent for this! Abhi's calm reaction revealed that it was normal for him to see this scenario. He insisted on staying the night at his home. On our way back, he sensed my dissatisfaction over his room's selection but assured me of getting the best deal; to live in Bandra at just 4000. Moreover, to uplift my spirits he narrated Shahrukh's story of his days of struggling in Mumbai which I already had heard and read several times but still listening once again to it in the streets of Mumbai left a big smile on my face.

"How is the Mumbai boy?"— Jahanvi asked, almost singing it. Matching the same rhyme, I said—"Same as Delhi girl"

Throughout the day, I was waiting for Jahanvi's call to discuss about how I felt when I saw Shahrukh's home, how walking at marine drive reminded me of the *didi* and me running to catch the other, how my childhood's school's building hasn't changed over the years, and finally telling her that a part of my childhood belonged to Mumbai. But she seemed to be less interested in listening to me and instead discussed Connaught place's famous milkshake, about the Palki bazaar she visited, and Udit missed the metro at Rajiv Chownk and she had to step down at the next station where he came in the next metro.

I got involved in listening to her story until she at last said—"I thank Udit for taking me there. You know how much I was getting bored in Vaishali?"

It irritated me to the core but I wanted to avoid any fights.

37.

I was at Bandra terminus once again waiting for my train to Delhi. I decided to give up on Mumbai in just 12 days. It's true that my first priority was ACTING but I had shifted it to my second preference for the time being.

The next day when I woke up after my first day ended in Mumbai, my uncle and Abhi had already gone to work. Being alone at home, aunty started to discuss the same story, with different screenplay, of Abhi giving up on the dream of becoming an actor. Somehow I prepared myself for the worst when she told me that Abhi was various times offered a role in tv-soaps at the cost of compromising with the directors or casting directors. Eventually, it broke his morale and with a heavy heart he gave up on acting dream. For the next week I was called every morning by my aunt and insisted on having breakfast at her house. Along with it, for the next week I was told the same story again and again of Abhi giving up on being an actor. I failed to find the difference between the need of telling the story to bring awareness in me about the industry or precisely for de-motivating me. Honestly, my heart believed in the latter reason.

A person like me who always preferred living in his own space when having to share a room with six strangers felt pathetic. Two Muslim brothers, who run an auto repair shop, were busy in their own life, a Marathi driver, who had moved from Buldhana, had a duty of 12 hours, two students of government polytechnic college would spend hours in library and would come back home just to sleep, a 62 years old inebriate man, who had come to Mumbai in 1978, was still uncertain about his job. The best rule established and followed at the house was that lights would be off after 10.30pm and anyone creating disturbance would be made to sleep outside the room. But the worst was the common bathroom where one big tub was filled in the morning to be used for works like bathing, brushing and filling the bucket for going to the community toilet. The unhygienic environment of the bathroom vexed me completely. After seeing people dipping the bucket they used in the toilet for brushing, I was left with no option but to do the same. Thus, for the next 12 days I lived a life literally opposite to how I lived since childhood. My mental harassment in that place was catapulted at the night when I got up in the middle of the night after smelling an unpleasant odour. The old man used to sleep to my right while the Marathi was at my left. I turned the flash on my mobile to see what it could be. On finding nothing on my left, I turned to the right and saw the old man's mattress being filled with his vomit. The liquid was just about to reach my mattress when I pulled it in force. Having no other vacant place for my mattress in the room, I spent the whole night watching the sky in the corridor.

I found auntie's story quite honest when after my audition in Mumbai, conducted by a casting director, for a role of protagonist's friend; I was hinted by the director for a compromise. His body language cleared it enough when he held my hand in his office when we two were alone and slid his fingers in mine. The forceful pull of my hand left his mouth open and he threw me out of his office.

Above all, during my days in Mumbai, my relationship with Jahanvi was becoming bitter because of our consistent fights. Someday she wouldn't talk because of her meetings and the other she wouldn't talk because of Udit and his family being around. When I was left all by myself in Mumbai, talking to her was my only way to find serenity but she was absent. A loner, frightened, demotivated became an insecure lover too after finding Udit being in Jahanvi's room at 8 in the morning.

After my calls went unanswered thrice by Jahanvi, it was Udit who picked the call and informed her being in the bathroom taking a bath and disconnected it. The incident led Jahanvi and me into a verbal fight for the next 12 hours before I was informed that I am coming to Delhi.

I failed badly in handling the chaos and I decided to sort my differences with Jahanvi first. My career seemed uncertain to me. Hence, I didn't want to lose what I had. I left destiny to decide my path. Jahanvi assured me of starting my career as a model in Delhi as it too has a huge fashion industry. For a while, I thought about it and believed it was an oasis.

Love makes us optimistic. That's the worst thing it can do to you; because after that calculations stop and we let love decide our fate.

38.

It left us two in a big smile after seeing each other after almost a month. Anyone's eyes mattered none to us and we hugged tightly that even air could not pass through us. Everything that was scattering into pieces for me suddenly combined together once I saw Jahanvi at the station wearing a parrot shaded one piece dress. The enthusiasm I was devoid of for days returned and I couldn't control my exhibition of teeth.

From New Delhi station to New Delhi metro we walked hand in hand. We could never experience roaming in the city with our fingers into each other when we were in Jalandhar due to the fact that family, relatives, colleagues or any other person could bump into us. However, there was nothing to worry about in an alien place to us. This new found freedom of exhibition of affection was making me feel exhilarated.

The coach of the metro was compact. She laughed when I complained about it to her for choosing metro over cab.

"Get adapted to life here."—she said and winked at me. She continued—"Metro is the spine of Delhi".

Within a second I heard the announcer—"Rajiv Chowk. The doors will open to the left"

The name was reminiscent of the day when Jahanvi narrated her story of being split from Udit at this station. As I was lost thinking about it, I felt Jahanvi tugged her hand in mine and took a step forward towards the door. As soon as the door opened, I had to do nothing and with zero effort I found Jahanvi, my luggage and my body with no organ loss outside the metro and I took a sigh of relief.

I said—"If the metro is the spine of Delhi, this station would surely be the lumbar vertebrae.

"Today it was very less crowded due to the weekday and noon

time."— Jahanvi said and walked ahead.

I had no doubt Udit and Jahanvi lost each other at this station when in the worst, it can be loss of life too.

Rajni *didi* was informed about my arrival. She assured me of leaving early from the office and picking me from Connaught place. The ambience of Wenger's, Jahanvi and my story of days in Mumbai kept us engrossed for two hours until Rajni *didi* didn't arrive. Jahanvi's eyes got filled and she held my hands tightly. Words didn't require its use that day to illustrate how apologetic Jahanvi was for not being around when I needed her most.

"Short hurdles prepare for big challenges"— Jahanvi said while looking at our clutched hands.

I passed a half smile to her and it made me think of Delhi being never on my cards but eventually I have arrived in this city.

While we were talking, Rajni *didi* arrived at the restaurant and she noticed me before I could. As she arrived at our table, she called— "Would you like to order anything else, Sir?"

A change from male waiter to female made me take my eyes off Jahanvi and look at her. Watching *didi* in front of me, we both were left in a big smile and we hugged each other.

"Jahanvi she is Rajni *didi* and *didi* she is Jahanvi"— I introduced both.

Both of them gave a half hug and *didi* asked—"Would you prefer to be called Bhabhi (Sister-in-law) or Jahanvi?"

Jahanvi's cheeks turned red as she heard it. Honestly, so did mine change colour.

As the women started to chat, another two hours passed. It wasn't until Jahanvi got a call from Udit for returning home that we left the place. I dropped Jahanvi at the escalator of the metro and sat in the car with *didi*.

I was thinking of asking *Didi* about Jahanvi. I thought it should be "Did you like Jahanvi?" or "How did you find her?" to start my conversation but before I could she popped the question —"Who's Udit?"

39.

"Where is the office of Star Media Pvt. Ltd?"— I asked a fruit vendor and he gestured to the East.

It was a long open street and its end was nowhere being seen. I lowered and knitted my eyebrows together with his pathetic answer. He could have mouthed the least by telling if it is 2 buildings ahead, 3 kms away, or in a different country altogether!

Jahanvi pulled me from my arm and we stopped by a man in his 50s to ask, he said—"It's round the corner."

****

While I was having a cup of tea with *Bhua* ji and Pankaj bhaiya, Rajni *didi* was gathering her needs to leave for the office. Already, she had missed the office cab and now the Ola driver was waiting for more than 10 minutes for her.

Bhua ji and *Bhaiya* were calm and gave no expression upon it as it was just another day for them. *Bhaiya* said—"Relax, it's normal for us. You too will get used to it."

Just then *Bhaiya's* phone rang with a beep message, he took his phone from his pyjamas and said—"Got it."

My sip of tea was half-way through when I paid attention to him. He continued— "I am sending you the number of a casting agent. Go and meet him"

As soon as I received the contact number and address, I messaged Jahanvi—"We need to go to meet a casting agent in the Central Secretariat by 1:00 pm. Get ready. We'll meet at Rajiv Chowk"

****

"Hi, we are here to meet Mr. Chirag Mehra"— I said to the receptionist and she asked us to take a seat.

The waiting area had 15 more people in the queue and they all were there to meet the same man. I know it's a competitive world.

Small hoardings were hung in the hall which showed us about his acting and modelling classes being conducted.

Jahanvi was being supportive, she said—"You are getting your speech ready for Tedx talks."

I chuckled as she said it.

After two hours my name was called by the receptionist. Jahanvi and I went in his office. The man in his 40s was wearing a tiger printed shirt with his upper two buttons opened. His first appearance reminded me of the casting agent I met in Mumbai but unlike that person Chirag didn't seem to be interested in boys.

"I got to know about Pankaj's cousin coming to meet me"— He said in his baritone voice.

I saw his last cigarette still burning in the ashtray and he picked his next from the pack and asked—"Do you mind if I..?"

Not waiting for a yes or no of ours, he lit his lighter and blew the first puff. Thanks to his office's ventilation system, we didn't choke in his room.

I narrated all my works that I did in Punjab and he was quite impressed by it, he said—"It's highly appreciable that you attempted something at the local level before stepping to a bigger city. This surely will help you."

Jahanvi and I looked at each other and smiled. Once my introduction was completed with Chirag, he asked Jahanvi—"What's your acting experience?"

Jahanvi was confused about his question as nowhere we had mentioned Jahanvi too being there for meeting him, she said—"No no no… I am not here for… I mean, I am not an actress."— And gave a smile.

He put out his cigarette and stood from his seat. Taking out a file from his small cupboard, he threw the file on the table, he said— "This Italian pathology laboratory is going to open their chain in India. For now they are opening their eleven laboratories in Delhi,

Mumbai, Bangalore, Chennai, and Kolkata. You can become their face, if you want."

Jahanvi looked at me. She had zero interest in acting and even had no knowledge about it. I read her eyes and it was clear she wanted to reject it but couldn't say Chirag on his face. I initiated—"Actually sir... with all due respect. She has no knowledge of acting and even has no interest in it. Her experience has always...."— I couldn't even complete my sentence when he interrupted me—"No no no... this isn't about acting. It's a print media shoot. You have the perfect face according to the client's requirement. And for this one day shoot you will be paid INR 10,000 rupees."

Without thinking for a second time, I said Jahanvi in her ears for accepting it. She still was confused but accepted the offer. Chirag was happy as he finally found what he required, I was happy that at least one among us had started getting work, Jahanvi was happy seeing a smile on my face.

We left the office and walked down to metro station. Throughout our way we were thinking of what destiny has in store for us. Never would I have come here, never could I ask Pankaj bhaiya for getting a casting director's number, and I became the link between helping Jahanvi and Chirag meet.

Jahanvi said—"Exactly, it's all about destiny. Things are written. Even if it wasn't you to be the bridge it would have been someone else."

I shrugged in acceptance of what she said. Once we reached the station, she said— "Pratik, you go from here."

I was left in a dilemma, so asked —"What happened?"

She replied—"Udit is nearby and had asked me to go with him"

Not a second passed and I felt a burning sensation split through my ears, I asked her in high pitch—"Do you tell him everywhere you go? Or do you take his permission before you go anywhere?"

The state of anger was now split into two halves and with irritation in her voice she said —"How can you talk to me like this man?"

We two were in our raised voices in the middle of the metro station's gate, I said— "What do you expect from me Jahanvi? That

I should act normal when my girlfriend leaves his boyfriend for some other guy? Or shall I say you leave your first boyfriend for a second or vice versa?"— With every question I asked to her I didn't realise that I almost shouted at her.

She noticed before me that every eye around was pointed at us. Her eyes got filled with tears and she left the place. As she left, I wanted to calm the storm in me before going back home so I bought a cigarette from a shop and lit it.

40.

In the last 10 days Jahanvi and I had a fight for almost seven days. Unfortunately, what was apparent to me was not to Jahanvi or the least possibility was she was pretending everything to be normal.

Udit offered a job to her in his office till the time she didn't find any in her own field. The reason which led us to fight was that she didn't discuss it with me prior to accepting the offer.

"I am going short on money, Pratik. Can't keep asking my family to pay for my bills"— she said.

"This is Delhi. You can get ample of jobs if you really want to do one"

"Oh really? What job can I get here?"

"Video editing, photography trainer, graphic designer and so on. Why do you need Udit's favour?"

"Will they allow me if on short notice I get a meeting? Will they allow me consistent leaves if I get a video shoot on my hands?"— I knew she was correct on her part but deep down I wasn't ready to accept the reality. I was in no situation to be empathetic on points like my girlfriend living in his house will now be spending her entire day with him at his office.

It was just then an idea clicked in my mind, I shared it with Jahanvi and to my surprise she accepted it—"Leave his house and live in a PG."

She smiled and pulled my cheeks—"Look at your face Mr. Possessive"— I took my face back to resist it, she continued—"But I'll have to take a PG in Vaishali itself. Can't step out of this area as of now."

I pulled a cigarette out of my pocket and lit it—"Do whatever you want to but get rid of his house for now."

She pulled the cigarette off my mouth and threw it away, she asked—"Hey… since when have you started smoking?"

I hesitated answering her question and looked away but had to answer when she repeated her question by stressing each word—

"Since when have you started smoking?"

Not changing my sight on her, I answered—"For the last 10 days since our fights commenced."

On noticing that I was answering without looking towards her, she stood right in front of my face and said—"That's no excuse Pratik. Even if we fight or separate tomorrow it doesn't mean you'll get addicted to cigarettes. It just shows you are a coward to face reality on your own, if you need stuff to make you high."

As she said the words of being separated, a flash of losing her appeared in front of my eyes and couldn't feel the earth beneath my feet. My knees became weak at a prompt and I lost control of my body. Thus, I held the handrail of the staircase leading to the metro station below. Luckily, all this happened within a blink of eye that no one noticed it, not even Jahanvi. I spoke nothing and we started taking the downstairs.

Once we reached the platform from where she was to take her metro for Vaishali, she said—"It was a nice experience today being in front of the camera instead of behind it". I passed a smile at her looking how happy she was after completing the shoot for Chirag and getting INR10,000 without any delay.

The metro to Vaishali arrived and she kissed me on my cheek and took steps forward into the queue of women. Whereas, I took some steps backward and watched her from a distance.

The metro got slower and she turned to look at me and noticed my facial expression, with her raised brows, she mouthed—"What happened?"

But till then she got a push by the girls behind her to step inside. Instantly, I took out my mobile and called her. As she settled on the seat, from the glass window I saw her taking her phone out from the pocket. Before picking it up she turned and looked at me again with a smile. She picked it, I said—"We'll never get separated no matter what it takes."

Her eyes were glued on me till the train started and left the platform. I disconnected the call and headed towards the yellow line to take my metro for Keshavpuram. With a beep sound, my mobile in my pocket vibrated. I took it out and it was a message from Jahanvi. It read—"I promise, we'll never."

41.

Rajni *didi* took me on a walk before it was 12 am. I heard her talking to Pankaj bhaiya to bring the cake but I pretended not knowing anything about their plan. So as *bhua ji*, Rajni *didi*, and Pankaj *bhaiya* were passing messages to each other via eyes, I noticed them doing so and smiled. It was my birthday and *didi* wanted to make it special for me, I knew.

Just before the clock ticked at 11.30 pm, *didi* stood from the chair and ordered me to accompany her till the ice cream parlour. I took my phone and walked along with her.

There were quite a few reasons behind making my birthday a special. Firstly, it was my first birthday with *Didi* and her family. Secondly, I was in Delhi after 12 years. Apart from this, it was special for me because of Jahanvi. It was the first time we were present on each other's birthday. Deep in my heart I wished for her being with me at that moment.

As we were walking, *didi* and I shared no conversation till the ice cream parlour. Post which she became the ice breaker and asked—"So how is your work hunt going?"

I smiled and said—"It's going smooth *didi*. Getting some leads from people and hope things will start falling in my basket soon."

"Great"

"And… How about Jahanvi? Has she found work?"

I took a pause before answering as I was in a little dilemma of whether I should tell her about she working in a friend's company but dropped the idea, I said—"She is in talks with a few advertisement agencies"—and smiled, turning my face towards her.

Silence prevailed longer after this… but she questioned further being hesitant—"If you don't mind… May I ask you something?"

"Of course *didi.* You don't need to seek my permission"—I said.

"How do you two get along?"— She asked, breaking every word with stress.

People generally ask this question with excitement and interest but her tone revealed there is something more that she needs to know than was just being shown. Thus, I asked her directly—"*Didi*, please ask directly what do you want to know?"

We were just a street away from the house. She stopped and turned towards me— "Jahanvi is four years elder to you. How did you meet and are you happy with her?"— It seemed to me that her concern for her brother was quite natural and genuine. I mused to myself that since we had come to Delhi, there wasn't a day that we two didn't fight. My odd behaviour also led *didi* to doubt our relationship.

Clarification on her doubts was required as it sets Jahanvi's image in her mind. Therefore, I started telling every detail of the story to her. From how we met during a shoot, Jasneet, Payal, when she planned to move to Delhi, how I landed in Mumbai, what happened there and lastly about the reason for our conflicts - Udit.

She listened to me without interrupting me in between and it worked for me as a therapeutic session. Nonetheless, somehow it helped my heart become lighter.

I asked in excitement—"How do you find her?"

She rubbed her face with hands before saying—"I still don't find her the best match for you. I feel like she hides truth"

I asked further—"You mean she doesn't love me?"

"No, it's not that. You can love a person for life and hide truths from them. She seems the same to me."— Her words drowned me in deep thoughts, she continued—"From what I have heard and noticed is that she loves you, no doubt about that. But this habit of hers, can be problematic for you both in the long run."

It was just then, the clock ticked to 12 o'clock and *didi* wished me Happy Birthday. We went home and the lights were off with only candles being lit. I called everyone to come out of the rooms. Just then Bhua ji and Bhaiya came out with balloons in their hands.

"Where is the cake?"— I asked.

Bhua ji spoke—"Girls… bring the cake"

I narrowed my brows to understand who was there to bring the cake and then I saw Dixita *didi* and Jahanvi walking with cake in their hands. As I was overwhelmed, I hugged Dixita *didi* because she came from Jalandhar only for my birthday celebrations. Then I gave a half hug to Jahanvi due to the fact of bhua ji being around but deep down in my heart I wanted to kiss her.

While hugging Rajni didi, I whispered in her ears—"Thank you for making this birthday the most memorable one".

Once we were done with the birthday celebration, Rajni didi, Dixita didi, Jahanvi and I went on the terrace. While both my sisters were at one corner, Jahanvi and I were in another.

"I have got the job in an advertisement agency in Noida"— Jahanvi said.

My body position changed from resting on the fence with one leg on it to standing actively on both my legs, I said in exuberance— "Wow… that's the best news to hear."

She smiled with her lips' edges parted till its extreme and said— "It's Udit's friend. They are working with some top brands in India and abroad."

When I noticed that Dixita and Rajni didi were busy talking to each other with their faces on opposite sides, I held Jahanvi from her waist, pulled her closer and kissed on her lips. She instantly pushed me and stood at a distance.

I said—"Love you to the moon and back."

42.

Jahanvi and I were in Kirti Nagar furniture market purchasing a home décor for my rented 1 BHK flat nearby Rajni *didi's* house, Keshavpuram.

****

It had been more than a month that I was trying my best to give auditions and find some work in acting and modelling but nothing, no apple was falling in my basket and finally I was led into the same condition like Jahanvi where I felt that I can no longer ask my family for paying my bills.

After uploading my resume for IELTS training on Naurki.com, I was getting calls from BPOs for openings in their companies. I wanted to find something in my own field but after finding the unpopularity among Delhiites for moving abroad, I acknowledged that demand in the industry is poor in this part of the country unlike my hometown. Thus, I accepted to work in a BPO because I had to sustain myself.

My first interview with Convergys went perfect and I started working there as a Customer adviser for their U.K based Orange process.

Due to my previous work experience, I was offered more than the others who were selected and with that I decided to move into my own house rather being a burden to *bhua ji* and family. Rajni didi castigated me for doing so but after two days of argument she agreed for my moving on the condition of getting a house near the vicinity.

When I finally settled on a house, I locked it and sent its pictures to Jahanvi. The next day she was there for me and we decided to shop for the house together.

****

We got a sofa cum bed, two bean bags, one folding almirah, utensils and other needful items. The task of purchasing became exhausting, but the cleaning of the house was still pending. The day started at 10am for us and finished at 9pm.

Rajni *didi* called Jahanvi and me for dinner at home but I refused because of *Bhua ji* as she shouldn't know about Jahanvi's stay at my place.

We ordered food from a nearby restaurant, ate together on our newly bought Chinese plates, laid down together in one sheet, and made love in our bed.

Jahanvi's half of the clothes and other stuff was at my home. Out of two keys, one was with her and other with me. The family opposite to my flat believed in our story of two of us being engaged. Our habit of watching movies every weekend continued as we started living together. For nearly half of the month she would live at my place and next half at her PG. She became tremendously busy in her work and so was I. In between balancing my professional life, from Monday to Friday, and personal life, with Jahanvi, I forgot about caring about my physique. Also, my family back in Punjab required financial help.

The thought of becoming an actor slowly and steadily started to die in me even without my realisation. It could have only been possible if I would have given some time for self-analysis but it never happened. My life became more about making everyone happy. At work my relentless efforts were being well noticed by the management. Weekends were booked with Jahanvi. On weekdays when I would get some free time, I would visit Rajni *didi*.

We celebrated Diwali together. Even, Jahanvi's birthday was celebrated at our flat where Rajni *didi* and few of my office friends were invited.

I somehow adjusted and accepted where life had taken me. I don't even remember giving any auditions once I started my job.

Jahanvi was out of town for her work so I decided not to spend the weekend alone and called my colleagues for a beer party in my flat.

I forgot to hide a collage of my photo-shoot from the days when I used to do modelling. They were left dumbfounded when they came across the truth that I once had six pack abs below the beer belly today!

Cigarettes, beer, and some new friends always engross into nostalgia. They wanted to hear how an actor from Jalandhar landed in Delhi and I, being drunk enough, unravelled the truth that I had concealed from months.

"Love makes people forget themselves"— Aman, one of the colleagues spoke. I smiled with my half opened eyes.

"It's true that in love people forget about themselves and what only matters for them is their partner's happiness and satisfaction."— Aman continued. I smiled after listening to him and missed Jahanvi. But Aman continued in the next second—"However, the only time they do something for themselves is the last ten seconds before they cum during sex.

43.

The New Year holidays were over and I needed to head back to the office. However, Jahanvi decided to stay back a little longer. After months when I took Jahanvi home, Dixita *didi* was extremely happy to see her.

We two even went together to meet our group from the theatre. When they saw us coming they ran into us to meet. What we found from their conversation was they already knew about us two being in a relationship but no one asked us directly.

Payal's presence there was obnoxious because I heard from a friend months ago about her exit from theatre. Another person confirmed to me about her visits at the theatre on alternate days and she sits at the stands all alone.

When Keshav confirmed the rumours of Pratik kissing Payal, I felt goosebumps. I denied any such allegations and asked him not to talk about it to anyone else.

Actually, I was just concerned about Jahanvi. I didn't want her to be listening to any such nonsense which was of no relevance anymore.

I asked Keshav—"Who told you about this?" He replied—"Payal herself told about it"

I wanted to go and talk to her directly but Jahanvi's promise kept me from talking to her.

"Who else knows about it?"— I asked Keshav with my clenching teeth. "Almost everyone"— he confirmed.

I felt lub-dub of my heart as I panicked that Jahanvi might get to know about it. But luckily nothing like it happened and I promised myself of not taking Jahanvi there anymore.

Jahanvi's brother and sister-in-law, who came to see off her at the station when she left Jalandhar in May 2015, invited me for dinner as they too knew about our relationship. Also, they gave a green signal to us. This made us fly high in the sky.

All in all for me and Jahanvi it was love, love, and love all over showered from all sides. With a smile on my face I boarded the train.

44.

Delhi without Jahanvi was making me suffocated. No doubt, I got more friends than before in Delhi to hang-out with but a part of me was with Jahanvi and I felt empty within when she wasn't around.

We were in the cafeteria at 11pm for our dinner when Aman received a call and headed outside. On his return he took me to a corner and asked—"Is Jahanvi in Delhi?"

I smelled fishy as he asked it because never in months he asked about her, I responded—"Mmm… no. She isn't."

His hesitation in asking something was vivid—"Would you mind doing overtime tonight? Actually, I have a friend who needs a night's stay. She'll leave by 7am."

I chuckled the way he asked—"You need to get your girlfriend to my room. Just get it straight." He laughed as I completed and didn't speak a word. Thus, it confirmed that what I said was authentic.

I resumed—"Don't worry. I'll do it. You should spend some time with her."

I informed him about the keys being kept in the soil of the Areca palm plant outside my house.

He confirmed it through a message once he found it. I replied—"Enjoy" with a wink.

****

And it was then when I started missing Jahanvi even more. Being miles away I could smell her fragrance when she was in my arms, I missed holding her from her waist closer to me, I missed naked bodies warming up each other in the duvet.

I was left smiling as I recalled the incident when we both had a fight over selecting the phone's back cover and ended up not cooking dinner and going to bed with our backs facing each other. Neither of us could sleep and at nearly 1am she called me in her softest voice—"I cannot sleep like this Pratik."

Never had I remembered her taking a pillow but my arm to support her neck, I knew she was missing it and couldn't sleep. Thus, I took her in my arms and hugged her.

The next minute she spoke—"Not this. I cannot sleep with an empty stomach. I could hear my stomach making sounds."—I laughed as she said, making a childish face asking something from his father.

I ran out to the kitchen and cooked eggs, curry and rice.

****

As promised, Aman had taken his girlfriend away before I reached home. I messaged Jahanvi—"Missing you a lot. Come back soon."

I didn't know back then that her travel to Delhi will instigate all the blunders in our life.

45.

Jahanvi had her reservation in Shatabdi express from Jalandhar to Delhi. Just to confirm she hasn't missed it, I called her at 7:30am. The call went unanswered.

Once I reach home by 7:00 am, it becomes difficult to fall asleep. But that day just to wait for Jahanvi's call, I climbed the stairs to the roof. The foggy day interrupted the view of the Metro station, which was opposite my house. I combined the two chairs kept there and laid back on it. I lit a cigarette and enjoyed the chirping of the birds.

The calmness of the city is one of the rarest moments that one can experience. The cigarette ended and I dozed off while waiting for Jahanvi's call.

After 20 minutes when she called me I woke up in haste and felt how cold my body went. I picked her call and ran down into the room.

"Hey"— she said in her sleepy voice.

I yawned before replying to her and said—"Hello... boarded the train?"

After hearing my voice of yawning, it stimulated Jahanvi's need for yawning too. Now, I realised yawning was actually contagious, even miles away! Once I completed a longer yawn than mine, she said— "No... I need to go to Chandigarh today. Need to meet a client."

I took a short pause as my heart felt heavier with the thought of "I won't be able to see her today too."

With a deep breath I said—"Miss you. Please come back soon."

The day seemed longer to me. I slept for 6 hours but it broke after every one to one and a half hour.

Just when I reached the office gate, Jahanvi's message about her arrival in Chandigarh was received. I called her back instantly—"I thought you might leave from there by now. It's already 6.30pm and you are in a different city all on your own. I don't think it is safe for you to travel now. Have you booked your ticket?"

I rained questions at her as soon as she picked the call.

"Hey hey hey… hold on Pratik"—she said and chuckled.

She continued—"I couldn't help it as this was the only time given to me by the client. It's not a strange city, I am well aware of it. I will take a room in a hotel here and will take the first bus to Delhi tomorrow morning."

The idea of staying back in Chandigarh sounded safer to me than travelling in the dark. Thus, I agreed to what she said.

I said—"Take care of yourself. Love you"

The traffic at the work was heavier that day than normal because of some technical issue with the internet. Hence, we had an influx of calls and couldn't take our breaks before 1am.

Once we got free, I took out my phone to check if there was any message from Jahanvi and yes there was about her checking in the hotel. To remind me, she had shared pictures of the room she was in and asked "Remember?"

I was left with a big smile on my lips when I saw she took the same hotel and same room where we stayed in Chandigarh.

After checking the time of her last scene, which was 10:57pm, I gave up on the thought of calling her.

Just when I opened the lock of my room once I reached home by 5.30am, I received a good morning from Jahanvi. I called her and on the fourth bell she picked it, I said—"Hey Good morning."

After a pause she said—"Good morning"— and grunted.

"What happened?"— I asked but I knew she might be struggling to close the zip of her overloaded bag.

She took a sigh of relief and said—"Phew… now its closed" I grinned as I heard it and asked—"So leaving?"

"Yes… just now." "Alright… see you then" "See you"

"Love you and miss you"— I said.

She didn't hear it and kept her phone aside without disconnecting it. I thought to disconnect the call myself but later decided not to do so and when she finds it out I'll tell her that I kept waiting for my response of "Love you and miss you."

"This will sound romantic"— I spoke in my mind.

I heard her talking to the room service to take her belongings to the reception, she filled the feedback form and after a while she asked the receptionist to ask someone to keep her luggage in the car.

I heard the car's door being shut and a male spoke in his tenor voice—"what did he say?"

"Nothing... just casual"— Jahanvi said.

"Did you tell him about..."— he paused without even completing the sentence. Jahanvi's response was quick—"Noooooo...."

As there was a pause on their side, I was still trying to think who the man could be with whom Jahanvi is talking to. My first guess of him being a cab driver went marginally wrong as the person seemed to be familiar to her.

No words were shared between them for the next few minutes and Jahanvi still hadn't noticed her phone, so I decided to disconnect and call her back to know about the man beside him.

I did the same and called her, she said in her low voice—"Yes Pratik?"

My chest could feel the thumping of the heart, I asked—"Reached station?" "Just about to reach in a few minutes"— She replied.

"Who is with you?"— I asked and there was a pause at her side. The silence at both the ends now made my ears easy to listen to the lub-dub sound of my heart.

In her shivering voice she replied after a while and said—"No one... I'm in the auto."

My suspicion grew stronger after she said it because what I already had overheard was that she was taking a car. Now as her white lie was caught, I somehow knew who the person with him would be. So

I threw a guess—"There is no need no need to hide now Miss. Jahanvi Sharma, I know you are in a car and the person you are with is Udit."

Their murmuring sound was audible to me, she said—"I can explain Pratik."

Her acceptance completely shattered my trust into pieces. I was left awestruck when it was confirmed that what I said was correct. I fell on my knees in my room and disconnected her call. My mind started to overthink of Udit and Jahanvi being in the same bed where once we were, her cheating me, betraying my love for him. All those promises we made to each other seemed worthless to me in that minute. It became difficult for me to breathe. With tears in my eyes, my vision blurred. To let my heart cry, I buried my face in the pillow and screamed aloud till my throat and lungs didn't choke.

The entire scenario made me recall the day when Jahanvi and I were in Chandigarh and her words pushed me to get my hands on cigarettes. The difference was back then I had to go to buy them, while today I had it in my bag. I turned off my mobile, sat on the balcony, opened the two beers I had in my fridge and smoked four out of five cigarettes I had. It was then when I fainted on the balcony.

I woke up after 4 hours with a heavy head and eye bags. The pain in the head was intense but still lighter than the one in the heart. I switched on my mobile to check the time if I have missed my cab. It was nearly 2pm and there were still two hours left for my cab. As the network got its signal, a message from the airtel was received which told about 27 missed calls from Jahanvi and on WhatsApp I received 71 messages from her. I just turned a blind eye to it all and smoked the last cigarette from the pack.

46.

Lack of sleep and overthinking had drained the entire energy from my body. In the last 24 hours I had smoked more than 18 cigarettes, which was more than I had in all since I started smoking. With my bag hung on my shoulder, I walked from the cab to my home with wobbling legs. It itched on my nose and I scratched it with my right hand. The odour of cigarettes was soaked in the nails of my index and middle finger. Thus, the need to smoke one more emerged. I searched in my bag and couldn't find any. Luckily, the grocery store round the corner of my street was lifting the shutter of his shop and I changed the direction of my legs from room to his shop. From the last 100 rupees currency I had in my wallet, I bought cigarettes and smoked the first till my room.

As I reached my room, I found the lock missing from the lattice door. I freaked out with the thought of an intruder breaking into my house. I opened the lattice door and pushed the second door but it seemed to be locked from inside. I doubted if I was on the wrong floor trying to open the wrong house. I checked the flats beside me and all were familiar. I went upstairs and the view was unrecognisable. I ran down quickly and rang the bell of my flat. On the third bell, I heard the sound of the door.

Jahanvi was standing right in front of me. I felt my ears burning as soon as I saw her and I wished an intruder would have been better than her. I passed her in the house and got into my bed. In the bowl, which I was using as an ashtray, I threw my cigarette. Watching me in this condition Jahanvi didn't question once.

In my hoarse voice I asked—"What are you here for?"

Standing with her back rested to the wall she answered—"We need to talk" I smirked—"Is there still anything left to talk about?"

Her soft tone was unchanged—"Yes, there is. You cannot punish me for something that I haven't done."

I laughed on her face as I knew that's the one thing that irritates her a lot; laughing in between serious talk—"So how was your night with Udit? Enjoyed?"

I saw a drop of tears rolling down her cheeks within seconds. To be honest, my heart didn't melt. Rather, it grinned.

She said—"You have no right to throw false allegations at me."

After a pause I said in the most sarcastic tone—"I don't even have any right to you."

She ran into me and hugged me and wailed. The anger against her evaporated somewhere and I felt sorry for making her cry with my harsh words. But still, I didn't apologise.

She left me after a while after she acknowledged that I hadn't responded to her hug. She sat beside me on the bed. She started speaking—"Udit's dad called me for helping with a presentation of his company's upcoming project. The meeting was scheduled and at the last moment their manager had to return from Chandigarh to Delhi because of his daughter's asthma attack. Thus, I was asked to demonstrate the project to the client. I couldn't turn down their request after remembering all the help they provided me. Once we were done with the meeting, I took a room in the same hotel we were in and Udit went back to his maternal uncle's house. Next morning, I came to Delhi with him."

Once she completed narrating the entire episode, I looked into her eyes, which were still filled with tears. I wanted to believe her but still my heart didn't accept it. I took the duvet over and went to bed. After a while, she joined me and hugged me from my back. Somehow, her touch gave my mind relaxation more than the cigarettes I was smoking incessantly for two days. I didn't even know when I slept.

After I woke up, Jahanvi wasn't beside me. I heard the sound of the screeching of utensils. I walked up to the kitchen and saw her cleaning utensils, whereas, rest of the things were at their places. Ever since she went to Jalandhar, I hadn't cleaned my house apart from the bed.

Our habit of kissing on the other's lips was a way of wishing good morning to the other which never happened that day. From the corner of my eyes, I noticed her watching me pouring the tea made by her in two cups. I picked mine and left the place.

She made a chignon out of her displaced hair, which was interrupting her from working, and picked up the broom. The balcony didn't require much dust unlike the room. She did the same, and started cleaning it. The bed sheet was changed and the bean bags were thrown in the balcony. On removing the covers from the pillow and bolster, she placed them on the bean bags under the sun. More than 12 burnt cigarettes were found while she was sweeping. If it wasn't for the distance created between us after the misunderstanding, we would have been fighting over the cigarette butts. I observed her murmuring something after the cigarette butts were found but she spoke nothing about it to me.

I finished my cup of tea and went into the kitchen to keep the empty cup in the sink. Her unfinished cup of tea was still on the shelf uncovered. Keeping hygiene in mind I threw the tea in the sink and kept the cup there. As I returned to the lobby, I found Jahanvi sitting on the floor beside my chair. I passed her and sat on the chair.

Not long after I sat, she spoke—"We need to talk."

Having no interest in doing so, I avoided responding to her.

She repeated her sentence with clarity and a bit louder—"I said… We need to talk"

This time, I folded the newspaper, kept it aside, sat on my knees and said looking into her eyes—"What do you need to talk about? That you weren't with your Udit in that room? That you haven't fucked your best friend or you haven't…"— I hadn't even completed my sentence when she brought a pack of condom in front of my face.

I was perplexed by what she wanted to say. I saw her eyes which had a combination of pain and rage in them. On the other hand, my mind started guessing what she wanted to denote.

I said—"What?"

She answered in her raised pitch—"That's what I am asking you about… What is this?"

Still, I couldn't understand what she was trying to say. I said—"It's a condom."

"Even though I know that Pratik, what is it doing here?"

I replied—"It might be left from the last time"— Unable to recall when I brought it and where it was kept.

She smirked with tears now rolling down her left eye—"Pratik, we used the last condom and I threw the empty pack myself."

Finding the discussion leading nowhere, I stood on my feet and sat back on the chair and said— "It might have been left in your bag from my honeymoon in Chandigarh"— I was purposely using these words to hurt her and honestly the more she was getting hurt, it was healing my pain. It was strange in a way.

This time, my words had hit right in the centre of her heart and she threw the pack of condom on my face which had hit on my right cheek. She yelled at me—"Don't you dare to speak with me like this. I found it in your room beside the table."

The minute she spoke "Table", it reminded me of Aman. He told me about some sealed condoms kept on the table. I clarified—"Oh… yes, these are of Aman. He came here with his girlfriend a couple of days ago," I said as a matter of fact.

She stood, walked into the room, and closed the door with a bang. I thought of her being angry with me for letting some unknown people use our bed but she returned with her bags packed and said— "Go sleep with the whore you brought here in my absence."

47.

I had no interest in clarifying to her about the unused condoms in my house. Actually, I felt better ever since I was hurt and was in pain after knowing she was in Chandigarh with Udit. It soothed my mind when I learnt it wasn't only me who was suffering but Jahanvi too was hurt after what she believed to be true.

Days passed and none of us had contacted each other. The urge to talk to her would emerge every morning when returned home after work. Many-a-times I dialled her number but could not press the call button. It became a routine to check her display picture on WhatsApp which was taken down by her. There was even a tint of fear in me after seeing her display picture of her blocking me but my misconception would get an answer after reading her unchanged status since 2013; "At work".

Rajni *didi* noticed that something was wrong between Jahanvi and me as my visits to her house became more frequent than before. My weekends which were occupied with Jahanvi shifted to spending time at her house.

Time and again she asked about her and I replied, without looking at her, of her being busy until she directly messaged Jahanvi one day. Without any filters Jahanvi narrated the complete story. On my special request *Didi* made Rajmah rice and fed me with her hand, as always. We went on a walk where she asked—"Why isn't Jahanvi coming on weekends with you?"

Walking straight and avoiding making eye contact, I said—"She got some project to be completed before…"— she cut me in-between and held my arm to stop— "She told me everything."

In love we are more concerned about our partner's image in front of our relatives than our own. Jahanvi's acceptance had left me dumbfounded and I knew now *didi* would never want me to talk to her again after knowing she was with her best friend in a hotel room.

After my non responsive behaviour led her to continue with the topic, she asked—"Who was the girl?"

My eyes shifted from looking down to look at her as the words struck my ears.

Both my hands were in my jacket's pocket and with raised shoulders and narrowed brows I asked—"Who girl?"

She took a sigh before speaking—"She told me about the packet she found…"

I cut her in-between and exclaimed in surprise—"Woooh woooh woooh… wait a minute. She told you about what she found in my room and not what she did?"

She looked into my eyes but didn't reply which clarified to me of Jahanvi telling half the story to her and portraying me as the guilty one.

I continued—"It was Aman, my colleague. He brought his girlfriend to my room when I was at the office."

She listened patiently to what I said and then asked—"What did she do to you?"

I was left shut at her question. I never wanted to discuss about Jahanvi and my problems with any of our family members but eventually I was left with no other option. I discussed about the details of her telling me the story of going to Chandigarh for a meeting with a client and how the next day I found of her being with Udit in the car on their way back to Vaishali.

I could read from *Didi's* eyes of how irked she was after getting to know that. Had it been Jahanvi confronting the story from a to z, it would have done less damage.

48.

Sunday used to be my day for dusting and cleaning. As always, a combination of Punjabi beat and pop music's list was made and I was on with my headphones with volume to its maximum. What was different this Sunday was a pack of cigarettes in my pocket where another was lit just after one got over.

The utensils were already cleaned and clothes were washed. The part I hated that day during dusting was the ashes of cigarettes would spread every time I would clean with a broom. Like a child I was running behind it to catch it. As I did so, my left leg slipped because of the water splashes that came from the wiper I had kept in the room. My head got hit on the floor and the headphones got removed and fell away from me.

Bang-Bang Bang-Bang

I could hear the knock at my door aloud. I sensed there were two hands beating the door in an arrhythmic tone. Somehow I managed to help myself rise from the fall, I grunted as my right knee was badly hurt. With wobbling legs I walked up to the door and opened it. Rajni *didi* and Jahanvi were together. With red eyes *didi* punched on my right shoulder and entered the house. Jahanvi followed her. Now there was nothing on the right side of my body.

Didi patrolled the whole house before sharing a word with me. Room, balcony, kitchen, bathroom were properly checked by her. Jahanvi and I stood still in the lobby away from each other without exchanging any greeting.

Didi walked up to me and with both her hands on her waist, she questioned— "What were you doing?"

I looked at Jahanvi before replying to *didi* in order to understand the reason behind the investigation. Jahanvi with her folded hands didn't turn her eyes towards us. I replied—"I was cleaning the house". After a pause, I asked—"What happened?"

Didi continued with her questions—"Why is your mobile off?"

I stuttered—"I… I… I… switched on the flight mode because I thought no one would call me in the morning and I was listening to music with my headphones on."

Didi looked at Jahanvi, Jahanvi looked at me and then at *didi*, I looked at Jahanvi and then at *didi*. *Didi* looked back at me and hugged—"Ohhhh… my sweet little brother. I am sorry. I doubted you."

"Now I understood the scenario completely. As they were knocking at the door from 15 minutes, when I didn't open it they thought of me being with a girl. That's why *didi* checked all the rooms."— I spoke in my mind.

I chuckled but didn't say anything. I saw from the corner of my eyes that Jahanvi bit her both lips and controlled her laughter.

As *Didi* and Jahanvi walked up to the kitchen to make tea, meanwhile, I completed the cleaning and arranged it with a new bed sheet and pillow cover.

Delhi's chilling cold, Sun's morning rays, and cup of tea helped us to relax amidst Sunday's chaos.

To kill the silence *didi* instigated the conversation for what she brought Jahanvi along with her. She spoke—"okay… so let me start with the reason I brought you both here."

Rather looking at *didi* as she spoke, Jahanvi and I glared at each other with a ray of hope.

"Misunderstandings and cancer are just equivalent. Both grow with time if not treated"— she said.

I knew she was there to resolve the difference which arose between Jahanvi and me and somehow I too wanted it. Her absence made me realise that I love her much more than I hated her. Although, I had no proof of her being with Udit in Chandigarh, yet I considered later what I said being in the heat of the moment. My heart wished her side of the story to be true.

Didi continued—"I have spoken to you both in person and I have concluded that it is a mere misunderstanding and nothing else.

Jahanvi showed me the chat between her and Udit and it proves her being innocent. Whereas, I know my brother when he lies or says the truth. Please don't ruin your beautiful relationship for the sake of a trivial reason."

Jahanvi looked at me and so did I at her. We had our eyes glued at each other for the next few seconds after which she crawled up to me and hugged me. It felt like the rock on my heart was moved away by her and felt much lighter and relieved. *Didi's* assurance stimulated my desire of wanting her back in my life. Thus, I hugged her tighter than she did and I whispered in her ear—"I missed you so much."

Without any delay, she replied back—"Love you a lot."

As we were in our own world, *didi* coughed to get our attention. We left each other soon as we heard and blushed.

Didi said—"I got to take mom to Jhandewalan Mandir."— And she stood to leave. At the door, she said—"Happy Valentine's day to you both."

Immediately after the door closed, Jahanvi and I started to kiss wildly there. I pushed her forcefully at the door and started to kiss around her neck. She moaned. I slipped my cold hands under the sweat shirt she was wearing and felt the heat of the body on my hands. She removed my hoodie and t-shirt and so did I. 7°C didn't matter to us and continued kissing there for next 10 minutes in our bare bodies. As we stopped, we looked at each other and grinned. Being unable to breathe she mouthed—"Happy Valentine's day"

I lifted her in my arms and took to the bed. We made love as it was our first. We made love as there was no tomorrow.

49.

A strong relation breaks several times before finally breaking.

Ever since our reunion, Jahanvi and I started spending more time with each other. Our love grew more than ever. The void created in our relationship was overflowing with love now. I realised how much fights are important in a relationship which multiplies the desire of wanting the other manifold.

Jahanvi took a promise from me to never smoke again. Without a second thought, I promised her. I didn't even feel the need to smoke as my mind found its tranquillity.

Jahanvi's mother wanted to meet me so we selected to go home together for Holi celebrations.

"Now that's the most beautiful surprise one can give"— my mother said that with a big smile on her face and ran down the stairs to hug me after seeing me from the balcony. Hearing her, papa and Dixita *didi* too came from their rooms and hugged me. Every time I would come back home after two to three months of gap my reverence would increase, for a day at least.

The list given by Dixita *didi* of the things to be bought from Delhi on my next visit required a different hand bag and so was passed to her.

As I was in Jalandhar only for two days, I wanted to talk to mom and dad about getting married to Jahanvi on the same day. Also, they needed to know about my visit to Jahanvi's mom tomorrow.

Throughout the day I was waiting for the perfect moment to initiate the conversation about the topic circling my mind. I didn't want them to judge my conscience. We both were having no plans of getting married before *didi*, but an assurance to her family had to be given.

Once when I gathered all my courage to talk to Mom but she was taken away by massi's(maternal aunt) call. Another time *didi* grabbed mom from her arm and wanted to show the Maybelline makeup kit palette I bought for her. Finally, after dinner I got the audacity to talk to mom and dad while we went for a stroll.

"I need to talk to you guys"— after completing three lanes, I ultimately spoke.

Mom replied in her softest tone—"I am so sorry. You wanted to talk about something during the day too and I got occupied."

"Aah... that's no issue"— waving my hand I said.

Papa spoke in his baritone after clearing his throat—"Is everything fine back in Delhi?"

Within a second I said—"Yes... Yeah... absolutely... all good back there."

We stopped at the T-point around the lane under the streetlight and I felt more frightened than minutes ago when I started the conversation. The panic stricken situation for me was because for the first time I was going to talk about a girl with my parents in a very official manner. Although, they met the girl already and they knew about our relationship too but today I was there to talk about getting to tie the knot with her. A boy of 25 with an unsettled career, whose elder sister is unmarried, who lives in a rented house when breaks the hierarchy and talks about his marriage – this entire background made me worry to know how they would react.

Mom read my eyes and asked—"Is it about Jahanvi?" Mothers will be mothers, I pondered to myself – they have that sixth sense always working for you.

I felt the lub-dub of my heart and nodded in acceptance. They waited for my words now. I spoke—"Jahanvi's mom wants to meet me tomorrow regarding our marriage."

Mom and papa looked at each other. I sensed that they had an opinion about this which surely wasn't a green signal. Papa spoke— "I hope you know you have an elder sister at home for whom we are looking for the best match."

I lowered my head and nodded.

He continued—"It is not that we are against your marriage with her. She is a sweet kid and if you two are ready we don't have a problem with it. But just that you are getting married before your elder sister is something which doesn't sound like a good idea to me."

I clarified the misunderstanding to them about which I was doubtful. They felt a bit relaxed about our decision of not getting married before *didi*.

Mom said—"*Beta*, but she is 4 years older than you."

I looked at her without uttering a word, she continued—"Will her parents accept it?"

Jahanvi's *bhabhi* (Sister-in-law) already knows about us and has no problem with it. To what Jahanvi and I guessed was that her mom and dad too will accept our relationship.

I nodded to her question and lied about them already in knowledge of it.

Papa questioned—"Does Jahanvi know that we live in a rented accommodation?" "Yes, she does."— I replied

"Will her family accept this?"—he asked.

I had no answer to this. After talking about it when Jahanvi came to our house, we never touched this topic again.

The next evening I was at Jahanvi's home. While Jahanvi was in the kitchen with her sister-in-law, I was sitting alone in the living area. On the opposite wall was the big fat Punjabi family photo, which was reminiscent of the picture from *Hum Saath Saath Hain* where the eldest members were sitting, hung with all the thirteen members; the children were standing behind and grandchildren were sitting in front of Jahanvi's parents.

My concentration was broken by Jahanvi's mother's entrance in the room and I stood to touch her feet.

With a broad smile on her face she said—"No need to do this, *beta*."— And gestured to me to take a seat. Sitting opposite to each other the basic questions about family, job, and career started till Jahanvi arrived with a tray of coffee cups and biscuits.

Jahanvi was dressed in the pink cotton straight suit we bought from

Moments mall, Kirti Nagar. I smiled at her as she was looking more beautiful than ever before.

She read my eyes and blushed.

Her sister-in-law then entered with some fritters and grilled sandwiches. We just smiled at each other because of the reason that we had already met before but Jahanvi's mom had no knowledge about it.

The coffee was accompanied with Jahanvi narrating the story of how we met in a shoot and finally became friends.

"Aunty, I can't see uncle around."— I asked in my low-tone voice with a smile on my face.

However, her reply was with a straight face—"He wouldn't agree to this marriage, I knew. So I wanted to have a word with you on my own before I convinced him."

I passed a half smile at her and then gazed at Jahanvi who diverted her eyes from me.

Jahanvi's mom and I were left to talk in person after a few minutes. A 24-year old failure who was unprepared for any marriage plans for the next few years was completely blank to talk about marriage, but still I was sitting right in front of my prospective mum-in-law!

With her left leg over her right and hands folded, Jahanvi's mother spoke—"So what do you do in Delhi?"

After clearing my throat I said—"I work in a BPO there"

And then her list of questions rained on me—"On what post?"

"As a customer associate"

"Hmmm… the lowest post. Isn't it?"

With a pause and being uncomfortable I nodded while biting my lower lip.

"What's your salary?"

I became conscious of answering that. What my mind predicted was her reaction that went exactly the same after my reply—"22,000"

She raised her brows that depicted how dissatisfied she was.

After leaving their home I felt embarrassed to even think about marriage at this stage. While directly heading to a betel seller's shop, her words kept playing repeatedly in my head and I could hear her voice clearly.

"You earn 22,000 and pay rent in Delhi, you have to send money to your family, your family lives in a rented house, how will you manage to survive the inflation?"

She hadn't spoken a single sentence which I wasn't aware of. All I was doing for years was running away from these questions. I understood the thin line between knowing the reality and facing the reality.

I bought a cigarette and blew the puff for the first time in the air of my home town. I chuckled at what I planned for myself and what I had become since last year. A career oriented boy who worked hard on his physique had an unshaped body today, a boy who'd rather than giving auditions is talking about his marriage, a boy who smoked cigarette only once in his college days today has become a chain smoker.

As the first cigarette finished, I bought the second, then third, and disconnected three calls of Jahanvi in between.

Although Jahanvi and my ticket were confirmed for next morning, I took a bus the same night to Delhi without dropping any message to her. Her calls and messages were ignored constantly.

50.

The question followed me till Delhi too and haunted me. The last quarter of Blenders Pride left in the house was gulped down as soon as I entered the room. Unluckily, the grocery shop in my lane hadn't opened but the urge to smoke forced me to knock on the owner's house and insist he sell me a pack.

The noise of door-bell ringing woke me up from sleep at noon, and with efforts of opening fallen eyelids I walked till the door. As expected, it was Jahanvi who threw her bag on me in rage and yelled at the door—"What is your fucking problem? How did you leave me alone there and came back last night?"

I took some time to settle myself and spoke softly—"Come inside"

She pulled her arm away from my grip and warned me to touch her. The people passing by slowed down to see the piece of entertainment for them. After my persistent pleas to sit and talk she finally gave in. While holding her hands, in the bed, I spoke—"Jahanvi, I had a word with your mother and I guess she isn't happy with our relationship."

She interrupted—"Listen…"

I interrupted her and insisted—"Let me complete…" She nodded.

"She is absolutely correct at her end. There are always expectations of parents for their children's future. No one can shut eyes after knowing the insecure future of their children."

She listened to me with her attentive ears and said—"It's nothing like that. It's true that they didn't agree with the proposal initially, but I convinced her late at night in our discussion."

A smile arose on my lips just like sunshine after a hazy morning after more than hours. I hugged her and she hugged me back. She questioned in her throat filled with tears—"Will you leave me every time in between without any discussion?"

I took her face in my arms and assured—"Never Jaan"

As soon as I said it, she broke into tears and said—"Do you know how frightened I became when you left me alone there? I felt ashamed of myself. I felt like the past was repeating itself"— and she started to choke. Listening to her gave me immense pain too. I was now all embarrassed and feeling pathetic for myself for bringing tears in her eyes and stranding her mid-way. To console her I took her in my arms again and kept her head on my left chest. I kissed her forehead. She continued— "Will you too leave me like my real parents did?"— I shook my head and couldn't speak a word.

"Will you leave me like Rohit did?"— I shook my head again and was on the verge of breaking into tears.

"Will this time too I won't become a bride?"— She questioned and I felt pain in my throat. I wished the emotionally immature me would break into tears and cry his heart out and exhibit to her the love I felt for her but it couldn't happen.

Being well aware of my habit of not crying in front of anyone, she experienced a change for the first time in me and heard pain in my voice as I just spoke a word— "No". As soon as she heard my unclear voice she left me and looked in my eyes, she said—"Please don't leave me Pratik, I can't live without you"

I replied—"I promise. Will never."

We were back in each other's arms and laid on the bed in the same position as always; her head on my shoulder, me holding her from my arm and fortifying her, her left leg on my lap and her arm around my stomach.

After some time I asked—"Did you assume I would come back to Delhi?"

She raised her head and smiled looking into my eyes, she answered—"I called your home last night."

For every day we were happy, we had to pay for it with hefty interest. This vacation of happiness lasted only for a week.

51.

Jahanvi wasn't responding to my phone calls and messages from two days. All I was thinking about was what went wrong or what wrong had I spoken to her. My out of focus mind at work led me to fall far behind my day's target. Her being online and not responding to my messages was irking my instinct to finally break the promise of not visiting her PG ever. Ultimately, my mind started to wander to weird thoughts and one such imagination was the scenario where Udit and Jahanvi were together in Chandigarh.

Be it Facebook, WhatsApp, Instagram, Snap chat, I flooded her accounts with messages on all and left no stone unturned to abuse her over ignorance. She read all the messages but didn't respond to any. This stimulated my anger and I threw the utensils from the kitchen to the lobby.

Doubts of her mother instigating her to break all contacts with me, her father refusing the proposal of our marriage, or brother being the barrier too crossed my mind but my heart believed Jahanvi standing strong with me in every situation.

I decided to message Udit on Facebook and ask for her. Udit and I neither spoke to each other nor were Facebook friends. Long back, once, he accidently liked one of my posts that I shared, and it didn't take him long to unlike it. Luckily, I was online and it got into my notification. Since then I have been checking his profile time and again.

But what surprised me that day was that I wasn't able to search his profile. There were chances that either he deactivated his account or he had blocked me.

Thinking about the second scenario catapulted my anger. To confirm, I called Rajni *didi* and asked her to search for Udit's profile on Facebook. Calling at odd hours, while she was at work and asking for stalking someone, and above all my tone made her suspicious. But before asking what happened she did what was instructed to her. When the list appeared she asked—"Is it the one where Jahanvi is a mutual friend?"

My legs become restless and I started to walk fast from one end of the room to the other and answered—"Yes, you are able to see it?"

With a pause and very softly she replied—"Hmm… I can"

This boiled my blood. Ironically, it shouldn't have mattered to me as we weren't friends but it irks me all the more as he had blocked me because of the same reason- we weren't friends.

I ran down stairs and bought two packs of cigarettes. While I blew one cigarette at his shop, the customers stepped away from me. I walked till the building and sat at the entrance. The empty house was suffocating me. Anyhow, Jahanvi never was always in the house but being far away too she was always with me. But today, I could find no trace of her after two days.

While thinking about this the first cigarette finished and I lit the second. As my mind relaxed a little, thinking about Jahanvi and Udit became passive.

Just then a car stopped in front of me and Jahanvi stepped out of it. I stood from the ground instantly without cleaning the dust from my jeans. She was wearing black ripped jeans with a pink flower printed white crop top. She was looking beautiful as always. As she stepped out, the car accelerated and left. My eyes couldn't take off from her face that I hadn't noticed who drove her there. All the anger for her that I had contained inside me since morning somehow evaporated after seeing her. I was assured if I had a tail; I would be wiggling it like the pets do after waiting for their masters throughout the day.

I hugged her tight. The change that I could notice in me was my eyes got filled with tears and I was on the verge of crying for the first time in front of anyone without being embarrassed or afraid. I wanted to share every drop of tear with her and thank her for returning back to me.

"I missed you so much…. You don't know what…"—I stopped completing the sentence as I realised that she hadn't hugged me back.

I left her but the smile didn't leave my lips. I asked—"What happened… are you okay?"

"Can we go upstairs?"— She asked with a straight face.

While going to buy cigarettes I forgot to shut the door and it was left open. I saw Jahanvi and thought she would scold me for this but she turned her face away without speaking a word. I found it obnoxious.

While entering she was staring at the lobby's floor which was covered with spoons, plates, bowls, and other utensils that I threw just a few minutes ago. To clarify it I sat on my knees to pick them and chuckled—"Actually, I was just…"— but she stopped me and said— "It doesn't matter. Let's talk."

My heart started to beat fast after her cold reaction. She was never this cold blooded. She didn't scold me downstairs for smoking, she spoke nothing of me being irresponsible for leaving the door open, the mess in the house had not affected her a single percent.

We walked in the room and I gave her space to sit on the bed, beside me, but she pulled the bean bag and sat away, yet another act by her which wasn't normal. The same thought arose in my mind that her family had outrightly rejected the proposal of marriage.

She pulled her phone out and showed me a picture of a woman, she asked—"Who is she?"

I took her phone in my hand and tried recognizing the face but failed, I replied with shrugging my shoulders—"Don't know"

She smirked with her raised brows. She took the phone from my hand and swiped the next picture and passed her phone once again— "Who is this child?"

The picture was of a 3-year old boy in his vest and short pants at the seaside.

Because the child was busy digging the mud, the picture couldn't capture his face properly. Thus, I was unable to recognize him too. Therefore, I slid my upper lip behind my lower lip, shrugged and shook my head.

She took her phone away from me again and showed the next picture—"I believe you would recognize this picture. At least", she said, putting stress on her words.

Looking at the picture and it stupefied me as it made me acknowledge the woman and the child as the picture included me. It was a picture taken outside the theatre, clicked by Payal, and the woman was kissing my cheek. But in what context was Jahanvi asking for it was still not understood.

I passed her the phone and asked—"What is this doing with you?"

She got tears in her eyes, she jibed—"Shocked to know that your lie has been caught?"

The word game was getting too far from my understanding and I asked her—"Be clear please. I am not getting you."

She stood from the bean bag and took a few steps to support her back with the wall. She kept her right hand on her forehead and left on her waist. The tears contained by her eyes now had started to roll down. In her choking voice she said—"You had an affair with a married woman when we were together…huh?"

I ran towards her and held her face in my hands—"Hey… Hey… there was nothing like that. I don't even know this woman. She said she was a fan and wanted to have a picture to be clicked. That's it."

She pushed me away, pointed her index finger at me and yelled— "Don't fool me Mr. Pratik Sharma. Who are you? A superstar that you'll have a fan dying to get a picture clicked with you. Huh? You are nothing Mr. Sharma, a failure in life who had run away from Mumbai within 12 days. That's your reality."

Her words hit me hard. My stomach started to churn. The only good memory I had from a short span of my acting career was the days I spent in Jalandhar and Mumbai. All those were broken with what Jahanvi said.

As I went numb, Jahanvi continued speaking—"You don't know her? Then what the hell were you doing with her in the hotel Country INN's room?"

My mind flew to the day when I went to see Payal in the hotel for the last time. I wanted to clear it to Jahanvi but couldn't tell her as I had hidden about my meeting with her. Thus, I said nothing.

Jahanvi came with yet another picture, which was of a register's data of the hotel. It read-

"Name- Mrs. Seerat Kaur and Mr. Pratik Sharma Time In - 5:00pm

Time Out- 5:55pm Date: 28/02/2015 Room Allotted- 224"

My jaw dropped as I saw it. What became clear to me was, I went to meet Payal and got trapped in her cunningness. From where to start and how to explain to Jahanvi, I fell short of words. My mind was running at a breakneck speed but my tongue was crawling. There were hundreds of ways in which I proved myself to be a scapegoat in my mind but Jahanvi couldn't hear a single word that day. The strong wall built between us was an obstacle for her to understand me.

This wasn't enough until the last picture was shown to me by her. This picture was where I was kissing a girl. The angle of the picture was where the back of the girl could be seen but not her face, but anyone could recognize me. It was a well-planned trap thrown by Payal. It was from the day when I went to see Keshav's show in the theatre and Payal and I kissed for a second, which was certainly accidental.

My head started to beat fast and I felt like throwing up. If once in our life we would have a veto power to go back in our life, I would have gone back and never met Payal. How subtly she executed her plan to break my relationship with Jahanvi had to be appreciated.

There were words spoken by Jahanvi that my eyes could see but for ears it was impossible to catch. This was one good thing that happened to me in that hour. If the process of listening to her would have continued, I am sure in guilt I could have killed myself. My soul left my body and I could see it standing in between me and Jahanvi. The soul smiled, the reason for the smile wasn't clear and I had no energy left to ask even. The body remained stoned until I saw Jahanvi passing through my soul and shaking me. I got back into consciousness. Again the thought of clearing the entire misconception to her arose in mind but my heart said it's too late.

Jahanvi asked—"Since a week this woman had been messaging me and she came to Delhi especially to meet me. I didn't believe her when she told me about it on the phone and I wanted to shut her mouth after the meeting. But guess what? Vice- versa happened."

My mind started to join the dots between the story and I even got a clue of why it happened now. I asked Jahanvi—"When was the last time we went to Jalandhar. Did you meet anyone from the theatre?"

While folding her hands with her chest she asked—"I am here to confront you and you still dare to ask me questions?"

"Just answer me. Please?"— I insisted.

"Yes… I met with my friends from the theatre."

"And you shared your number with them. Haven't you?" With a pause and a shaken voice she said—"Yes. I did."

I hit my right fist on my left palm as hard as I could, I spoke in an excited tone to make her understand—"It's all been done by Payal. Since you shifted to Delhi, there wasn't any threatening call, a stalker, no intervention in our life but as soon as you shared your number with your friends in the theatre she got your number again and the whole game started."

She put stress on her mind to re-think what I just said but within a second she said—"I am not here to listen to any of your stories Pratik and again fall in your trap. I spoke about it with Udit too and even he thinks you to be a cunning person."

My awakened enthusiasm drowned again and this time it died. I knew Jahanvi was in no condition to listen or understand anything because of the assumptions she had made about me these days.

She said—"I want to break this relationship."

In no time I hugged her and pleaded—"Please… Please… Please Jahanvi. Don't do this. Don't leave me. I can clear things. We can sort this out…"

She repeated more strongly this time—"I have decided. I want to break this relationship."

She released her from my arms and stepped back. Within a second her phone rang and she picked it—"Yeah Udit. Coming"

I walked towards her and held her from her shoulder and said— "Let me talk to Udit. I am sure he can understand me. Main mil loon use? (Shall I meet him?)"

With a smirk, she said—"Tum us layak nahi ho ke kisi se milwa sakoon(You are not worth to be introduced to anyone)"

My legs gave upon me and froze there. She walked past me but I couldn't stop her. I lost two things to her that day; Love and trust, and one thing to myself; self- respect. Only two voices were audible to me that moment; one of my heartbeat and the other was of her footsteps heading towards the door. A little energy contained in me was exhausted with no will of regaining it. I felt the acute pain of loss that day. Neither it was in the heart nor in the middle of the chest, it was right in the centre of stomach and liver; pancreas. It was severe.

The sound of the door closing was heard, and my last percent of energy left me after which I fainted.

52.

"Tum us layak nahi ho ke kisi se milwa sakoon (You are not worth to be introduced to anyone)"— Her words echoed in my ears for three long months, not even a single day passed when I could not hear those words ringing in my ears. To unlisten it, cigarettes and alcohol became my regular partners. Burnt cigarettes and empty bottles of alcohol could be easily found in my home more than bread to eat and water to drink.

I found myself being blocked by Jahanvi, on the same day she left my home, from WhatsApp, Facebook, Instagram, and whatnot. The graph of calling her per day plunged in the next few weeks from eight calls to two calls per day and ultimately zero.

From the list of best performers, my name got shifted to poorest performers. Thus, many times I was instructed by my team leader to improve my performance or else he won't be able to save my job. When I couldn't close the given target of 28 cases in the bracket of 8 hours, I sat for the next 4-5 hours but only could close just 17 cases. Another visible effect was my eye bags when my sleeping hours shrunk to just 3-4 hours. My weight fell by 6 kgs in two months because of a diet and over- drinking.

Rajni *didi* heard my entire story after 3 days when I stopped receiving calls from her and went back home. Pankaj *Bhaiya* and Rajni *didi* had to break into my house as I wasn't coming to open the door either. They found me lying on the floor with a cigarette butt in my finger, I could hear the door being bashed and the bell ringing, but I wanted complete isolation with no one interfering in my life. I guess a slap from *didi* was all I needed to wake my dead spirit.

Bhaiya and *didi* patiently heard my entire story and immediately after *Bhaiya* packed my bags and I was taken to their home. My wallet was taken by her and so were my house keys. All they wanted was for me to stay away from cigarettes and alcohol. However, the urge to smoke or drink didn't pop-up in my mind. The numb me would stare at the wall for hours.

I wanted to cry but couldn't do it. Of course, I couldn't get my personal space to cry but even at home for three days, not a single drop of tear shed from my eyes. Actually, my mind wasn't able to calculate the exact reason to cry for; was it Jahanvi leaving me, she realising me that I am a failure, or she considering me worthless?

Meanwhile, a week's absence from office without any intimation made them think of me being absconding.

I wished *didi* to revive the day and succeed in clearing the misunderstanding between the two of us. But the day she told me to forget her, it was crystal clear to me that by no means Jahanvi is going to return.

Rajni *didi* allowed me to stay back at my room on the promise of not smoking which lasted for 3 hours and I was back to my basics. After every day the suffocation in Delhi's air increased for me. Either my lungs started to give up after dozens of cigarette's smoke or it was Delhi's smog. I consoled my heart that the latter was the reason for my worn out lungs and continued smoking.

Every day the company's cab would come to pick me up at 4:30pm and I would reach the main road by 4:00pm. I wouldn't miss any chance of leaving the house as it would only remind me of Jahanvi. Honestly, the few metres distance from the building to the main road would feel like inches, but on the other hand, from main road to building would feel like miles.

I decided to leave the city because every place would just remind me of the days spent with her. Be it Moments Mall in Kirti Nagar, Rajiv Chowk Metro, Wenger's in Connaught Place, Metro Walk, Rohini and each and every place had a memory of her.

Ultimately, I called my school friend Gagan Atwal to pick me up and take me back home.

53.

"Where have you reached?"— While packing my bags and collecting all things, I called Gagan.

While honking long, in his irritated tone he yelled—"Bhenchod eh Kanjar gaddiya ch apni dhui jma ke beh gye lagda. Hilde hi nahi pye (These assholes got their bums stuck to the car's seat. They aren't moving)

I laughed at his tone. The words weren't something that I hadn't heard before, but it was missing from my life for a long time.

I asked with a smile still attached to my lips—"Where are you exactly?"

He took a pause and then replied—"I have entered Kurukshetra but got stuck in a jam here."

"Hmmm… it will take you nearly four hours to reach here"— I said with a sigh.

"Mmm… consider it six. I don't think; this will scatter anyway soon."

I thought of going to Jahanvi's PG before going back home to deliver her bag that contained her clothes and other stuff kept in my house. As Gagan was already behind by 6 hours, the second thought of delivering it to her myself arose.

After thinking about what to do and what not to do, I finally made my decision and left the house with her bag on my way to Vaishali.

As I climbed the stairs of Keshavpuram station, memories of Jahanvi appeared to me when she would come to the station and call me to help her get the bag till home. I would mock her for being a complete drama because she is the same girl who dragged the bag all the way from Vaishali to Keshavpuram by changing the metro at Rajiv chownk and taking the yellow line.

"So…? I got it from so far; can't you take it from here?"— She would say in her childish way.

Although the seat was vacant, still my preference was to stand in between the area where two coaches are joined. That was the same area where Jahanvi and I would prefer to stand every time we would go somewhere. I never understood what logic drove her to choose that spot.

"Why do we always stand here?"— I asked her, whispering in her ears.

The five feet 2 inches would pick her resting head from my left chest and would say—"Shhhhh… you talk so much."

I wished the coach was empty, actually, the complete metro to be empty, all the stations to be vacant, and there were my memories of me and me commuting together from Keshavpuram to Vaishali.

The announcement for the opening of the door for Rajiv Chowk station broke my memories and I stepped out.

I walked till platform 3 where I would get the metro to Vaishali. This was the path where Jahanvi wouldn't leave my hand and would hold it tight.

"Why do you get scared so much? You do travel alone too on this path many times"— I asked her with a smile looking at her who held my sweaty palm tight.

"When I am alone I am not scared but when we are together I get anxious of being separated from you." — She said holding my left hand and arm with her right and left hand respectively.

I passed the coffee shop at platform number 3, my eyes fell on it which used to be our landmark to meet when she would come to Vaishali and I would come from Keshavpuram.

Also, the day I was standing at the end of the women's queue staring at Jahanvi appeared too and gave a smile on my face.

The metro to Vaishali arrived and I stepped in. Once I was in the metro, my mind started to tell me to give up on the idea of visiting her.

Tum us layak nahi ho ke kisi se milwa sakoon (You are not worth being introduced to anyone)"— Her words echoed in my ears yet again.

"Had it not been her stuff with me, I would never have gone to her"— I tried convincing my mind in defence.

The metro reached at Vaishali station, so I took an auto to Sector 4c to find her PG. It wasn't difficult as the address sent by her was well known to the driver.

And there was me, standing outside her PG with trembling legs. Half of me wanted to see her once before leaving Delhi, and the other half didn't want to see her. With the confused mind, I walked till the gate and asked the watchman if any Jahanvi Sharma lives here. The 40 year old man wore his spectacles and scanned me from head to toe before asking—"Who are you?"

I hesitated to answer that because, technically, I was her Mr. No One now. I hated getting into any conversation with him and wanted to run away leaving the bag there.

"I am her family."— I replied.

With a smiling face she said—"Oh acha acha… let me call her"— He said and ran inside the building.

I shouted— "No… Please… just give her this bag."— But the rotund man ran briskly.

Perspiration started instantly and I felt an instant drop in my blood pressure. When in the next five minutes there was neither Jahanvi nor the watchman returning, I thought of dropping the bag and leaving. But destiny had some other plan, as soon as I kept the bag on the ground to leave; I saw Jahanvi standing in front of me. The awkwardness on her face depicted that she hadn't expected me to visit.

She was wearing a black coloured jumpsuit and was barefoot. The white coloured round earrings gave a hint about the colour of the shoes she will wear; white, definitely.

The watchman's presence prohibited her from speaking a word. Luckily, he was called within a minute in the building again. Jahanvi spoke— "What brought you here?"

The smile from my face escaped. I was assured her reaction would be aggressive or too cold but still there was a minuscule proton in me which was somewhere expecting a positive response like she was running towards me and taking me in her arms! Good, that it didn't have to wait too long to burst.

"I came here to return your bag."— I replied.

She pulled the bag towards herself and picked it, she said— "thanks"— and turned to go back.

I called a bit loud—"I am leaving Delhi."— I saw her legs stop.

My heart asked—"Please stop me… I swear I will drop the plan if you ask me not to leave. Does this impact you? A little?"

Without turning her head, she said—"Good"— and left.

I felt an unseen slap on my face. My mind was already prepared for it but still I hated myself for getting hurt. Another second of being there could be fatal to me, thus, I ran from there. I ran till my ribs hadn't started to hurt more than my heart. I ran till I didn't escape from her vision. I ran till I hadn't escaped from my own embarrassment. I wanted to run till I didn't faint and fall flat on my face.

Three streets later I gasped and sat on the footpath. I wanted to cry as the feeling finally emerged in me that IT'S OVER PRATIK. The water tank from the Chandigarh's hotel was exactly what I wanted. Hibernation I wanted to go into. As soon as a drop rolled down my cheek, I felt I got all the eyes from the surroundings. Thus, I had no other option but to take a cab.

The OLA driver arrived and I got into the back seat.

"Keshavpuram, just drop near the metro station"— I guided and lay in the back seat.

"Are you okay, sir?"— The cab driver asked.

"Yes, just increase the AC's fan and play the music aloud"— I replied.

He did what was asked of him to do. I hid my face inside the shirt I was wearing and created a semi-hibernation cell for myself that helped me cry. My head started to spin fast. My days spent with

Jahanvi started to play in my head in flashback; from where we met, how we started talking, our first love making, getting house in Delhi, shopping together, talking to her mother, fighting and finally breaking up.

The pain of the loss was so intense that not for a single moment my tears left me; as it was waiting since long for it to rain. I wanted to scream and burst my vocal cord but couldn't do it remembering the driver. The bubble blown from the nose was time and again wiped with the shirt. After a while I started feeling suffocated but I wanted it to continue and it helped me die there. The pain of parting from Jahanvi was growing and becoming unbearable.

The driver shook me hard and said—"Sir... Sir... We have reached."

I woke up with my heavy eyes and with difficulty faced the brightness of the day. The wet shirt reminded me of what just happened and ultimately I got into my consciousness.

"420 rupees sir"— the driver said.

I handed him the note of 500 and walked away.

54.

Though Gagan had brought me back into my city, I realised the bigger mistake I made. I ran from Delhi as each and every place was reminding me of Jahanvi.

However, I forgot that Jalandhar was no different. Restaurants, cinema halls, malls, stores everywhere my friends; Babu, Sarabjeet, Gagan, Aarohan, Kanav would take me to entertain, it would still remind me of Jahanvi.

Dixita *didi* started to spend more time with me than ever. She left her evening job in an academy and rather devoted that time to me. Her efforts were visible to me; many-a-times I would even smile at her jokes to make her feel good but the emptiness was killing me from inside and I didn't want anyone to be around.

13th August also reminded me of last year how Jahanvi was with me but this year she wasn't. The day would kill me as much as nights and a night before my birthday I didn't want to be alone. Hence, I insisted *didi* to sleep in my room. But she refused as she had some presentation to prepare for school, and that she would go to bed late. Not insisting further, I laid back watching the fan rotating. As the needle struck 12, didi, mom, papa entered the room with a cake, birthday hats, and blowers. In no time, there was THE BORED PANDAS outside the house. They too enjoyed the family party. I had people around me who were doing all this for my smile, they were doing it to make me feel special, and most importantly they were doing it to fill the void.

I sensed my enthusiasm was dead and I, literally, had no feeling in me. I wanted them to be around me but silent. I wanted them to enjoy it but without forcing me to.

At 12.30pm, my phone rang as Jahanvi called. "Hi"— I said smilingly.

"Happy birthday Pratik"— she said in her soft tone. "Thankyou"—

I too replied softly.

"I want to say something."— She broke the ice when there was complete silence at both the ends. Hence, I was brought back into consciousness.

I spoke in excitement—"Yes yes… please"

"I want to meet you. I am missing you."

I said—"Sure… I will come there in two days." She sniffled—"I'll go now."

Her sniffling made me sceptical, so I asked—"Is everything fine?" Sniffling again she replied in her soft tone—"I think so"

I knew she was crying, I knew she too was broken by the separation, I knew her rigid behaviour of not accepting it, I said—"Love you"

She replied—"Hmmm…"

That was the beginning of my 25th birthday.

55.

There were not one but two gifts I received on my birthday. First, of course, was the reunion of Jahanvi and me, and second was *Didi's* marriage was fixed with a guy named Ameer Sharma, living in Australia. The news had to be shared with Jahanvi but I hid it till I didn't meet her in person.

Rajni *didi* was informed about my Delhi's visit but she nowhere sounded excited to me.

After months I was on cloud nine. Coming to Delhi with two latest happenings in my life made the proximity appear more distant.

We decided to meet at our favourite place; Wengers. The ambience inside the restaurant looked more appealing than ever. There was a standard smile fixed on my lips since I departed from Jalandhar.

To kill the time waiting for Jahanvi's arrival, I checked our complete album on my phone.

With her first step in the restaurant, I felt her presence. The five feet two inches Punjabi girl in her white top with culottes and black coloured striped bitter-lime pants was puzzled searching for me.

I waved at her to make it easy to find me. She smiled and walked to me. I was confused whether to shake hands or to hug her as the mini-separation chapter had created little differences. Nevertheless, she made it easy by doing nothing and taking a seat directly.

I watched her face as I never watched it ever before. The unsettled storm that was in me a few days ago found tranquillity.

She spoke—"So how are you?" "Good. How about you?"— I asked. "Fine."

And there was a pause. We both looked at each other for the next few seconds. Her eyes were speaking more than her lips. Her eyes had stories to tell about her sleepless nights. Her eyes were telling me

Jahanvi still loves you the same. While I was busy reading her eyes, Jahanvi spoke—"I wanted to speak to you"

"Yes... please."— I said and leaned forward on the table to pay attention to her.

By taking a sigh, she said—"I couldn't imagine you betraying me. My world was shaken. This has done more damage to me than my past relationship."

My heart was extremely sorry for hurting her, for making her cry, for leaving her alone, and therefore it also wanted to explain to her how she has been misled by Payal. But I was there to listen to her and not to tell mine.

She continued—"I want to give a fresh start to this relationship."

To shed tears, smile, and dance or hug Jahanvi, I wasn't sure of what to do. But I remind myself of the cost I have to pay every time when I am extremely happy.

Tearing my lips to its extent, I gave a big nod to Jahanvi and said— "I promise to make the second innings the best."

She passed a half smile and nodded.

"There is another good news I needed to share with you."— I said with a fixed smile.

She nodded.

"Dixita *didi's* marriage has been fixed."— I said with an extensive smile.

She smiled and congratulated me but the reaction was cold which was quite unexpected. But, I couldn't understand how to ask about it.

At 6 pm, I went to *Bhua ji's* house. Rajni *didi* was waiting for me on the terrace; walking from one corner to the other. I was aware of her habit of doing this whenever she is tensed.

As I climbed the stairs, I waited for her to complete her round. She turned and her eyes fell on me. She stared at me from a distance and didn't approach me.

Therefore, I walked towards her.

I hugged her and walked to share each and everything about today. But I realised her hands weren't on my back. Her behaviour was peculiar. I left her and held her from her shoulders—"What happened didi. Is there anything wrong?"

She spoke—"Did you go to meet Jahanvi directly?"

The tone she used to ask was deeply unaffectionate. I took my hands off her shoulders. The smile decamped from my lips.

I asked—"Is there something wrong didi?" "I asked you something. Answer me?" With a little hesitation, I replied—"Yes."

"What did she say?"— The heaviness in her voice rose as she asked it. The apprehension in her voice made me feel like a cat on hot bricks.

I asked—"Please get to the point didi. What is it? You are making me nervous."

She yelled—"Are you insane? I am asking you something and you are questioning me instead."

I was blank. She was never like this with me. The polite and caring sister for the first time in all these years shouted at me. Thus, I answered her question—"She said she wants to give this relationship a new start."

"And what did you say?"— She asked in haste.

"I agreed to it… Why is that even a question?"— I smirked.

She turned towards the other side. I was in complete vacuity. I walked near her and stood beside—"What is it, didi?"

She took a deep sigh before telling what she was concealing in her heart—"Last week, I was in Saket City Walk with some friends and there I saw Jahanvi. I could have gone and met her but I found her being accompanied by a boy. I thought it to be Udit but it wasn't him. I even thought of them being casual friends but their chemistry wasn't allowing me to believe my own thoughts. Thus, I followed them to the showroom of Massimo Dutti. The way Jahanvi was changing dresses and taking his opinion to make a purchase increased my doubt on the relationship they shared. It wasn't friendship for sure the way they held hands…"— I stopped her. I walked away from her and the world seemed swinging to me.

My heart was in no condition to accept what she said. My mind spoke—"Why even is it bothering you? You know your Jahanvi better than anyone else."

I turned to didi and assured her in a heavy tone—"From the condom scenario that happened with me, I have stopped believing eyes and so should you."

She yelled at me—"Are you so dumb to not understand how cunning she is?"

"What do you expect me to do?" Spy on her"— I asked Didi with a straight face and a louder tone, which was unlike me with her.

My answer left her in shock, she said—"How stupid are you Pratik. Here I am trying to save you from that witch and rather you are…"— she waved off her hand at me and turned aside.

The word 'witch' echoed in my ears for the next minute. Honestly, it provoked anger in me. I felt my ears burning. "How can someone call her a witch?"—This question kept haunting my mind.

In spite of spitting the anger filled in me, I decided to infuse it in her by my words. Thus, I reacted—"Instead of saving mine, it would have been better if you saved your relationship."

Within a second she turned towards me. Surely she heard it at first but asked again aghast with disbelief —"What did you just say?"

Crushing her expectations in pieces, I retorted—"This habit of yours of poking nose in other's matters and doubting people led you to lose the man who loved you. If you could…"— just when I was in the flow of speaking my heart out, actually a part of my heart knew Rajni *didi* being the reason behind the broken relation of hers with her boyfriend, I received a tight slap on my face, before I could register anything else.

I looked at *Didi* who was filled with anger and tears at the same time. I realised I crossed my limit but still a part of me was happy to pass on the pain, by words, successfully to her that she just did.

Sobbing, as she was, she yelled—"Get lost from here and never show me your face even if Jahanvi leaves you."

Not being apologetic for anything I said, I went downstairs and sat in Pankaj bhaiya's room. For the next hour, the only thing to do for me was to cool the fury. Eventually, I succeeded after a while and wore my flip-flops to walk in the living room.

Having no knowledge of my presence, *Didi* yelled at me when she saw me—"How shameless are you to still be in the house from which you are asked to get out!"— *Bhua ji*, standing aside, had a blank expression as she was completely clueless about the verbal brawl which had just happened between the brother-sister duo.

I had no knowledge of being asked to leave the house. Rather, I thought it was her vision from where I was instructed to be walking out.

"Just G E T O U T "— she stressed aloud this time on every letter as if a child is being given a pronunciation class.

This time *Bhua ji* intervened and asked—"What has happened to you both. What are you fighting for?"

"Either this boy or me, only one can stay in the house"— she spoke in her unshaken voice and raised brows.

Anger and embarrassment, both clutched me at that moment. Without even listening a single word of *Bhua ji*, who tried saying something, I went into the room and started packing my bag. After a while, I opened the door of the room and pulled my bag along. I passed *Bhua ji*, who tried stopping me, didn't turn towards *Didi* and walked out of the main gate.

I was out-of-knowledge of where to go. Jahanvi would be at PG and Aman at work. Having the train for the next day at 7.20 am, I had a full night to spend. Either calling someone or staying on my own, I was dicey between the two options. My mind gave the best advice— "Are you ready for one more embarrassment if someone denied help?"

I got my answer and took an auto for New Delhi Railway station. I bought 10 cigarettes before walking into a dusky old building guest house which had a night's rent of meagre 700 rupees for a single room and 300 for sharing. Since the night in Mumbai, sharing rooms became a nightmare for me. Thus, I chose a single room.

Actually it was a hall with 20 beds and four rooms were added at a corner with wooden fencing and uncovered roof, this is what they called — PRIVATE ROOM.

When I heard voices of men complaining of mosquitoes, I didn't complain as the cigarettes I was smoking worked as mosquito killers. 10 cigarettes in 8 hours helped to kill the night. Also, I realised the capacity I had built over the time for getting low- blood pressure after a second cigarette in a day to smoking 10 in 8 hours and still unaffected. Being proud or cautioning myself, I didn't stress myself to get an answer.

I called Jahanvi at 5 am to meet me at the station before I boarded the train to Delhi forever because returning to the city was no longer on my list.

She was there at the station. Now after the reunion, there wasn't a single difference in our bond before the short-term break up period. Hugs were as warm as before, jokes were as funny as before, as so was our love and fondness for each other. Once when the inner me wanted to clarify her about the entire misunderstanding which had been created by Payal, I was stopped then and there by her—"Please, I have come long here to forget all that happened. Rather than discussing the past, why not focus on our future?"— She said and winked at me. Though my lips caught a smile for a while, my brain was still processing her words.

I asked, with a sustained smile—"What does that mean?"

Acquiring a bigger smile than me, she proceeded—"Let's get married."

I was short of words because for me it was all dreams; Jahanvi, mom, dad, and me together in our small happy world. It was such words said by her which became impossible for me to even think about.

"Say something, at least"— Jahanvi said in a louder tone than the last, with the same smile.

Still dumbfounded, I still couldn't say a word but nodded to reply at least.

All my way to Jalandhar I was only thinking about her, precisely, about us. The only confusion was the question of the city now; where to continue our further life; Jalandhar or Mumbai. Delhi by default was removed. The second was the least option but still in the list as with the reappearance of Jahanvi in my life, there was a wake up of the dead enthusiasm too for becoming an actor. Now I wanted everything to go better than ever so that the hurdles could be passed smoothly.

54.

Preparation for didi's marriage started in full swing. Resort booking started and so did the list of invitees. The increasing count of relatives was directly proportional to the addition of little things for ceremonies. Papa seemed tense for two days to me. On asking the reason, he would deny it by saying it to be exhausting days.

Mom finally came to me late at night and said—"Your dad was expecting money to be returned from his friend whom he had given a year ago as a form of help."

I waited for her to continue the story. Thus, I didn't speak a word but nodded with my frowned brows.

She continued—"He completely denied when asked to return it." Waiting no further, I asked—"What's the amount?"

She hesitated initially on responding and moved her eyes.

Softly, I held her hands and repeated my question—"Look at me maa! What's the amount?"

"7 Lakhs"— she said, in a low and hopeless tone.

For a family that lives on rent, the only son earns nothing, daughter who left her job for marriage, a father whose business could hardly give food to eat and a mother, who teaches in a school with a salary of not even touching five digits, has a marriage of daughter coming in nearly a month's time! All these thoughts raced through my mind all at once, creating chaos.

To be honest, all our life's savings was invested for this marriage and arranging 7 lakhs in a month's time was just next to impossible for us. I had saved Rs. 84,000 from my job in Delhi that was undeclared money to my family. I thought of giving it to papa so as to help in relieving his worries.

"Even if it's given, there is still a massive six lakhs left to be covered."— I said in my mind.

The reality was hidden from *didi* as we didn't want her happiness to subside. The night papa, mom, and I didn't speak a word but were only listening to *didi* while she was telling about her after marriage plans that she discussed with *jiju.*

The next day, my first call was to my friend Ashween, who works with HDFC bank, and asked about the criteria for personal loan. Luckily, because of my job in Delhi where my salaried account was with HDFC, loan availability was showing 8 lakhs rupees on my account. Not thinking of a second, I asked him to apply and got 6 lakhs credited in my account within a minute's time.

I withdrew the money and handed it over my papa. His eyes were perplexed and full of exhilaration at the same time, he asked— "Where did you get this money from?"

Hereby, I hid the truth from him—"I had a savings of 4 lakh rupees and the remaining 2 lakhs I got a loan from the bank, Ashween helped me in it."

He cried his heart out and hugged me tight. It was at that time I understood what a father goes through to make life's end meet. Also, I understood there are roles we play in our life and responsibilities that we fulfil. His stress got free from the cage that it was in. Whereas, mine was captivated as an EMI of 15,000 was fixed to be paid for the next few years now.

Anyhow, the halted preparation started yet again. Whereas, I became doubtful about my decision of getting married to Jahanvi as 15000 EMI, 7000 house rent were in total 22000 that was supposed to be my contribution to the family. I felt myself got stuck in a bog and getting sunk slowly bit by bit.

55.

Where days were meant to be subjected to two things; one preparation for marriage and second for job hunting, I kept my night occupied with writing scripts for a movie. I contacted Mohit, who works with a famous production house, through Facebook. They produce Punjabi movies and songs and have been quite successful with their last few releases. Randomly while scrolling Facebook one day when I sent a request to Mohit, it was accepted by him right then. Without wasting my time I messaged to have a meeting with him. Unlike other people from the industry, Mohit seemed much grounded to me despite tasting success. He requested to come over to their Kharar based office and discuss the story. Not even having a clue about the genre of the movie, I spontaneously responded that it was a romantic-drama family movie after he confirmed what the project was about.

Therefore, I had precisely 11 days in hand to write a story.

Story writing was never in my wish list of dreams. I approached Mohit with it to get in the industry by hook or crook. However, writing dialogues and screenplays for theatre were something I used to do seldom, but professional writing was not my cup of tea. I still did it so that I could get a break, at least. With this I could possibly earn the amount to pay that figure of Rs.22,000 a month.

Eventually, I was able to create quite a good story line and I was more than confident of him liking it because the Punjabi movie industry was more focusing on comedy than any other genre since its second innings.

With a warm greeting, Mohit offered me to be seated in his cabin— "Please, have a seat Pratik"

"Thank you so much"— I took the seat opposite to him.

The nearly forty-five minutes of intuitive story-telling convinced Mohit of it being a commercially successful project. Somehow I realised that my talent of telling stories is more applauded than my acting. Thus, I got clearance for my alternative career option other than acting.

"I really loved your story Pratik"— He said with an extended smile.

I nodded while keeping a short sustained smile so that he doesn't acknowledge my over excitement. Also, I didn't want to be euphoric as my bad luck woke me up from the slumber and messed everything up.

"A helpless poor is more afraid of losing his good days than the time when he was in bad days"

"But only my perspective cannot be considered for making a movie. The company's MD and senior creative directors' opinion are more than important."— He completed.

Mohit noticed the anxiety on my face and clarified instantly— "Hey… don't worry, I have been in the company for the last few years and I am well aware of the kind of project they would accept or reject. And this one, I'm damn sure will be on the floor very soon because of the freshness of the script."— The smile with which he appreciated me was now used for assurance.

For a long time the happiness that I was stalking was somehow found after walking down the building. The ray of hope was now tearing the clouds of misery from my life and was starting a new title— **Writer**. Perhaps, I was even happier to not be waiting long for paying off the EMI and delaying my plans of getting married with Jahanvi.

I called Jahanvi soon after I got the bus back to Jalandhar. It was busy.

Meanwhile, my inner self suggested that I not tell anyone and wait for the final response from Mohit. I found the suggestion quite suitable.

Jahanvi called back—"Hey… You called?"

"Yes… just wanted to know about the dress that you have selected to wear at the wedding. I am supposed to go shopping tomorrow with mom and dad so I will buy something matching."

The sound of background horns and cars disrupted my voice. I asked—"Are you out somewhere?"

She in a higher pitch—"Yes. I am out for a shoot actually." Excited to know, I asked—"That's awesome, what is it?" "It's a Punjabi song"— High pitches continued.

She continued—"Can't hear you clearly. It's better to text."

She cut the call and within seconds she messaged—"In Chandigarh for a Punjabi song's shooting."

Kharar to Chandigarh is just 20kms so after knowing that she is so close, I wanted to tell her of me being nearby Chandigarh. But the question of what I answer to her when she would ask the reason behind me being there, I preferred to keep mum.

I typed—"Who is it with?"

"There is a new male singer. I got the opportunity to assist the director. Actually, I wanted to learn what directing songs are like and to be honest, it's a lot different than movies."— She replied.

I asked—"This is awesome. Proud of you, really. How did you find this project?" "A friend from Swaggy Records is directing it actually. He offered to assist him."

As far as I knew about Jahanvi and her contacts, she had no friends working with Swaggy Records.

So this got me curious to know—"Which friend?" "Ankush Katyal"— she replied.

I stressed my mind a lot to think about this person if I had known or met him, but failed. Just then she messaged—" Got to go. Catch you later. Bye"

56.

It was Didi's bangle ceremony that day. Since morning there were people pouring in from everywhere, the house was thronged with all my cousins, *didi's* school and college friends, some girls and ladies from the neighbourhood. Despite being surrounded with nearly a half a hundred girls, my eyes were desperately looking for Jahanvi to enter from the main door. At first, my cousins walked to me and asked if Jahanvi was arriving. Later, it was relatives and a few of *Didi's* friends who were added with me on Facebook, and at last mom, who asked me that question. I realised Jahanvi's and my relationship to be unhidden from anyone. I smiled before replying everyone the same answer—"Just coming in a while."

The bangle ceremony started. It was all cousins who were supposed to first get clicked with *didi* and slip bangles in her hands. Followed by some married women and then it was mom and dad. They called me to join for a picture while I was at the door, looking outside to see Jahanvi entering. I dreamt of making this picture a complete family picture with Jahanvi accompanying us. "Dammit, where are you?"— I muttered, and proceeded for the picture.

"Can you please smile for the picture"— *Didi* whispered in my ears and laughed to fake it. Actually, she wanted to portray it as if she cracked a joke.

I followed her instructions. After some randomly changed places, and pictures getting clicked, I kissed Didi's forehead to shower all the blessings and happiness on her. I finally got the feeling of her leaving us in a few days. She was surprised because she didn't expect this reaction from an reticent brother like me.

"Sorry, got stuck in a meeting with the director of Swaggy Records. It's going to take more time here. I am afraid I cannot reach it."— Jahanvi's message arrived. I read it while I was sitting with *Didi*. This ruffled my feathers. So, without replying, I locked the phone and slid it in my pocket.

Just when the bangle ceremony was about to get over and almost everyone was done with gifting bangles, questions were again rained at me by a couple of Didi's friends—"The function is about to end. Where is Jahanvi? Isn't she coming?"

Without looking at them, I replied—"She couldn't make it today. But there will be another function."

I believe there should be a limit of questions that we can ask someone and this should be a law. Because there is always a last question after which we don't have answers. That's exactly our peak of patience and if in case after this we have a right to slit the person's throat and wouldn't be jailed, this is exactly how I felt at that point of time.

"What happened to her?"— One of Didi's three friends asked.

I controlled my patience till then but couldn't do it for much long, so I spoke— "Periods aate hai jab, pet mein cramps padhte hai naa, kuch teekha-chatpata zyada khaya ho toh dard bhi hoti hai, and kamar dard kaisa na ho. Bus yahi hua hai usse"(during periods, people get cramps in their stomach, doesn't it? If one eats something out of routine, then it would be painful too. And how can we forget the bad back in periods. She is suffering exactly from these things currently!)

The outcome: Three of them left the function without having lunch.

57.

My cousin Divya stood with me while the ring ceremony was going on. She held my arm softly. We both were looking at the joyful faces of *Didi* and *Jiju*. There were smiles all around us. The boy's family was happier than us, and this is for the obvious reason. On another side, I could notice teary eyes of dad and mom, standing in a corner, in their own little space, where they don't want anyone to interrupt while they watch their princess getting engaged. Phones, cameras, video shots, drones and what not were taking pictures of the two, but my old parents reserved the day to be captured through their eyes and keep it secure in their hearts over any device.

I didn't message Jahanvi that day too for asking to come. Since the day of the bangle ceremony not once has she mentioned or asked anything about *Didi*, marriage, functions or anything. Where I needed her to be with me, her video shooting schedules, in Delhi and Chandigrah, were given priority by her. I had given up. But this wasn't something new, I knew it well. Her over-practical behaviour and too realistic approach on shoots is what attracted me to her. After struggling with the two sides of me and ending up convincing myself of her being the same way ever since I have known her, I decided to stay as calm as I could.

However, Jasneet was with me while the ceremony was going on. She was more excited than me to see videos and pictures of Dixita *didi's* engagement. Just as once we decided over the phone of her being present along with me during each and every ceremony, she was virtually there for me.

It was then when I got to know how fucked up situations life can create for us. Jasneet could be available if invited; Jahanvi wasn't available even when invited.

I switched to Jahanvi's chat box many times but she wasn't seen to be online to me even once.

58.

Punjabi, Hindi, Punjabi, Haryanvi and again Punjabi— One after another requests were made to the DJ to play songs. The crazy night saw confident, under confident and some overconfident dancers thumping their legs on the dance floor.

I realized I was so much engrossed in my own fucked up life from a few years that never realized the school going cousins were in college and college goers were working. I believe the ambience of the night blended well and there were young ones offering alcohol to me that they had hidden somewhere in their car.

The drinks had hit me powerfully that waves of emotions all together came running in me. I was sparkled with *didi's* marriage, anxious with Mohit's response, hurt with Jahanvi's absence and embarrassed with Jasneet presence after what I did to her. These all stimulated me to have one after another drinks without keeping a count.

After 1 am, DJ stopped, cooks were off to home, lights were turned off apart from the lights installed at house for decoration, family and relatives walked up to their rooms.

I was still outside the house, feeling the air. Honestly, as the silence prevailed, I became scared of whether the question of Jahanvi's presence would still be asked by anyone. Therefore, with that fear and embarrassment I sat in a quiet corner.

Jasneet's message arrived with a good night. I replied instantly— "Haven't slept yet?"

"I guess that's how I am messaging"— the message was followed by a wink. It left a smile on my face. I further asked—"I thought you were sleepwalking."

She was online and read the message too but didn't reply for a short time. However, some laughing emoticons were received thereafter and she replied— "Near the well."

Nostalgia had hit me hard. My heart got filled. I knew well if my heart was filled on the other hand Jasneet's eyes would be. Although I enjoyed the conversation with her at that time of night, I also knew after all the blunder I did, the conversation would only leave her with more scars.

The chaos in me wanted a cigarette as there wasn't anything else that the heart and brain could cope with. I called Rajiv *jiju* to accompany me and he was there within a minute. Just when we were to leave for a cigarette, on two wheeler, we were stopped by Rajni *didi*.

"*Jiju*, your wife is calling you."— *Didi* said. "Tell her we are coming in a while"

"I am not going upstairs right now you go and tell her" He took a sigh and said to me—"Wait. Coming in five"

As soon as Rajiv *jiju* went upstairs, Rajni *didi* sat behind me and said—"Go go go…"

I drove to a nearby market where tea and coffee were served late at night.

I realised that in the last 25 minutes, since we left the house, we didn't talk about anything.

I got two cups of tea, Parle-G biscuits and used the scooty's seat as a table. I rubbed both my hands as the cups were too hot to hold. Didi opened the pack of biscuits and we both dipped one biscuit each in the tea and took a bite.

Didi—"Ummm… can I tell you something?"

I didn't respond to her but moved my eyes at her. She got the answer and proceeded—"You know, I am eating chai-biscuit for the first time after you left Delhi."

I realised the number of people I have hurt in the last few months are more than I ever collectively hurt people all my life.

I said—"I am sorry *didi* for everything that I said and I did to you… I was just being childish and stupid."

She responded, after taking a sip of the tea—"As if I don't know!"

I looked down in embarrassment because I knew how hard it was to face her after all the ill things spoken.

She asked—"I got to know that Jahanvi didn't come in any of the functions"

I looked away and took a sip of tea. I didn't want to answer that question because I too didn't have any genuine answer for that. However, I also knew that I couldn't completely evade the question, at least in front of her.

Thus, I began—"I don't know what is going on in my life. The moment I think everything is fine, the moment I get to know 'no it's not'. The more I try to gather everything, the more it goes out of my hands. Just when I think I have achieved what I had desired and now I can settle, the very next moment I get to know it was momentary. I feel like a dehydrated and starving traveller who is lost in the desert, he sees water but ends up finding it to be a mere mirage. "

The answer was something that anyone apart from *Didi* and I wouldn't understand. But we understood well. We didn't need a clarification on that. Nothing more and nothing less to that was required to explain.

59.

"Humans are highly selfish; I bet on that. Our whole life we desire to be surrounded by a person with a beautiful face, attractive body but on deathbed it's the most beautiful heart we look for."

At 9:00am, I was woken up by mom as she was running from one end of the room to another end, searching for something. With my puffy eyes, I asked her—"What happened?"

"Wake up you idiot, you have to go to Dixita's in-laws to give them *shagun*"— she said, with continuation of her search.

"I thought we already had given all the *shagun* yesterday"— I questioned.

"That *shagun* was for a ring ceremony, today is marriage"— she found a red satin cloth in which something was wrapped that I couldn't even guess.

Rubbing my eyes, I asked—"Ohh! *Shagun* has categories.?"

She closed the room's door from inside and opened the locker in which her jewellery was kept. As soon as she opened her jewellery box and took out a heavy gold necklace, just as the ones we see in movies of kings and queens, my puffy eyes were wide open, I asked in a strong voice—"You are going to give this expensive jewellery? This is not *shagun* but it's called dowry"— and I stepped out of the bed to take a hold of it.

She slapped my shoulder and said—"Nakli hai pagal yeh(It's artificial). The originals are kept with Manipuram Gold as we took loan from them."

"And what's in this cloth?"— I asked and did not wait for the answer. Instead I opened it myself, it had some raw rice, sesame oil, some grass, and turmeric.

I was confused. So I looked at her. She kept her artificial jewellery back in the case and said—"Go and give that to your *jiju's* mother. Its *shagun*"

On my way to *jiju's* home, I got a call. The name stopped two things at the same time; the car and the heart.

"Hi"

"Hi"— I said.

"I hope I didn't disturb you" "Not at all"

And the silence prevailed for quite a while. "So…"

"So…?"— I questioned.

"Just wanted to check if everything is fine" "Hmmm…"

"Don't forget sending me pictures of *didi* and *jiju,* and a video of *jaimala*" "Sure"

"Take Care"— and Jasneet disconnected the call.

Loving unconditionally to anyone is not what everyone can do. I could feel Jasneet's and my condition to be at the same place. She loves me; I love Jahanvi whereas Jahanvi loves her work. A failed relationship includes n-number of factors in it. However, the blame taken on themselves for a failed relationship can kill without cuts and poison.

Just as I was thinking about all this, I received a call from papa, who was at Lovely Sweets.

"Pick all the sweets' boxes and drop them at the resort"— he said "I am going to *Jiju's* house. In return, I will do this."

Just when I reached *jiju's* house, I was taken to the living area and was offered with different sweets— at last it was the bride's brother who came.

I got a call from an unknown number. Getting an excuse to leave the house, I faked it being the resort owner calling me. By the time I greeted some a dozen uncles and aunties and got into the car, the call had already gotten disconnected.

I called back at the number but it went unanswered.

From an unanswered call, I reminded myself of calling Mohit who didn't reply to my last couple of messages as well as calls. To my surprise, he picked it on the third ring—"Hey Pratik, I am so sorry for not replying to you. Actually, we are in pre-production for Diljit's next movie and I was on recce for that."— he completed the practised dialog in the first take.

That day I understood that it's more irritating to talk to the person who doesn't pick the call and later does.

"Any response on my script"— I asked in a straight voice.

"We do have our next meeting on your script in two hours' time. I have gotten the confidence of three out of five directors of the company. Now it's a collective YES that we are looking for. I know it will work"

This gave me some hope. I wanted to announce the news of the movie getting selected to everyone at the marriage so as to tell them that the failure PRATIK has finally succeeded. Among the entire cousins and friends list, the first person who struck my mind was Jahanvi—"Finally, I will be LAYAK for her."— I said in my mind.

I picked up the boxes of sweets and delivered them at the resort. Already, the decorators started unloading their props to be used, and tents to be installed in the resort's garden area were being drilled. As the resort was in the countryside, chirping of the birds, fresh air, zero honking horns, and presence of strangers convinced me to stay there for a while. There was no one to disturb, no one to ask questions, no one to inquire about my future plans.

Just when I was engrossed in the thought, the stage where *didi and jiju* would sit was getting its final touch. I clicked its picture and sent it to *didi*. Within a minute she sent some blowing kisses after seeing the message. Then I thought of sending it to Jahanvi who also saw it in a minute and replied—"We'll click pictures here in the evening". My heart skipped several beats at the time she sent the message.

More than for *didi* and *jiju*, I wanted the stage to be decorated with the best flowers for Jahanvi and myself. Right there, I sent one of the labourers with extra money to bring fresh roses. Until the time it wasn't brought, I didn't feel like being seated.

From entrance to stage, I checked everything to be just perfect. My excitement was unsettling. It continued till the time I reached home too. When the ladies began getting ready from 4pm, men were waiting for the next cup of tea ordered.

The ladies one after the other would call any young child to get hair pins, safety pins, makeup brush and other equipment required for getting ready. The young ladies were discussing sarees, hair style, matching footwear, and makeup while the olds ones were busy back-biting their own daughter-in-laws and others' daughter- in-law. On the other hand, men were also discussing laws but these were state laws, central laws, and international laws. In between the babbling of the two groups, I received a message from Jahanvi once again—"Bhaiya and Bhabhi are coming in the evening". Precisely, forgetting others', now I had my own in-laws to be taken care of.

I ran to Rajni *didi* to inform her about Jahanvi's brother and sister-in-law coming along with her. I went straight to the room where all the cousins were getting ready. I knocked and heard a voice saying—"Aaaaayiiiiii(coming)" Having no one to open it in next five seconds, I banged the door with my fist, harder, and asked— "Rajni didi?"

I saw the door knob turning to the side and there was just a head that peeped out and one of my cousins, Sheffali asked—"Kya hai?

I tried my best to see inside but she closed the little door she opened, and I heard her voice from the other end—"Rajni didi nahi hai yahan bhaag jaa yahan se(Rajni didi isn't here, go away."

I ran into the other room but still didn't find her to be present.

"Rajni didi bhua ji ke saath pandit ji ke pass gye hai(Rajni didi has not with bhua ji to see the priest"— a young 6-7 years old girl came walking to me while her eyes were stuck to mobile's screen to inform it. I never saw her before; neither had I had the curiosity to know.

I waited at the balcony to see if mom and *didi* return from meeting the priest. 5 minutes standing there felt like 5 hours. Thus, the jumpy me decided to go myself towards the temple. So, I ran down the stairs and kick started my bike. I saw mom and Rajni *didi* sitting on

Activa and parking it.

"Where are you going?"— Rajni *Didi* asked me. I held her from her hand and took her to the side.

"Her family is coming in the evening"— I told her over-excitedly.

She frowned her brows to better understand the noun here—"Who her?"— She questioned in a low voice.

"Jahanvi… aur kaun(Who else)"— I said.

From frowned to normalised, her brows rested back at the position but her eyeballs widened up. She had some thoughts running back in her mind but she cared less to say those.

Without any answer she started walking inside the house. I kept staring at her for her cold response. To be honest, it irritated me.

"At least say something?"— I shouted standing at the same place which stopped her moving legs.

I anticipated her to turn back and say something but she remained unresponsive. That annoyed me a lot. For which I decided to not talk to her unless she initiates.

At 7:00pm, I called Babu, Sarabjeet, Gagan Atwal, Kanav, Divyanshu and Aarohan to bring their cars and work as chauffeur to drop guests from home to the resort.

In a queue when six cars decorated with flowers were parked, I clicked a picture of it and sent it to Jahanvi.

The message to her was delivered but was unseen. Even after 4-5 minutes when she didn't see the message, I called her and the call went unanswered.

"She might be getting ready"— I told my mind.

"Reached the resort?"— A message from Jasneet arrived.

I switched the chat box and opened hers. The same picture that I sent to Jahanvi, I sent to Jasneet. She received, saw, and replied within a minute.

"Oh my my… the *kaafila* looks so amazing"— Jasneet said, followed by a few happy emoticons.

I typed— "Would have been happier if you could be here"— but the message remained unsent as I was called by *bhua ji* to come upstairs. I locked my phone and slid it in the pocket.

"See your dad is crying"— *bhua ji* took me to the room where papa and mom were.

My heart felt heavy as I rarely had seen my father crying over anything. There were tears in my mother's eyes too but she was consoling dad.

"I never felt this much empty"— He said in his shivery voice.

My father's love for my sister was more than for me, I knew. I hugged him. I think it was the first time in years when I hugged my father. This father-son duo relationship remained unsaid and unexpressive.

I patted on his back, even rubbed to cheer him up.

"Let's go papa. We are *ladki waale.* We ought to reach early"— I said. The words *Ladki wale itself* were enough to stop the rolling tears. I understood how responsibilities overpower our emotions.

We reached the resort at 8:30pm after passing by the heavy traffic jam in the city. Not before that I realised that 10th October, 2016 was really a big day as almost every resort and hotel was booked for a wedding. There were cars decorated with flowers everywhere on the road.

Where mom and dad, along with other relatives were left at the entrance to welcome guests, I walked in to check the arrangements done, food, camera setups, parking, lights, and above all the stage for *jai-mala,* at last it was Jahanvi and I who are going to click a picture there.

I unlocked my phone and read the unsent message to Jasneet. Thereby my emotion changed and I deleted the message typed. I sent a few pictures clicked of the resort to her. As always, without a second, she saw them all and typed—"Wow! This looks so so amazing."

On the other hand, Jahanvi still had not seen my last sent message to her. Thus, I called her again. Her phone was busy. I disconnected the call.

I felt a hand on my shoulder. I turned around and saw Rajni *didi* standing there. She wore a wine coloured gown. I looked at her from down to up. Having seen a never before look of her, smilingly she said—"Ab bta bachu kaisi lag rhi hoon?"

I said nothing but held her from shoulder and mouthed— "beautiful"— she had a broad smile.

My phone rang and I knew it would be Jahanvi. I picked it up with complete optimism but it was Dixita *didi*—"I am ready. Send someone to pick me up."

I then called Sarabjeet to ask where he was—"Kaha hai?(Where are you?) With his mouth full of food, he said—"Pizza Pizza"

I walked to the garden area and snatched pizza from his hand—"I am dying with hunger"

Eating a full slice of pizza somehow relaxed my stomach which was making a gurgling sound. Once the eating was done I licked the oregano spread on my index finger and thumb, and asked—"Where is Babu and Aarohan?"

Sarabjeet slapped me hard on my hand which literally fell down, I looked at him with popped up eyes, he said—"Behenchod shadi pe aaya hai domino's mein nahi jo paise poore karne lagga hai"(You are at a marriage not dominos where you are to recover the bill paid)

I kept staring at him and raised my brows. He realised after a minute and said— "Haan paise bhi toh apne hi lagge hai shadi pe, karle paise poore(I forgot that the money spent too is ours, go recover the bill"— and picked up more oregano, poured it on my hand, and walked.

I looked at my hand, then at Sarabjeet, then my hand again. I thought of pouring all the oregano on him but his 6'2" height and 17 inches biceps stopped me from attempting anything, so I just asked—"Where are you going?"

Without being bothered to turn around, he said—"Aarohan and Babu ke pass(Going to Aarohan and Babu)"

I questioned back—"And where are they?"

He kept walking and shouted—"Gol-gappe kha rhe hai(They are

having water balls)"

To be honest Aarohan and Babu eating gol-gappes being 25 years grown was not something that pissed me off but Sarabjeet over proudly telling it aloud to everyone did more.

Literally, there were eyes looking at me with a SORRY face of having friends like them.

In between golgappes and Pizza I forgot *didi* to be picked up from the salon. I received a second call from her, she said in her sarcastic tone—"Tere jiju phere lene salon mein aayenge jo mujhe leke nahi jaa rhe tum?(Is my husband coming at salon for marriage due to which no one is bothered to pick me up?)

"Coming in 5"— I said and disconnected the call before anything else to be heard from her end.

I called Gagan to confirm where he is—"Where are you?"

He said in his straight voice—"Drinking" "Where?"

"In the resort"

"But there is no stall of alcohol in the resort"

"We bought our own"

"Who are WE?"

"We are 15 people here"

"And who is the host?"

"Your Chachu(Uncle)"

And I spoke nothing for the next few seconds. He continued—"You want to drink?"

"Shut up. Its *didi's* marriage, I can't drink today"

"So may I continue drinking if you disconnect the call?"

Yes, Sure, absolutely, of course… I said nothing but disconnected the call.

I took Divyanshu's car and drove to pick up Dixita *didi* alone. The 35 minutes' drive was interrupted with 8 calls from her. When I finally reached outside the salon she was in, she told—"Wait for 10 minutes, the eye liner needs a final touch- up"

My tone got irritated with that—"Why the hell were you calling for the last hour then?"

She took a pause that made me think she disconnected the call, she said—"tujhe jaana hai kahi? Nahi naa. Keep waiting.(Do you have to go anywhere? If no, then keep waiting.)"— And I realised she had a point.

After 10 minutes, it was more than 10 minutes she asked for so my mind added another 10 minutes even when she didn't say so.

I received a call from an unknown number. I picked it. A lady from the other side said—"Hi Pratik"

"Hi"— I said.

"I am Jahanvi's bhabhi(sister-in-law)"— I gulped down the water that instantly collected in my throat.

Namaste, pairi-pona, Ram-Ram, hello, hi what exactly to be said was not fitting the blank in my head. However, I ended up saying— "Good evening"

She had a small laugh, I heard it, but replied—"Very good evening. We have reached the resort. Where are you?

"I am just coming in a while. Came out of resort for some work" "Okay, not an issue"

"Please help yourself with food and drink. I'll be there soon"—I said.

"Jahanvi and family has reached, rush now Pratik"— I said to myself. I locked up the car and started walking towards the salon. I opened the door and saw a girl sitting at the reception. I asked— "Dixita Sharma?"

The receptionist was about to call the makeup artist to confirm but just then the door opened and I saw *Didi* walking out. She was dressed in red bridal wear— LEHNGA. I kept staring at her. She kept smiling at me. She knew she was looking beautiful. I knew I had imagined her exactly as beautiful as she was looking.

She walked up to me. I kept looking at my beautiful sister. She came close to me and raised her brows and smiled. She gestured to ask for a compliment. I kept smiling as her excited eyes wanted to sooth her ears with comments like— ADORABLE, OUTSTANDING, ELEGANT, and all. I took a step back, went on my knees and touched her feet. Out of her expectation and imagination, this response left her speechless. She held me from my shoulder, lifted me, and hugged. I hugged back and said in her ears—"You are the best thing happened to me"

We left for the resort where the Baraat had already reached. So instead of going from the front gate, we were taken through the back door.

Didi was taken to the room reserved for the bride on the first floor and was surrounded by relatives and her friends in no time. I saw her getting busy with everyone and I quietly placed my footsteps outside the room.

My eyes were looking at Jahanvi and her family. I wanted Jahanvi to walk by with *didi* when she would be taken to the stage where the ritual of *Jaimala* will take place. I took out my phone to dial her number but one of my uncles came to wish me for my sister's marriage.

Uncle—"Bohat sohna function kitta hai tusi yaar. Tere papa-mummy di mehnat taan hai hi tusi bachya ne vi poora saath ditta apne ghardean da. Proud feel ho reha aj.(The function is extremely beautiful, my son. Your dad and mom had worked intensely hard for the day to happen. But along with them you kids too supported your parents in every situation. You guys have made us all proud)

I thanked my uncle and continued with the search.

I opened the call log and clicked on favourites to get Jahanvi's number. As I was walking through the passage, I observed a few eyes on me. My cousin Sakshi and Divya were staring at me. I could sense their gaze that something was fishy with them, I passed a half smile and kept walking to not to wait anymore to meet Jahanvi. But a few more eyes on me started arising the anxiety in me. Ranju *didi* at the corner with her folded arms carried a glum face. I wanted to stop by and ask, however, this wasn't something my brain signalled to do. I think it might have sensed the catastrophe coming ahead.

I kept walking straight. My fingers just needed a touch to call Jahanvi but I failed to do so. I wanted to escape the eyes staring at me; I wanted to breathe in the open. The Air conditioned hall failed to not let me suffocate. My heart wanted to arise from the long hibernation it went into and hinted at what happened; I ignored it trying not to listen to anything. I was almost at the door when I saw Babu, Sarabjeet, Aarohan, Gagan, and Kanav standing together in a group and looking at me in a similar way. My legs stopped moving. They were standing at a corner, a few steps away, but neither they nor I had the audacity to walk close. My ears didn't want to listen to what they were to tell, so was the part with the lips which preferred staying mum.

I closed my eyes and took a deep breath before finally walking towards them. I chose to nod than to speak. Sarabjeet looked at the rest of them and unlocked his phone which he already had handy. The direct page opened was of Jahanvi's instagram account. It had a picture of her and a boy, who I never saw. They both had a half hug and the picture was a selfie clicked by the boy. The caption read—

"You make me feel happy when sad, motivated when low, on cloud 9 when taken away with miseries, and sorted when I am scattered. To meet you was by chance, to love you is destiny. I love you Ankush."

My stomach wanted to push out and make me vomit if anything I had in the moment. Unluckily it was empty. I don't know why but the DJ slowed the volume of the music, however, I saw people still dancing on the dance floor with absolutely no music. I observed everyone's lips were moving but they weren't able to speak- is that how an apocalypse starts? Because not everyone could be dumb altogether. I turned my head to look at Sakshi and Divya, they were running towards me but extremely slowly- I got to know they had gotten some problem with their legs. Ranju *didi* gave car's keys to Gautam and instructed him something before running towards me- again everything was so slow that I counted her 23 steps before she reached me. Why was time becoming slower was something I couldn't understand. Apocalypse! I was assured. I was finding everything funny, thus, a smile appeared on my lips. When all this was happening, it was a single breath I took. Wow! I was able to count my breaths between observing people in the hall doing their things. Sarabjeet held me from my shoulder but his hands couldn't be felt. I wanted to tell him to meet a doctor because he lost his power to touch things, is he a spirit? I thought. But when Kanav did the same, touching me in spite of being felt, I wanted to tell them both the same. I guess it was only Babu and Aarohan who understood that the world is ending because they were stoned, and hadn't moved an inch. I heard a voice that might be the DJ was playing, so I turned my head towards him. It sounded—I am sorry Pratik. Please don't do this.

Please don't leave me. I will try to change myself. I am really sorry. Please don't go. Please Pratik.............................. "

I took my third long breath and returned to my senses. The DJ was continuing to play loud Punjabi music. I could feel Sarabjeet's hand; everyone got their voice back. However, I was feeling suffocated. I had my forehead, face, neck, back everything wet due to perspiration. Gagan returned with a bottle of water. He opened the cap and passed it to me. I gulped down the whole bottle in one go. I couldn't feel the dried GI tract and the water passing through the throat, chest and finally reaching the stomach.

My phone rang which was of papa. I picked up and he said—"We have to walk along with Dixita from the room to the stage. Bring all brothers."

I disconnected the call and looked at everyone. I said—"Ranju didi call Gautam and tell him to reach in *didi's* room with Shivam. Guys let's go, we have to bring *didi*. Sakshi, Ranju didi, and Divya, be with Dixita *didi*. I dared not to look at anyone once I completed it. I knew they all found my behaviour to be odd but no one wanted my clarification of Jahavi's picture. We went to the room. All my cousins and my friends held the chunni under which *didi* along with sisters were walking to the stage.

On the stage, the groom's family occupied the stage with a *dhol*. On the ground, we were bringing our sister. Even though there were nearly 350 people surrounding me, I felt like I was on the side lines. I felt like my presence would not matter to anyone— "Am I laayak enough to even be here? — I questioned myself.

When we reached near the stage, I couldn't take a step to climb it as the thought of Jahanvi being with me struck me.

I watched the *Jaimala* ceremony standing with everyone—downstairs. But once it ended, I walked to Gagan and said—"I need your car"

Gagan—"We'll go with you"

I didn't have the energy to explain the reason why I needed the car. Thus, I simply nodded. Gagan and Sarabjeet speculated me to drive the car at Jahanvi's house and yell at her or something kind of the same. However, I wanted some space alone. I unlocked the car, opened it and lay down at the back seat, all alone, covered the windows with window covers, and played a random music as loud as I could— the perfect hibernation required. Having no one around me helped my tears roll down at the speed they wanted to. I screamed as loud as I could. I wished the voice of music dominating my yelling so that Gagan and Sarabjeet who are standing outside don't hear it. I cried to my fullest. I cried my heart out. The vomit-like feeling emerged inside the hall, re-emerged when I was in the car. But it was my saliva that managed to come out of mouth. Where the watery nose made it suffocated for me to breathe, my tears made the vision blur. I wanted to escape the embarrassment of everyone. I wanted all this to appear a bad dream. I wanted my heart stopping to work so that I do not have to face anyone. Above all, I wanted to ask Jahanvi—'Why???"

I took out her number and wanted to call her but it couldn't go further than the first ring. I tried again but it was still the same. I opened her Instagram account of hers, and a picture of the boy and her appeared. I was left with no energy, my stomach started paining, and a pain that was becoming unbearable. From being broken, my emotion shifted to being angry and I shouted again at the picture. The aggressiveness was so high that my cords tore. I could feel a losing voice.

I checked two of the pictures she posted with me last year had been deleted. My tears had no plan of stopping anyway soon. My head started spinning, hands became cold, legs became powerless and it was my stomach paining the most. The urge to puke re-emerged and saliva found their way again. I choked on my nose being watery and coughed three times that stimulated further coughs and coughed some fifteen to twenty times more. My kidneys gave up the strength to bear a single cough more. I picked up a cloth that was in the car for cleaning and inserted it in my mouth to stop feeling anything.

Unhygienic lover is in a far more serene situation than an unloved lover.

The tears continued, the visions of Jahanvi continued, and so had continued her voice echoing—"Tum is Laayak nahi ho ki kisi ko milwa saku"

The door of the car opened. My wet eyes had blurred my vision so I couldn't understand who opened it. Someone stopped the music, picked me up and helped me sit. My eyes were being wiped, the cloth in my mouth was removed, and my hair was being combed. I tried hard to open my heavy lids to get a clearer view. But till then eye bags and heavy lids had met each other at the end.

"Take my goggles and make him wear it"— I could hear Kanav's voice. "Is he drunk?"— Babu asked.

"No he isn't"— Gagan said, and I acknowledged him being the one to pick me. "Everyone is searching for him inside"— Aarohan said

Gagan pulled me out of the car and grunted.

Just when everyone was around my tears stopped from being displayed, legs got its senses back, the blocked nose got one side opened to breath, and cough halted.

I walked inside in the hall with goggles on as if nothing had happened. "You cannot ruin the special day of your family"— my heart said to me.

I ran to the dance floor and started dancing, watching the same some of my uncles and aunts joined me. My friends and cousins were worried about my strange behaviours— I could see in their eyes.

I pulled each and every one on the dance floor. All I wanted was to have no eyes on me. But some still were on me— Ranju *didi* standing in a side kept watching what I do.

Our family along with the groom sat around the table to have dinner. I sat with everyone and laughed at every joke cracked, responded to every question asked, clarified every doubt raised, supported India whenever my NRI *jiju* insulted it jokingly. My over-normal behaviour was getting everyone's eyes.

My parents thought I was drunk, Dixita *didi* thought I was over excited, and the groom's family thought I was Ranveer Singh 2.0.

Once the dinner ended, I felt a hand on my shoulder while I was in talks to an uncle who was about to leave. I turned around and it was of Jahanvi's *bhabhi*.

I closed my fist as tight as I could so that the pain stays till a different body part and doesn't reach my heart— a stupid and silly lover unlover thing.

"Congratulations…"— she cleared her voice. Her eyes contained the embarrassment that I carried out throughout the wedding. I finally found someone with the parallel emotions.

I clarified— "Not your fault mam. She made her choice"

Embarrassment holds words to emerge. Thus, she softly placed her hand on my shoulder and said—"Bless you"— And left.

I saw her walking till she crossed the door of the hall. I saw her wiping her tears while she was on her way out.

"Why didn't Jahanvi come with her?"— My mom asked me while she walked up to me in a hurry and kept searching for something in her handbag.

I made up some answers in my mind so as to hide the real truth. Within a minute, without waiting for a reply—"Yeh rahi chabi (Here is the key). Go to the room allotted to us, bring Dixita's bag, and keep it in jiju's car. Ask your jiju's father to send someone along"

I snatched the keys and walked fast to the room. The empty room instigated me to find the hibernation again and to continue with the cries.

"Isn't this perfect? No one is here. I could drain all the emotion I wanted to."— My mind spoke to me.

I walked till the window and saw the depth of the room. I was on the second floor and the other side of the resort was the parking area.

"Wouldn't death be the perfect hibernation?"— Thought arose.

"Wow! This is something permanent just as the pain of Jahanvi's betrayal"— An answer within me arose.

Thud-thud

There were two hard smashes on the door that broke the conversation going.

"Uncle sent me to pick the bags"— *Jiju's* cousin came to help me out. "Yes. Hi. You carry this, I'll bring the other one"— I said to him.

When the bag was done, I was called to the area where the wedding ceremony—

Pheras— were to begin.

I sat with Sarabjeet, Aarohan, Gagan, Babu, and Kanav. Ranju *didi* joined me and sat beside me. We all were focusing on the rituals taking place or at least were pretending to be focused.

It was 2:30am. I looked at the sky. The sky was clear. There were stars twinkling and the moon lightened up everything.

I took out my phone to click pictures of the wedding. I unlocked it and saw 8 messages from Jasmeet

"Hey"— 10:03pm

"You were to send me pictures"— 10.41pm

"I am still up. Whenever you are free please send me"— 11.18pm
"How is *didi* looking?"— 11.32pm

"At least you can reply, *Aari*"— 11:34pm

"Ohhh! I am sorry to ask for anything. I thought you can...." — 11.45pm.

"Just send a picture of jai-mala. I won't ask for anything"— 11.48pm.

"Sorry to disturb you"— 12:48pm

Just when I read her messages I replied back at 2:44am —" Hey, sorry… Sorry just saw your messages"

Her whatsapp displayed her being online again in a second.

"I am sorry to disturb you, I should have known that your girlfriend could be around"— she sent.

I didn't feel the pain at that point. A deep void created in me in the last few hours was failing to be filled with anyone's name anymore.

"Sending pitures. Wait"— if I was in a situation to give an explanation? No I opened the chat box of the family group and downloaded all the pictures and sent the same to Jasneet. As there were videos included of all rituals and traditions, some 54 files were sent to her.

I kept my phone aside.

The *pheras* ended and the chirping of the birds started as the clock hit 5:00 am.

It was the time for *didi* to leave her own home and move into her husband's now. The *doli* was to be taken now and everyone gathered around the exit. Ranju *didi* didn't leave my hand and held it tight. Dixita *didi* met mom and dad first, followed by cousins and some relatives. She kept searching for me who was standing in the middle to let others meet her.

She saw me and hugged as tight as she could and I hugged back.

Never had I ever allowed a single drop to roll down in front of anyone, but there were many which actually did.

I dared not to look at anyone but to keep my face hidden in *Didi's* collar. "Take care of yourself"

"Hmmm…"— I replied keeping my face hidden

"Don't trouble mom and dad. Try keeping your room tidy yourself"— She said "Hmmm…"

"Don't let anyone hurt you. They are not worth it"

I released myself from her and looked directly at her face.

She wiped my tears with her hands and said—"Not everyone in

your life can understand you. Not everyone who understands can be in your life"

I gulped down the water in my throat and kept looking at her.

She was called by her in-laws to leave for their house. I took my phone out and clicked a picture of her sitting in her car. I thought about sending the picture to Jasneet. Thus, I did so. As always, she saw in seconds and sent an emoji of a heart.

I was asked by my father to push the car in which the newly wedded was sitting. Along with me, there were THE BORED PANDAS and my cousins doing the ritual. The car exited the resort. I took my phone out to tell it to Jasneet. A message from her arrived.

"Finally *didi* got married. Yippee!! I waited for this day for a long time. However, it was not in this way I thought to attend the marriage but destiny has its own plan. You know *Aari* I always loved you and will also keep loving you. But the thought of you being with someone else just doesn't allow me to stalk you…tbh it is killing me every day. I wish you to become the biggest actor of this country. I will keep praying for you to Ekam. I even promise to watch the first day first show of all your movies. But if I don't take this step today of walking away from your life, I will just do something unfair with my own life that Ekam has given me. I am leaving your life forever Aari. Take care of yourself. Love you!"

Once I finished reading her message, I started to type and her message appeared.

Meanwhile I got a message from Mohit and the notification popped on my screen. I quickly swiped the notification to type to Jasneet.

Before I could think, type and send, she messaged-"Don't type anything" And I stopped typing but she continued.

"Any clarification, any apology, or any message would break me completely. Please don't say anything"

"Byye Aari"

Her last message arrived and she blocked me.

Another message from Mohit popped on the screen, I opened,

it said- **"Hi Pratik. Sorry for being late in messaging as the meeting went almost overnightfor your story. Honestly, it has the strength to be made and among all five directors, we almost impressed three. But after a deep discussion they rejected stating the story wouldn't be liked by Punjab's audience. I am really sorry.**

 Hope to work with you in future on some other project."

Without even replying to him, I locked the phone and slid it into my pocket. I saw *didi's* car leaving the resort.

On the same day Jahanvi left me, I lost Jasneet, *didi* moved into her new life, and Mohit rejected my story. I knew now I will have to start all from scratch since now I don't have a job, love, loving friend, and dream of becoming actor. I kept standing there all alone wondering who was wrong, what went wrong, how everything started and how everything ended.